THE GOOD THIEF'S
GUIDE TO VEGAS

Also by Chris Ewan

The Good Thief's Guide to Paris
The Good Thief's Guide to Amsterdam

THE GOOD THIEF'S GUIDE TO VEGAS

CHRIS EWAN

MINOTAUR BOOKS

New York

THE GOOD THIEF'S GUIDE TO VEGAS. Copyright © 2010 by Chris Ewan. All rights reserved. Printed in the United States of America. For information, address St. Martin's Press, 175 Fifth Avenue, New York, N.Y. 10010.

www.minotaurbooks.com

Library of Congress Cataloging-in-Publication Data

Ewan, Chris, 1976–
  The good thief's guide to Vegas / Chris Ewan. — 1st ed.
      p. cm.
  ISBN 978-0-312-58082-7
  1. Novelists, English—Fiction.   2. Thieves—Fiction.   3. Magicians—Fiction.   4. Las Vegas (Nev.)—Fiction.   I. Title.
  PR6105.W36G69 2010
  823'.92—dc22

                                                    2010012877

First published in Great Britain by Pocket Books, an imprint of Simon & Schuster UK Ltd, a CBS Company

First U.S. Edition: August 2010

10   9   8   7   6   5   4   3   2   1

In loving memory of Carole Norton

thief: bandit, burglar, cheat, cracksman, crook, housebreaker, larcenist, mugger, pickpocket, pilferer, plunderer, robber, shoplifter, stealer, swindler.

Jeez, talk about a bad reputation . . .

THE GOOD THIEF'S
GUIDE TO VEGAS

ONE

Stealing a man's wallet is easier than you might think. The trick is to wait for just the right moment and to make your move without hesitating.

Not convinced? Well okay, imagine your target is leaning across a roulette-table in Vegas when his trouser pocket gapes open. And let's pretend that you're standing beside him with a bottle of Budweiser in your hand, so that even if he feels something brush against him, he'll think nothing of it. Believe me, it only takes a second to slip your spare hand inside his pocket and whisk his wallet away.

Maybe you doubt it can be that simple. Perhaps the most you'd concede is that it's possible, but only if the target is a real chump. If I tried to pull that move on *you*, say, you'd be sure to catch me.

Well, that's an understandable reaction, but I'm afraid it's plain wrong. For starters, I'm good. And I don't mean take-a-punt-and-brazen-it-out good. I mean talented good. I mean fast, nimble, experienced good.

Then there's the psychology involved. After all, I don't look like a pickpocket. I'm cleanshaven and smelling of cologne. I have on a sports jacket and smart jeans. My shoes are polished, my nails are clean, my breath is toothpaste-fresh. Plus, we're in a classy venue, the Fifty-Fifty casino in the very heart of the Strip, across from Caesars Palace, along from the Venetian Hotel. And we're at a high-stakes table in a high-roller area, separated from the hoi polloi by a velveteen rope and a raised plinth. You've been chatting for some time with my good friend Victoria. She's immaculately groomed and kind on the eye, and smart and witty and a whole bunch of pleasing characteristics besides. Oh, and did I mention that we're British? What ho! Tally pip! Hardly criminals, right?

So let's just settle on the idea that I'd have stolen your wallet in half the time it's taken us to get this far and that you wouldn't have come close to catching me. And hey, don't feel glum about it, because neither had the guy whose billfold I'd just lifted.

He was of average height with a cultured mane of dark, Hollywood hair, a wholly artificial tan and a keen awareness of his own minor celebrity. His name (if you can believe it) was Josh Masters, and he was the Fifty-Fifty's resident stage illusionist, star of the casino's second-string theater for twelve performances a week, forty-eight weeks a year. His speciality was in making things vanish—showgirls, tigers, the Stratosphere Tower, his own credibility—and his capped smile and intense blue eyes gazed out from billboards and flyers all around the casino complex and the wider city beyond.

My reasons for taking his wallet needn't delay us right now, but as a mystery writer by trade, I should probably let you know that I'm not a complete cad. So allow me to put on record that I don't make a habit out of picking people's pockets. I've done it in the past, and no doubt I'll do it again in the future, but it's nearly always as a means to a somewhat complicated end and never for the sheer hell of it. It wouldn't be worth my time—a man can only use so many driving licenses.

True, I'm a thief, but I'm what you might call a high-end thief. I tend to work on commission, and since I try not to work too often (in order to keep my chances of being caught as close to zero as possible), I only accept a job if I'm going to be handsomely paid. Usually, that means I steal from two kinds of people—the rich or the corrupt. And while that hardly makes me Robin Hood's spiritual successor, I like to think that it nudges my moral compass away from the zone marked *absolute scum*.

But anyway, the defense rests, and you'll no doubt recall that Josh Masters' wallet was out of his pocket and inside my own, courtesy of a neat piece of sleight of hand that Masters himself might have appreciated, if only he'd had cause to study my technique. And with my prize secured and my Bud set aside, I fled the scene of my crime by stepping down from the high-stakes area onto the main casino floor.

The Fifty-Fifty is one of the more recent mega-resorts to have been built on the Strip. It has a theme, like almost every other Vegas casino, and the subtle clue to the theme is in its name. Fifties America was what the place was all about, with the casino floor dedicated to the gangster world of *noir* movies, pulp films and popular imagination.

Take the cocktail waitresses as an example. They sported pageboy hairstyles, make-up that was heavy on the foundation, blusher and lipstick, and sequined bodices of a cream shade, over black micro-skirts and long, nylon-sheathed legs. Likewise, the pit bosses were dressed in gray sharkskin suits with wide lapels and trilby hats, and the security staff were kitted out in vintage cop uniforms, with blue polyester shirts, black slim-jim ties and gold, five-pointed badges. Over by the cashing-out cage, the staff behind the gilded security bars wore green tinted visors, while the croupiers were dressed in white collarless shirts with black waistcoats, and spent their time calling the female patrons "dolls" and "twists" and "frails," and the men "Mac" or "chum" or "buddy."

Swing numbers were playing over the sound system, but the tunes were lost in the noise of the gaming floor—the trill and ding of the slots, the whoops and cheers around the craps table, the riffle of cards, the clack of the roulette ball, the general hum and chatter of the vast number of suckers laying down money against all odds.

With so much happening around me, it took a few moments until I spotted the security desk (which for obvious reasons had made an impact on me when we first checked in), but once I'd logged its position, I set off toward it, remembering that the main elevators were located just beyond. Sticking to my route was easier said than done. For one thing, there were a lot of people in my way, but more to the point, the casino appeared to have been designed like a maze that continually led me back to an area where I might like to risk a considerable amount of money.

I passed through corridors of kidney-shaped gaming-tables, all of them fashioned from walnut veneer, cream leather and burgundy felt. Blackjack, Blackjack Switch, Casino War, Pai Gow Poker and Texas Hold 'Em eventually gave way to the craps-tables and the roulette-tables, and afterward the video poker games and the penny slots being played by elderly women in velour jogging suits.

As I walked, my feet beat down on a gaudy nylon carpet that charged my body with a frankly inhuman level of static electricity. I'd already learned to my cost that whenever I came into contact with anything metal I functioned much like a lightning rod, and the same was true of the call button for the guest elevators. I reached out a tentative finger to press it and . . . *zzzzzz* . . . a charge raced up my arm. Damn. I snatched my hand away and yelped, and meanwhile the doors parted on a nearby carriage and a tubby black man in a baseball cap and shin-length denim shorts stepped out. Taking his place in the elevator, I removed Josh Masters' wallet from my pocket.

I slid a key card from his billfold and popped it into the magnetic reader in front of me. I selected the button for Floor 20, and as the elevator climbed and a recorded voiceover encouraged me to buy a ticket for the *Josh Masters Magical Spectacular*, I took a tour through the remainder of his wallet.

He only had around sixty dollars in cash, which didn't surprise me because everything he could desire inside the casino would be complimentary. He had a platinum credit card, a gold credit card and a black credit card, all issued by Nevada state banks. He had a glossy signed photograph of his own good self and a valet ticket for his car and a folded paper napkin with a telephone number scrawled on it. He also had something that only the very lucky are prone to find and the very dumb are prone to keep—the neat cardboard sleeve that had originally contained his key card. It had the Fifty-Fifty's emblem on the front of it—a spinning fifty-cent coin—and his name just below. Oh, and it also featured his room number.

Suite 40-H.

I guessed it made sense. Star talent is treated like royalty in Vegas, and Floor 40 was one of the most exclusive in the hotel. And while I might have queried the application of the words "star" and "talent" to Josh Masters, it was clear from the bewildering success of his show that I was in the minority. But what did I care? I'd just saved myself the trouble of trying his key card in the 3,499 other bedrooms it might just possibly have unlocked.

The moment the elevator reached Floor 20, I coaxed it on to Floor 24, which was as high as it could go. Then I stepped out and walked along another stretch of carpet toward another bank of elevators, where I poked the call button with the corner of Masters' leather wallet—no flies on me—and made my way to the fortieth floor of the hotel. And there I reached a dead end. Because a short distance ahead of me was a concierge desk with an arresting blonde standing behind it.

The blonde had on a tailored black silk blouse that was elaborately ruffled and pleated beneath her very fine chin. Angular spectacles were balanced upon her nose, and diamond studs kissed her earlobes. She looked like she belonged on a catwalk and I wished to hell she was on one right now.

I suppose I should have seen it coming. In a resort like the Fifty-Fifty, the finest suites are nearly always serviced by a special type of concierge. They're the smartest, most attractive, most motivated hotel employees. They remember the variety of flowers you like in your room, the vintage champagne you require on ice, the location of your favorite table in your preferred restaurant, the names of your kids, your wife, your mistress, your cat . . .

I could go on, but the point is they memorize a whole bunch

of details, and they're prone to excel at it because that's how they score the really big tips. So there was no way this particular angel wouldn't know that I didn't belong on her floor. And that was a major problem.

By sheer coincidence, when she glanced over at me I happened to be acting a little gormless, so I hammed it up by turning on the spot, frowning at the number above the elevator and scratching the back of my head. I even gazed at the room card in my hand and slapped my forehead for good measure.

Then I stepped back inside the elevator and disappeared.

TWO

So all right, I didn't disappear. I went down five floors. But as far as the elegant blonde was concerned, there wasn't a marked distinction.

Floor 35 of the Fifty-Fifty was very nicely appointed. The area outside of the elevator doors was lit by an ornate chandelier, the walls were papered an agreeable shade of blue, and there was a good deal more of the lush nylon carpet with the low-level electricity running through it. But most appealing of all, there was no concierge desk.

Setting off along the carpet, feeling a lot like a balloon being rubbed against a woolen jumper, I walked for something like the distance of a half-marathon before I came to a door marked *Emergency Use Only*. I checked both ways and then I pushed through the door onto the service stairs beyond.

No alarm sounded, though perhaps a small one is going off in the back of your mind. It could be you're thinking about security cameras. Because security is what Vegas is renowned for, right? The countless fish-eye lenses covering your every move, the teams of finely drilled security staff watching over color monitors and analyzing your skin temperature and pupil dilation? Well sure, all of that is true, and more besides. But 99 percent of the surveillance is focused on the casino floor.

Yes, the mega-resorts along the Strip offer five-star accommodation, and naturally, every room is stocked with flat-screen televisions, gold-plated taps and walk-in power showers. But that's just the backdrop to where the real money is made—the gaming tables. And while the management would like you to have a good vacation and come back for more, they're not going to waste time monitoring your route through the hotel hallways to your bed. They'd rather watch you gamble.

So I felt pretty confident as I climbed the service stairs that my movements weren't being tracked and that I wasn't about to run into a team of security guards. I also didn't expect to meet any guests, since a city that features a replica of the Rialto Bridge with an escalator running up it isn't somewhere that fitness fanatics come on holiday. And hell, even if I bumped into a member of staff, there wasn't a great deal they could do. After all, I was a paying guest and I had my own room card to prove it.

As luck would have it, I didn't run into anyone, and after tackling five flights of stairs and poking my head out into the rarefied atmosphere of the fortieth floor once more, I was relieved to find that there wasn't a soul to be seen or a sound to be heard. Some 200 meters ahead of me, the corridor kinked right, and if my calculations were correct it would kink right once again before the alluring prospect of the blonde's rear profile would come into view. But I could only speculate, because the door to Suite H turned out to be located just before the end of the first stretch of corridor.

Loitering outside, I removed a pair of disposable plastic gloves from my pocket. There was nothing unusual about the glove I slipped onto my left hand, and it fitted nice and snug. The glove for my right hand was a little different. I'd snipped two of the fingers clean away, and I had to be careful the plastic didn't disintegrate as I eased it on. I needed the customized glove because my middle and fourth fingers were bound to one another with surgical tape. I suffer from sporadic attacks of arthritis, and just lately it had gone to work on my knuckles. Finger number four was especially bad. It had curled to the left, hooking over its buddy, and since it was more than a little painful, I'd taken the decision to tape them together. The upside was that my index finger and thumb were unaffected, and with the tips of my dud digits wrapped in tape, there wasn't much danger of my leaving any prints.

Since my index finger and thumb were still willing to participate in my felonious activities, I put them to work by sliding Masters' key card into the electronic reader on the door to his suite. After a beat, I removed it. A green bulb shone briefly and I heard a clunk as the electronic lock disengaged. Drawing a cautious breath, I reached for the handle and—

Zzzzzz . . . A blue spark snaked between the metal and my ungloved fingers. I gritted my teeth and growled, and then I leaned some weight onto the handle, swung the door open and stepped inside.

The moment I crossed the threshold, I experienced a buzz of electricity 100 times more powerful than anything the hotel carpets could conjure. It's always been that way for me. I guess if I spoke to a psychologist about it, I might learn some ugly truths about myself. Then again, perhaps if I broke into that same psychologist's office after hours and ripped the good doctor off, I might enjoy the biggest thrill of my life.

Analysis aside, I nudged the door closed and stood in the tiled entrance hall to the suite, whistling at the sight before me. Let me tell you, my own room had been plenty impressive when I first checked in, but this guy's suite was a whole different story.

Ahead of me was a compact kitchen with sleek, illuminated glass cupboards, a sizeable American fridge-freezer and a granite breakfast bar. Beyond the kitchen was a sunken area that featured a glass dining-table capable of seating twelve people, a large L-shaped couch in black leather, a wall-mounted television not a great deal smaller than the dining-table, a corner wet bar and a sturdy writing desk with a telephone and a fax machine. The desk was positioned beneath a brightly lit standing lamp and in front of some floor-to-ceiling windows that looked out over the rear of the hotel complex, the cross-streets and highways running behind the Strip and the red-hued mountain peaks beyond. A lighted passenger jet was coming in over the mountain ridge to land at McCarran International Airport.

The room was still and silent, save for the rumble of the air-conditioning unit. I shook my head in wonder and moved down onto the thick carpet of the living area. I shook it even more when it occurred to me that I was yet to see a bed.

I snuck across to a pair of double doors on my right and tried the handles. The doors were locked, and I got the impression they connected with a neighboring suite. There was another door on the opposite side of the room, just beyond the desk, and I breezed right through until I found myself gawping at a super-king-sized bed adorned with fine cotton sheets, quilted eiderdowns and woolen throws, not to mention enough pillows to stock the home-ware section of a strip mall Macy's.

A pair of teak cabinets flanked the bed, and on the nearest one a lamp with a fringed shade cast its light upon an alarm clock, a paperback book and a spiral notepad and pen. A water glass was positioned beside the notepad, its rim covered with a paper disc bearing the casino's logo.

Behind me was a double closet, and I threw open the doors, quickly discovering just how many leather jackets and pairs of stonewashed jeans one man could possess. An entire shelf was stacked with neatly folded white T-shirts, and another with gray. Masters' briefs were arranged just so, and his socks, I noticed with a shudder, were embroidered with his initials.

I must say I felt a good deal happier when I looked toward the bottom of the closet and found the room-safe. That may sound curious, but a safe can save me a lot of time. Without it, a guest might hide their possessions among their clothes, or their shoes or their luggage. They might find an obscure spot in their dresser or under their bed. They might even keep their valuables with them when they go out for the day. But more often than not, a safe eliminates those dangers, because most people think that it's a secure place to store their belongings.

It's not. Hotel safes are susceptible to the charms of most burglars, and that includes absolute beginners. They tend to be guarded by a simple electronic code, and it's often quite easy to guess the code a stranger has selected. If you don't believe me, try letting yourself into somebody else's hotel room and entering one of the following sequences—999, 911, 000, 1234 . . . You take my point. Oh, and if that doesn't work, try the number of the guest room itself. That baby's a frequent flyer.

But here's the really neat part. In certain American hotels, the safes are even more accommodating. For your own personal gratification, they offer you a choice. Sure, you can enter a good old-fashioned code, but if you're wise to the risks and you want a little more protection, you can opt to swipe your credit card through an electronic reader on the fascia of the safe. Secure, right? Well yes, unless the scoundrel who broke into your room happened to do it by lifting your wallet. Because if he has your wallet, then chances are he has your credit card too.

I had Josh Masters' credit cards and it was his platinum American Express that did the trick. As soon as I'd swiped it, I heard the whir and whiz of the locking motor, and the word OPEN flashed across the red electronic screen. Being a sucker for commands, I did exactly as I was told, and eased back the door to the safe before letting go of a variety of sigh that I usually reserve for somewhat more intimate moments.

The base of the safe was lined with a cushioned foam mat, and balanced on top of the mat were stack upon stack of some delightful casino chips. Most of the chips were purple, with flecks of lilac and mauve around their edges, but a few were painted plain, old-fashioned silver. Each purple chip was worth five hundred dollars in the Fifty-Fifty casino, and there were ten to a stack, six stacks in all. The silver chips were worth ten thousand dollars each, and there were three of those. Even my math was capable of running that sum. Sixty thousand dollars. It seemed to me like karma. No doubt it would seem to Josh Masters like an outrage. But to be perfectly honest, I didn't care, because I was more than happy for this to be one vanishing act that he'd never forget.

I filled my hands and had started to fill my pockets before I realized the error of my ways. The last thing I wanted was to lose a chip or to have them click against one another as I walked around the casino, and now that I considered the matter in more detail, I thought that one of the cringe-worthy socks bearing Masters' initials might make an ideal chip-holder. I reached for a sock and stuffed it appropriately, then tied off the end and gave it a shake. The sock worked beautifully, muffling the chips. I congratulated myself on an elegant solution, slipped the sock inside my jacket and pondered what to do next.

I weighed Masters' wallet in my palm. It was tempting to take the thing with me and try to return it to his pocket without being caught. All things considered, it would be the neatest outcome imaginable, and I felt pretty confident that I could pull the move off. But it was risky. A more sensible option was to dump the wallet in a litterbin elsewhere in the hotel. Yup, that was the clever play. Which probably explains why I decided to be a smart-arse and toss his wallet into the safe.

Of course, I couldn't lock the safe with one of his credit cards, because then the card in question would be separated from his wallet. So in the end I used a code. And since I considered the code I'd selected to be mighty clever, I had a sizeable grin on my face as I closed the closet doors and made my way back through the magnificent sitting room to the kitchen.

Helpfully, there was a peephole in the middle of the front door, so I could check that the coast was clear before making my exit. And making my exit was just what I was in the process of doing when I happened to glance to my left and spot something that prompted my brow to furrow.

Another key card.

The card in question was inserted in a plastic receptacle on the wall, and a tiny green light was shining beside it. Come to think of it, a good many lights had been on in the suite—the ones in the kitchen cupboards, the standing lamp over the desk, even the bedside lamps.

Hmm. I knew from my own room downstairs that unless a card was fitted in the slot, the lights couldn't work and the climate control couldn't function. But the lights were on in Masters' suite and the temperature was uniformly chill.

Now, it could be that Masters had two room cards, and if he was as environmentally concerned as the rest of Las Vegas, it wasn't too outlandish to suppose that he liked his air-con to be running while he was out and his lights to be on when he returned.

Or it could be that somebody else was inside his suite.

But I tended to believe that I'd have noticed if someone was watching television or taking a nap on the oversized bed while I ransacked the safe. And then it hit me.

I hadn't checked the bathroom.

All right, if you want to be picky, I hadn't even seen the bathroom. But there had to be one, and in all likelihood it was annexed to the bedroom. I hadn't noticed a door when I'd been in there, but then again, my attention had been focused on the safe.

I backed away from the peephole and drummed my fingernails on my teeth. Thinking logically, I was confident that if I found my way to the bathroom, there wouldn't be anybody inside. I mean, if there had been somebody there, I would have heard them moving about or they would have heard me and said something, because they would have assumed that I was Masters. The other alternative, the notion that somebody could have heard me enter the suite and had hidden in the bathroom, was too crazy to even consider.

So why was I considering it? And why was I dithering? Even assuming there was somebody in there (which there patently wasn't), there was absolutely no sense in me hanging around for a moment longer. I had the chips and my getaway was clear. The bathroom really shouldn't have bothered me in the slightest.

But the sad truth is, it did.

Call me a perfectionist. Call me obsessive compulsive. Call me an utter bloody fool. Either way, I had to know that the bathroom was empty. I had to prove to myself that I hadn't slipped up. It would bug me all night if I didn't make sure—just as it bugs a lot of misguided folk if they don't check that they've locked their front door before heading out for the day.

So I returned to the bedroom and I immediately saw the door

that I'd missed. It was white and bevelled and located on the far side of the bed. I approached it and set my ear to the wood—and there wasn't even the faintest murmur of a sound. And that *definitely* should have been enough.

But the peculiar impulse to be certain had me in its grip, and so I reached for the handle and edged the door open just a fraction.

And do you know what I found?

No, of course you don't, and I'm not going to tell you yet, either. Because right now I can feel my hack instincts tingling away, telling me that this is a choice spot for a crafty cliff-hanger. So if you'll forgive me, I think we'll leave things where they stand for just a moment while I leap backward and explain how it was that I'd found myself in this situation in the first place.

THREE

"Ah, Paris," I said. "There's nowhere quite like it in the spring."

Victoria groaned and rolled her eyes. If there was one thing I'd noticed about Victoria, it was her extensive repertoire of eye movements. This particular hitching of the pupils was one I'd become familiar with during our flight across the Atlantic to Newark, our two days in Manhattan and our hop onward to McCarran Airport. From what I could tell, it betrayed a monumental disappointment, perhaps even a regret, at my latest attempt at humor. The gag, you see, was that we weren't in Paris at all. We had been, only a week before, but right now we were in a taxi cab cruising along the Las Vegas Strip, and with a friendly nudge of the arm and a wink, I'd drawn Victoria's attention to the replica Eiffel Tower outside the Paris-Las Vegas casino. And then I'd delivered my punchline, and been left in no doubt that I was fortunate to avoid a punch of my own.

Being a perceptive type, I'd begun to suspect that my personality was beginning to wear a touch on Victoria. I thought that was understandable, considering we hadn't spent all that much time together before. Yes, we'd known one another for years, and Victoria had been my literary agent and confidante throughout what might charitably be referred to as my writing career, but Paris had been the first time we'd met in person, and much to Victoria's distaste, she'd discovered that my face didn't look anything like the author photo in the back of my mystery novels. The portrait in question was of a dashing chap in a dinner

jacket, and it was as fake as the sham Eiffel Tower I'd so fool-
ishly drawn her attention to—though now didn't seem like an
opportune moment to mention the parallel.

I suppose, with this kind of background, you may well ask
what we were doing together in Las Vegas in the first place. And
in response, let me just say, in an obscure and rather mysterious
way, that there were a number of reasons.

Not good enough? Okay, the truth is that I'd been invited to
leave France (by which I mean that I was told to get out and
never return), and at the time of my departure I happened to be
holding some merchandise of a somewhat dubious provenance.
Now, there aren't too many markets for the type of goods I had
hidden in my luggage, but I knew of a dealer in Brooklyn who
might be inclined to take a look. And by coincidence, Victoria
had recently agreed to represent an author based in New York,
whom she was keen to shake the hand of, following what she'd
taken to referring to as my *deception*. So, in short, we had come
to America. And after I'd sold my wares for a respectable profit,
and Victoria had glumly confirmed that her latest scribe was indeed the mirror image of his rather unfortunate mug-shot, I'd
suggested that we might be entitled to a little fun. And fun, to
me, meant Vegas.

In all honesty, persuading Victoria to come to Sin City had
been far trickier than I could have anticipated. To begin with,
she'd given me a flat-out refusal, insisting that she needed to return to London for the sake of her clients. Then she'd told me
that she couldn't afford a vacation.

"Piffle," I told her—largely because it was a word I'd always
wanted to use. "You deserve a break. I can't even remember the
last time you took a holiday."

"Try a few days ago. In Paris."

"Piffle," I replied—because I really felt like I'd mastered the
use by now. "You can't call that a holiday. It was a business trip,
of a kind, followed by an adventure, of a sort, and not a vacation by any stretch of the imagination."

Victoria closed her eyes and drew an audible breath. Then she told me, in a caustic tone, that if I said "piffle" once more, she'd be forced to cause me some damage of a rather unfortunate and testicular nature. And she added, quite calmly, that she positively didn't gamble. That it was, in fact, a Newbury family rule never to bet on anything.

"Not gamble?" I said, as if she was mad. "Are you a Mormon?" And believe me, I was careful to pronounce the second "m" very clearly.

"No, Charlie. I'm just a responsible adult. And anyway, what would I wager? I'm hardly going to fritter away the less than jaw-dropping commission I earn on your books."

"I'll stump you. I have more than a fistful of dollars from my Brooklyn contact. By rights, half of it's yours anyway."

"Then buy me a ticket home."

"But Vegas will be fun, Vic. You could do with a little frivolity in your life."

"Oh believe me, seeing all those Charlie Howard fees pile up in my bank account makes me quite giddy enough."

Her little barb caused my jaw to drop, and once it had struck my kneecap, I uttered what can best be described as a gasp. "Sometimes, I think it's lucky for you that I'm not precious about my writing."

"Not precious? Or not serious?"

"Ouch."

"All I'm saying is that it's been more than a year since you've given me anything new. And from what I can gather, your latest Faulks novel has hit the buffers."

"Not true. It's just that the Cuban section's proving a little tricky to develop. But give it time and it'll come together."

"Time? Well, if you spent half as much time at your desk as you do breaking into people's homes, it might be finished already."

I twirled a finger at my temple. "My subconscious has been toiling away like you wouldn't believe."

"Yes, but it's your conscious I'm worried about. That's the part that does the actual typing. Can't you at least pull together a short story? Something I might be able to place in an anthology? We do need to keep your name out there."

I paused for a moment and tried to gauge the turn our conversation had taken, my gray cells running through all kinds of complex and intricate thoughts.

"I don't mean to sound like a conspiracy nut here, Vic, but are you just nagging me in the hope I'll become so annoyed that I buy you a ticket to London?"

"Devious, *moi*?" She wafted her hand in front of her face and fluttered her eyelids.

"And you'll quit bugging me if I do?"

"I'll give you a month's grace."

"Done." I slapped my fist into my palm, as if I was banging an auction-house gavel. "And cheap at the price. You may even find yourself traveling first class."

Except she didn't, and neither did she find herself on a plane to the UK. Because left to my own devices, I went ahead and booked us non-stop to Las Vegas, together with connecting guest rooms at the Fifty-Fifty.

Now, it will come as no surprise to the more worldly among you that my subterfuge didn't go down all that well. In fact, it went down about as badly as you could imagine. But unfortunately for Victoria, it wasn't until I'd hustled her as far as the departure gate at JFK that she rumbled me, and by then she was so stupefied and so enraged that I was able to bundle her onto the plane before she thought better of it.

A flute of post-take-off champagne helped to thaw her out, and a good deal of manly pleading persuaded her to talk to me by the second hour of our flight, but now that we were motoring along the Las Vegas Strip, no amount of cajoling could get her to see the humor in my rather weak joke about the Eiffel Tower.

"Listen," I said, trying yet again to strike a reasonable note. "Surely it's not the meanest trick in the world. Just think of it as a thank you for all you've done for me over the years." I placed a hand on her knee. "And I did buy you a ticket home for the end of the week."

"Hmm," she said, and folded her arms.

"Is that a 'Hmm, yes I forgive you?'"

"No, Charlie. It's a 'Hmm, let's see how quickly we can change my flight so that I can get away from you before I kill you.'"

I checked on our cab driver in the rearview mirror. A toothy grin had slashed his face in half.

"At least wait until you see the hotel. Stay a night and see how you feel."

"I suppose I'm going to have to."

"So you might as well enjoy yourself, right?"

"Hmm," she replied, and turned from me to study the shimmering lake outside the Bellagio. The famous dancing fountains weren't performing their hourly routine at that particular moment (it would have been too much to ask), but it was an impressive sight all the same.

"We're almost there. Trust me. You're going to love it."

And do you know what? She actually did. A lot of that had to do with how staggered she was by her first glimpse of the Fifty-Fifty, and her reaction was easy to understand. The main hotel building was a curved fin of smoked glass, fifty stories in height, that happened to be topped by a revolving restaurant. Above the restaurant, and spinning in counterpoint, was a giant 50-cent piece.

It was really quite something, as were the Broadway-style marquee bulbs above the main entrance and the vintage American roadsters that gleamed and shimmered in the marble foyer. And it didn't hurt that the service we received at check-in was impeccable, nor that our junior suites were plenty capable of rendering us speechless.

Happily enough, things only improved when I treated Victoria to dinner in a kitsch hotel restaurant. The Test Site Trailer was designed to look like the interior of a classic Airstream caravan, with vinyl seating booths, chromium-edged tables and, appropriately enough, a Mushroom Cloud Soda Fountain. Our Atomic Burgers and Fallout Fries had been delivered to our table by a waitress on roller skates, and by the time I'd ordered a second round of boozy Meltdown Milkshakes, I might even go so far as to say that we were on the very best of terms.

So of course, I chose that moment to spoil it all by telling Victoria how I planned to conclude our evening with a game of no-limit poker.

"Oh, but you mustn't, Charlie," she said, in a surprisingly earnest tone.

"Oh, but I must. This is Vegas, Vic. You practically have to play poker here. I think it's the law."

Victoria pursed her lips around her drinking straw and slurped her milkshake. "But you don't know how."

"I do."

"Since when?"

"Since I began playing online."

Victoria gagged and spluttered, and I feared a stream of milkshake might spurt from her nose.

"I'll have you know I've made fifty-eight dollars since I first started out."

"And when was that?" she croaked.

"Six months ago."

She dabbed her lips with a paper napkin and cleared her throat. "How peculiar that your writing seems to have stalled during that time."

"Pure coincidence."

I pushed the remains of my hamburger aside, reached for the bill and scrawled my room details in the appropriate spot.

Victoria rested her fingers on my good hand and gave me a searching look, seemingly unaware of the gob of milkshake on her chin. "You know I don't agree with gambling, Charlie."

"That's why I'm not asking you to take part."

She frowned and contemplated the depths of her milkshake, as though she might find a more compelling argument somewhere beneath the vanilla froth. Just as she went to speak again, the mock window to our side bloomed with a flickering white light and our table began to tremble and shake. I wasn't alarmed. An information sign beside the entrance had promised a simulated atomic explosion every half-hour. Sure enough, a thunderous rumble played over the stereo system, interrupting the early rock 'n' roll we'd been listening to, and our waitress shrieked and trundled beneath a nearby table in a truly woeful piece of acting.

In time, the noise and the shaking faded away, and our waitress reemerged and dusted herself down, leaving Victoria to continue as if nothing had happened.

"Has it occurred to you that you could be exploited? There is such a thing as professional gamblers. They come to places like this and they prey on novices."

"It's a reputable casino, Vic. There's a staff dealer on every table."

"You still need to be careful."

"Point taken."

"Know how much you're prepared to risk before you sit down. And don't even consider exceeding your limit."

"Okay, Mum."

Ah, the narrow-eyed assassin's glare. I'd been waiting for that one to make an appearance.

"I'm only looking out for your best interests, Charlie."

"I know that, and I appreciate it," I told her. "But what do you take me for? A complete idiot?"

FOUR

I was a complete idiot.

No, the poker didn't turn out as well as I'd hoped. In fact, the poker went very badly indeed. I still had my shirt and my complimentary Budweiser, but I didn't have a great deal else, and one thing I positively didn't have was any of the money I'd made in New York. Every last cent that my Brooklyn contact had paid me was gone, and while some of it had already been spent on our trip to Vegas and Victoria's ticket home to London, the rest had been scooped into the arms of a mirthless cowboy with a Buffalo Stetson, a bolo tie and a handlebar mustache. Seriously. It was one thing to lose, but losing to a cliché was really tough to swallow.

It's hard to pinpoint where it all went wrong, short of my sitting down in the first place. I suppose I didn't play tight to begin with—for which I blame the Meltdown Milkshakes—and my opening stake was gone so quickly that I felt compelled to buy back in. Some dumb part of my psyche figured it would be embarrassing to stand up and walk away early in the game, without considering how daft I'd feel leaving with nothing a half-hour later. In my defense, I had some bad luck, and it's not often you see a straight flush (as held by the cowboy) and a full house (as held by yours truly) in a game of Texas Hold 'Em. I had the guy figured for Trips at best, which is why I went all-in after he raised me on the River. Hell, I don't know, maybe my errors had something to do with playing real opponents for once, instead of a collection of pixels named *Dark Dawn* or *Amarillo2000*.

Whatever the explanation, I was a good deal poorer than when I'd last seen Victoria and I was in a pretty foul mood to boot. I idly considered circling the tables to see if anyone was enjoying better luck, but it didn't strike me as the surest way to cheer myself up. A more tempting option was to head outside for one of the free Strip spectaculars—the erupting Volcano at the Mirage, perhaps, or the saucy female pirates waging naval warfare at TI. Practically anything had to be better than returning to my room and having Victoria drop by to say, "I told you so."

On the subject of Victoria, I was really quite confused by her attitude to gambling. Sure, I'd just become the latest casualty of the vice, but I couldn't deny the thrill I'd taken from that final hand—at least until I'd lost. And if her objection was a moral thing, her thinking was mighty peculiar, because she'd never seemed very troubled by my sideline in burglary. Then again, she had mentioned that not gambling was a family rule, so perhaps it was something that had been drummed into her in childhood. She'd once told me that her father was a judge, which didn't exactly suggest a relaxed upbringing.

In any case, she'd been very clear that she didn't approve of my foray among the gaming-tables, so you can imagine my surprise when I heard a raucous whoop and a squeal, only to glance to my right and find someone who looked just like her leaping in delight from behind a high-stakes roulette-table.

I knuckled my eyes. The woman had the same shade of brown hair as Victoria, cut to the same length and curled in around her shoulders in the same style. She had on a similar green blouse and charcoal pencil skirt, teamed with a familiar-looking green handbag. Her height and frame were strangely alike, and she had some of Victoria's mannerisms down pat.

The doppelgänger held her arms above her head and bounced on her toes while the croupier smiled at her indulgently. He wasn't alone. There were six players seated around the table and they all seemed utterly charmed. Most enchanted of all was a guy with dazzling white teeth, a flawless tan and showpiece hair. He wore stonewashed jeans over alligator cowboy boots, a plain white T-shirt and a tan leather jacket.

The handsome hunk wrapped Victoria's double in his gym-muscle arms and lifted her clean from the floor. She giggled and beat down playfully on his shoulders, meanwhile bending her legs at the knee.

In almost no time at all, I seemed to be standing alongside them, and so I reached out and tapped the woman on the shoulder. She whipped her head around and blinked, and then she covered her mouth with her hand and said, "Oh God, Charlie," with the kind of alarm I might have expected if I'd just broken into her home.

"Who's your friend?" I asked.

Victoria blushed and gestured to be set down. She straightened her clothes and adjusted her handbag strap and gingerly motioned toward her muscular beau.

"Charlie, this is Josh. He's an illusionist. You've probably seen the posters for his show."

"Nope, I don't think so."

"Hey, Charlie." He clapped me on the shoulder. "It's sure great to meet you."

Now, allow me to come clean and admit right away, just in case you haven't picked up on the subtle clues that I've weaved into my account, that I disliked Josh Masters instantly. When Victoria introduced us, his greeting was about as genuine as the medieval knights inside the Excalibur casino, and his eyes weren't even pointing in my direction—they were angled toward the roulette-table, calculating the bets he might lay.

Here's the second reason I didn't take to him—he was winning very handsomely. Stacks of purple chips were neatly arranged in front of him, looking like the ramparts of a mini-fortress. He also had some of the blue one-hundred-dollar chips, though not as many. They were scattered carelessly around the perimeter of the purple fort like a moat. But then I imagine you can afford to be a little blasé about century tokens when you have something in the region of eighty thousand dollars to wager.

Right at that moment, it was around eighty thousand dollars more than I had to my name. And his left hand, which featured a gold signet ring and a set of finely manicured nails, was resting in the small of Victoria's back. Now true, we weren't an item. Victoria was my literary agent and my friend, nothing more. But Josh Masters didn't know that. He didn't have the faintest idea. And he evidently didn't care.

"So, Josh," I ventured, "Victoria mentioned you have some kind of magic show?"

"Right here in the magnificent Fifty-Fifty," he drawled, his attention fixed on the roulette felt.

"So what would you call yourself? A children's entertainer?"

"*Charlie.*"

I swear, Victoria actually spoke in italics. She also gave me a warning look. It was a pretty severe kind of warning look.

"What?" I said. "I like magic, as it happens."

"Since when?"

"Since I was a kid."

It was true. In my boarding-school days, I'd taught myself a whole bunch of card tricks, and before too long, I'd reached the stage where I was able to invent some tricks of my own. That was just how my mind worked. I was a kid who liked puzzles, and magic was exactly the kind of activity that entertained me when the other boys were out playing rugby or cricket or kiss-chase (and this despite, or maybe because, it was a single-sex school). Well, magic and learning to pick locks, but you get the idea.

As it happens, I was quite proud of my card play, and every so often I'd put on a small performance in my dorm. Over the years, I developed a reputation as a bit of a conjurer. So perhaps in some ways Josh Masters and I were kindred spirits. I guess that could be another reason why I hated his guts.

"Let me show you a trick," I said. "It's a real corker."

"Thanks, buddy, but I'm good."

"Humor me, why not. Do you have a deck of cards and a pen I could borrow?"

Josh sighed and rubbed his face with his hand. "Listen—Chaz, is it?"

"Charlie."

"Right. I'm kinda busy here." He jerked his eyebrows toward the roulette wheel. "So . . ."

"So?"

"Maybe another time."

"But it's a good trick."

"Hey, I'm sure it's terrific."

"Then why don't you let me perform it?"

"Charlie," Victoria cut in. "Josh has a very successful show here at the casino."

"And?"

"And he must get people wanting to show him tricks all the time."

Josh slapped me on the arm, as though that was the end of the matter, then turned to the roulette felt and started to lay some bets. He placed ten purples on red, plus another eight scattered across the numbered squares.

I pointed my thumb at his back and leaned toward Victoria.

"What's his problem?"

"He doesn't have one. He's offered us free tickets for his show tonight. Which is really generous of him, don't you think?"

No, I didn't think it was spectacularly generous, not when I considered the amount of chips he was setting down. But at least there was one consolation—as he reached across the table, I thought I could see hair plugs dotting his scalp. I was about to mention it to Victoria when he turned back and pressed two more purple chips into her palm.

"Get lucky." He lifted her hand and kissed her fingers.

Victoria chewed her lip and gazed at him excitedly, before turning her attention to the table. After a moment's hesitation, she laid both chips on the corner between red 16 and 19, and black 17 and 20. A thousand dollars, at odds of eight to one. I was about to ask her what on earth she was doing when every other player at the table stacked their chips on top.

An elderly woman in a gold lamé jacket caught my eye. She gripped the pearls that ringed her turkey-flesh neck.

"Your friend is a real lucky pill."

"Is that right?"

"Oh sure. She's been on a hot streak."

The croupier spun the roulette wheel clockwise and flicked the ball in the opposite direction. I watched it whiz around in a pale blur until it began to lose momentum.

"No more bets," the croupier murmured. He was a scrawny type with a slicked-down side-parting and an acne-scarred face that was perfectly in keeping with the gangster theme. "Bets are closed."

"Thought you didn't gamble," I said to Victoria.

"Not my money," she replied, as if that explained everything.

The ball clacked and bounced off one of the tiny metal spurs that dotted the wheel, then pitched and dropped into red 19.

And then it popped out.

"Red Eighteen," the croupier mumbled, leaning forward to gather in the losing chips with his spindly arms.

A collective groan went up from the table. Victoria winced and offered an apologetic look to the elderly lady.

"I'm so sorry."

"Don't be, honey. You won me plenty." The lady gathered together her not-inconsiderable pile of chips and tossed a hundred-dollar marker to the croupier. "Goodnight, y'all."

Victoria turned to Josh. "Apologies to you, too."

"Hey, don't sweat it. We won on red, remember?"

Victoria swiveled and gawped at the table. She clapped her hands in delight.

"How much did we win?"

"You doubled your stake," I said, trying not to sound too bitter.

"Came out even," Masters corrected me. "Allows us to dance another day."

He winked at Victoria and I swallowed down the bile that had just risen in my throat before reaching for the strap of her handbag and giving it a tug.

"Shall we go?"

"Oh." She glanced at Masters. "I think I may stay for a while. And like I said, Josh has given us tickets to his show."

"Front-row seats," he added.

"Yes, front-row seats. His assistant has come down with a bug, you see, and he needs a volunteer to help him with one of his illusions."

"And what—that volunteer is you?"

"I thought it might be fun."

Victoria and Masters shared a look. It wasn't the type of look I relished seeing them share, and I sure as hell didn't want them to share anything more.

"Hey, Chaz, how'd you like to run a bet with some of my chips?"

"It's Charlie," I told him. "And I don't bet with other people's money."

"Is that right? Well, you know the minimum stake at this table is five hundred dollars?"

I was just about to tell Masters where he could shove a handful of his purple-colored chips when Victoria interrupted us.

"Roulette's not really Charlie's game. He's more of a poker player."

"Is that right? Say, you're not one of these folks who plays on the Internet, are you? A lot of newbies get caught that way."

I fixed a smile to my face. "Thanks for the warning."

"How did you do, by the way?" Victoria asked. "You haven't been gone very long."

"Oh, I decided to pass in the end. Thought you might fancy a stroll around the Venetian. Maybe a drink in St. Mark's Square?"

Victoria scrunched up her face. "But I've already said that I'll take part in Josh's show. It starts in an hour—right, Josh?"

"Uh huh. Unless you win big enough for me to quit."

He pressed two more purple chips into Victoria's palm. She looked between us.

"You don't mind, do you?"

"Mind? Why would I mind?"

"And you'll come to the show with me?"

I wanted to say no, but she was giving me a new variety of look, a doe-eyed effort that would have made me feel like an absolute heel if I'd said no.

"If that's what you want. But I'm going to take a tour of the Venetian first. So I'll see you inside. Okay?"

"Perfect."

Josh snapped his fingers. "Chaz, I'll have your name put down on the ticket counter." He flashed a grin at Victoria and wrapped his arm around her shoulders, guiding her back to the table. "Now, sweetheart, how about you tell us what number is going to win?"

As Victoria debated where to set her wager, Masters leaned forward to lay a chip on black number 6. In that instant, his trouser pocket gaped open and I caught sight of his wallet. I felt my hand twitch, and before very long, I'd reached out and made magic with his billfold.

So all right, I lied about having a good reason for ripping the guy off. But then, what did you expect? I told you I was a thief.

FIVE

All of which brings us back to that pesky bathroom door.

You'll recall that I'd coaxed the handle down and nudged the thing open, being careful to do so as soundlessly as possible. You'll also remember how unnecessary it had been for me to check on the bathroom in the first place. I'd given the matter a good deal of thought and I'd concluded, not unreasonably, that it would be ludicrous to think there could be anyone inside.

In support of my logic, the door hadn't been locked. Now, if there really had been someone in there, and if they were hiding from me, they would have bolted the door. But I'd eased down the handle and it had opened without any resistance. So all things being equal, I was as certain as I could be that the bathroom would be empty.

But of course it wasn't.

It was very large, in keeping with the rest of the suite, and it was stylish and expensive-looking. The floors and the walls were done out in gray marble tiles and there were two circular sinks, with gold-plated taps, set into a slab of black granite that was adorned with fluffy white towels and monogrammed toiletries. There was a toilet, a walk-in shower cubicle large enough to accommodate an NFL team, a flat-screen television, and a bath (or a tub as our American friends like to call it) that was perhaps a little smaller than your average swimming pool. The bath was square-shaped and very deep and it was dotted with plastic Jacuzzi nozzles. It was also filled close to the brim with water. Oh, and there was a naked woman inside it.

Now, as this isn't a piece of erotica, allow me to add that while she was slim and petite and nubile, she was also face down in the water and she wasn't moving in the slightest. Her arms and her legs were floating out from her torso, just below the waterline, and her head was fully submerged. Her flame-red hair was congealed on the surface in sodden knots and tangles, like some extraordinary plant from the South China Sea. The bathwater was as still as her body, and she looked as though she might have been floating there for many hours or even days.

Just then, I caught my reflection in the mirror behind the double sinks. I looked fairly shocked, which wasn't altogether surprising, but I also looked kind of shifty, poking my head through the gap in the door like that. Even so, in the seconds that followed, I was really quite stunned to see my reflection moving through the door and approaching the bath.

One thing I absolutely wasn't going to do was to check for a pulse. I'd touched a dead woman before, not so very long ago, and I'm not ashamed to admit that it was one of the most unpleasant experiences of my life. The sensation of her cold, lifeless skin was still very real to me, and I didn't doubt that it would linger for a long time to come.

By way of compromise, I removed my left glove and slid my index finger into the water at the end of the bath, as far from her toes as I could get. The water was cold. If she'd drowned while taking a bath, the temperature suggested that it had been quite some time ago and there wasn't a hope of saving her. And if she'd been killed by someone else, well, then they would have made sure that she was dead in the first place. And to be blunt, I wasn't all that keen to take my involvement any further. What could I do, after all? Telephone hotel security and explain that while I had, admittedly, committed one misdemeanor by breaking into Masters' suite, they had no reason to trouble themselves with the notion that I might have committed another, more heinous crime?

Listen, if there'd been a chance that I could have saved her, I would have given it my absolute best shot, and to hell with the consequences. But she was way beyond that now, and I couldn't risk hanging around. Over the years I've come to appreciate a number of hazards associated with the line of ungainful employment I've tended to pursue, and while being caught is one of the least appealing, being caught in the vicinity of a floating corpse is even worse.

So I'm afraid I turned to leave, and it was only as I did so that I noticed a hotel robe lying crumpled on the floor behind the door. The robe was burgundy in color, matching the felt on the gaming-tables downstairs, and it had a fifty-cent coin embroidered on a chest pocket in silver thread. Tangled up with the robe was an item of clothing of an altogether skimpier design, fashioned from pink Lycra. I prodded it with my foot and discovered that it was a one-piece leotard with a short, frilly skirt. It seemed like the type of thing a Vegas showgirl might wear. I looked again at the body in the bath. She had the athletic build of a dancer, though perhaps the legs were a trifle short. But if it wasn't a showgirl's costume, then what could it be? It certainly didn't remind me of any of the outfits I'd seen on the casino floor.

And then, all too gradually, my thoughts clicked into place like the slowing drums on a slot machine. What was it Victoria had said about Josh Masters' show? Something to do with volunteering during one of his tricks because his assistant had come down with a bug? Well, Christ, it must have been some variety of super bug if it was capable of sweeping a redhead off her feet and drowning her in a tub of bathwater.

Leaving the robe and the costume and the girl where they were, I closed the bathroom door behind me and raised my hand to my forehead, asking myself if I should put the casino chips back where I'd found them. And of course, the sensible response was absolutely, no question, but it was being drowned out by the buzz of fear and panic swarming around my head. And my feet, the traitorous little blighters, had already carried me through into the sitting area before my rational self could take control of the situation, and by the time my rational self had gathered its senses, my irrational self had sided with my feet and was yammering away about how I should get the hell out of Dodge before I spent the rest of my days rotting in an American penitentiary for a death I'd had nothing to do with.

Next thing I knew, I was scurrying along the hotel corridor toward the service stairs, and by the time I was careening downward and hauling myself around the banister rail, the game was truly up and there was no way my brain could conceive of a set of circumstances in which it would be sensible for me to break back into a hotel suite with a dead woman inside it.

So the casino chips were still in my jacket pocket, and not in the closet safe, and Josh Masters' wallet was in the closet safe, and not in my pocket (or indeed, his). And I guess I should have been a bit more troubled by all of that than I presently was, but strange as it may sound, I could just about glimpse the merits in holding onto sixty thousand dollars' worth of chips. Heck, if nothing else, it was going to make a mighty useful getaway fund, because fleeing Sin City was the first thing I intended to do once I'd found Victoria and brought her up to speed.

There was no way we could stay in the hotel, you see, because as soon as the body was discovered, I'd be in a great deal of trouble. Yes, I'd thought it fair to assume that security didn't spend their time watching over closed-circuit cameras in the hotel corridors, but that didn't mean those cameras didn't exist. And once the body was found (which might not take very long, considering there was a nightly turn-down service), the cameras would be checked and my face would be seen. And with every member of staff briefed on exactly who to look out for, I wouldn't be in a position to order room service in a hurry.

To make matters worse, I'd checked into the hotel under my own name, with my own passport, and short of inventing a time machine, it wasn't a mistake I could easily remedy. All I could really do was run, and if that meant that the USA was forever shut off to me and that I'd need to spend the rest of my days living under an assumed name in a country I'd never even heard of, then maybe that was for the best. After all, Victoria had been suggesting that I write something under a pseudonym for quite some time.

Victoria. I had to find her, and quick. And not just because I needed to make myself scarce, but also because I had to make sure that she was safe. The redhead in the bath might have drowned accidentally or she might have committed suicide, but there was also the possibility that she'd been killed, and either way she'd died in a suite belonging to Victoria's new best friend.

I'd lost count of how many flights of stairs I'd rushed down in my panic, but judging from the way my lungs were burning and ominous black spots were beginning to cloud my vision, it had to be a fair number. I leaned against the wall and tried to catch my breath, meanwhile stuffing my gloves inside my pocket. Then I moved out into the corridor, trying my best not to appear like a murder suspect to the first person I ran into.

As it happened, I didn't run into anyone until I reached the elevator bank, and there I met a collection of guests all at once. They were a family group, ranging from grandparents through to sullen teenagers, and they turned and muttered greetings as a set of doors parted on an empty carriage. I squeezed in after them, feeling conscious of the heat and sweaty odors radiating from my body, and then my stomach lurched as the capsule plunged downward and a gushing infomercial encouraged us all to come revel in the captivating aura of the great Josh Masters.

SIX

The theater was undeniably impressive. True, an even grander stage on the far side of the casino hosted the nightly Rat Pack extravaganza, but this was no school assembly hall. The seating was tiered, running through rows A to W, and from my position in the front of the auditorium I couldn't see the entrance doors unless I stood from my chair.

As it happened, I was standing right now, and I was turning on the spot and covering my eyes with my hand, but no matter where I looked, I couldn't spot Victoria. She wasn't in the seat that had been reserved alongside me, and she hadn't been at the roulette-table, or wandering the gaming floor, or waiting outside the theater. No message had been left for me at the ticket booth, and when I'd hurried up to my hotel room, I hadn't found a note slipped under my door or a light blinking on my telephone. I was completely in the dark, and now that the lights had gone down, so was everybody else.

A hush passed over the crowd and I dropped into my plush theater chair and scratched my head. At the rear of the stage, a twinkling silhouette of the Vegas skyline became visible against the black velvet curtains. I could see the pyramid of the Egyptian-themed Luxor at one end of the curtain and the needle-shaped Stratosphere Tower at the other. The silhouette began to flicker in and out, as if the wiring was dodgy, and then the sound system kicked in, playing a big band number loud enough to make my kidneys shake. The music was all strings and brass, like the

opening score from an old black-and-white movie. Puffs of dry
ice billowed across the stage and silver spotlights cut through
the smoke, sweeping left and right before settling on the upper
left corner of the curtain. From somewhere above the gathering
music I heard the roar of an engine, and then Josh Masters appeared on a flying motorcycle.

A flying motorcycle? Yup. I might have witnessed some pretty
daft sights in my time, but I'd never seen anything quite like this.

It wasn't simply that Masters was dressed like Marlon Brando
in *The Wild One*, right down to his black leather jacket, white
T-shirt and peaked biker's cap. It wasn't even that his teeth gleamed
more brightly than the chrome on the motorbike. No, what really
topped it all was the way flames spurted from the exhaust when he
cranked the engine.

It looked plumb idiotic to me, but the crowd seemed en-
thralled. They gasped as Masters dipped and soared and twirled.
They whooped at the noise and the fire and the lights. And when,
at last, Masters lowered the motorbike to the stage, the acclaim
he received was beyond anything I'd ever experienced.

He milked his bow and tipped his hat, then clicked his fingers
and jumped from the bike to gather a glittering silk cape from
the floor. He showed us the cape, front and reverse. He snapped
it in his hands in time with the music. He tossed it into the air
and allowed it to fall gracefully over the motorbike.

He raised his fingertips to his temples and closed his eyes, as
though fighting hard to concentrate. Then, after a short pause,
his eyes opened and he thrust his hands toward the motorcycle.

But the motorbike hadn't moved. Its outline was still visible
beneath the sparkling cape.

The show music ceased with an abrupt screech, as if a stylus
had been yanked away from a record, and Masters fixed a look
of wry confusion to his face. He cupped his chin. He tapped his
foot. He even went so far as to shrug his shoulders. Then he
reached out and whipped the cloth away to reveal a rusted old
bike with a dented front wheel and bent handlebars.

The audience hooted and whistled and clapped. They stamped

their feet and pumped their fists and cackled joyously. But none of them enjoyed it anywhere near as much as Josh. It might have been the five thousandth time that he'd pulled off the trick but he gave the impression that it had never happened so perfectly before. And as he removed his biker's cap and tossed it out into the audience, I had to admit that the goof knew how to put on a show—and that he gave no indication of being the least bit concerned for the welfare of his poor assistant.

Eventually, the acclaim began to fade, and Masters grinned sheepishly and rubbed his hands together before speaking into a flesh-colored microphone bud. He welcomed us all to the magnificent Fifty-Fifty and wished us a swell vacation, and then he told us, in an intimate tone very nearly as authentic as his tan, how as a kid growing up in Utah his big dream had been to appear as a magician in Vegas. People clapped and others sighed. Josh acknowledged them with a humble smile and a wave, and then in a hushed voice, he added that his dream had grown. It was no longer enough to simply appear on a Vegas stage. Now he longed to make his act bigger and more spectacular than any magic show that had ever appeared on the Strip before. But, he added with a raised finger, some of the very finest tricks involved the kind of close-up magic that he'd started out with all those years ago. And so, after meeting my eye with uncanny accuracy and pulling a deck of cards from his pocket (an ordinary deck of cards of the kind used in the Fifty-Fifty casino, no less), he waded into some sub-David Blaine shtick that filled a good ten minutes.

I quickly lost interest and turned in my seat, scanning the dark recesses of the theater for any sign of Victoria. I was feeling more than a little anxious by now. My every instinct was telling me to flee the hotel as quickly as possible. Sure, it'd be nice to cash in my stash of casino chips before I left for good, but every minute I stayed was a minute longer for trouble to brew. It was trouble I couldn't readily afford. But despite it all, I remained in my seat, willing Victoria to show so that I could be certain that she was okay.

I suppose if you'd asked me to speculate on the precise danger Victoria might be in, I would have found it difficult to give you a satisfactory answer. One thing I would have conceded, however, was that it was unlikely that Masters could harm her during his performance. Which was all well and good, until my brain suddenly caught up with his act and I noticed that he'd summoned a volunteer from the middle of the audience, and that the volunteer in question was Victoria.

She passed me without even a wave and accepted his hand as she climbed onto the stage, her green blouse shimmering in the bright lights. The audience welcomed her with polite applause, and then Masters asked her a series of questions. In response, she told him her name, that she was visiting from London and that she happened to be staying in the Fifty-Fifty.

"Which room?" Masters asked, with a devilish wink.

Victoria blushed. "Never you mind."

"Hey, no worries, maybe you'll tell me later, as a thank you for the trip I'm about to send you on. Say, Victoria, how'd you like to pay a visit to Rio de Janeiro, Brazil?"

The audience cooed.

"Sounds good, huh?"

"It sounds wonderful."

"And you have your passport with you tonight?"

"Er, no."

"Well, don't sweat it. I'll get you there without your passport. Without even an airplane." He paused for dramatic effect and wiggled his eyebrows disconcertingly. Then he gestured toward the wings with a sweep of his arm. "Bring on the teleporter."

A crescendo of music sounded and a burly, bald-headed stagehand appeared, dressed all in black and dragging what looked to be an old bedroom closet toward the center of the stage. The closet was tall and narrow and rudimentary in design. It had brass castors on all four corners and two hinged doors at the front. The wood enamel was chipped and scratched, but when the stagehand twirled the closet before us, it seemed to be solid right the way around.

The closet didn't have a room safe inside it. In fact, once the stagehand had made himself scarce and Masters had flung back the doors, it didn't appear to have anything inside it at all. The interior was pitch black, like every other magician's cabinet I've ever seen.

"You like my teleport machine?"

"It's . . . delightful."

The audience tittered at Victoria's quaint English ways.

"Would you like to step inside and begin your trip?"

Victoria slipped off her heels and did as she was asked.

"You have packed your bikini, right?"

She raised a hand to her mouth, as if scandalized. Masters offered the audience a palms-up gesture and another of his trademark grins.

"Can't blame a guy for trying," he said. "Now, Victoria, you want to be secure in case of turbulence, right? So I need to strap you in nice and tight."

He reached inside and fastened Victoria to the rear of the closet with a set of black fabric straps that fitted across her chest like a parachute harness. Then he stepped back and closed both doors. There was a circular porthole through which we could see Victoria's face. She didn't appear altogether comfortable, but that was nothing to her expression when the stagehand returned and passed Masters a pair of sizeable metal blades.

Josh slapped the blades together, demonstrating that they were real. Then he beamed inanely at the audience, like some Hammer Horror bloodsucker.

"Can't teleport you all in one piece, Victoria. So I'm going to have to send you in chunks. Okay?"

For the first time, Victoria zeroed in on my eyes, and for just a moment she looked almost as alarmed as I felt. Then she squared her shoulders and set her jaw and nodded as though having somebody threaten to run her through with razor-sharp blades was an everyday occurrence.

Masters held the blades in one hand and used his spare hand to flip down two hatches, revealing a pair of slots at around the height of Victoria's waist and neck. Victoria gazed toward the ceiling, as if she was trying to avoid an unpleasant scene in a gory movie.

"Don't worry," Masters bellowed. "This is top quality steel. Hardly ever snags."

The audience snickered uncertainly but I didn't join them. I had a fair understanding of how the illusion worked, so I was aware that there was an element of risk. And if you're wondering how I knew that, might I encourage you to invest in a paperback edition of my second Michael Faulks mystery, *The Thief in the Theatre*?

The novel is available in all good remainder bins and it tells a diverting little tale about the theft of a very fine necklace from an operatic diva who happens to perform in a nightly West End variety show. As with all of my burglar novels, things don't run smoothly for Faulks. Some way into the story, at around the point at which Faulks has developed a seemingly flawless plan to steal the diva's necklace, he's alarmed to learn that she's agreed, for one night only, to participate in the show's magic act. And not only that, but she's prepared to allow her precious necklace to be placed inside a velvet bag and smashed into a thousand tiny pieces with a claw hammer.

Now clearly, the necklace isn't really smashed. We've all seen that particular trick too many times to believe that it could be. But imagine the shock on the face of the diva, not to mention the sheer panic displayed by the magician, when our hapless conjurer reaches the moment of his big reveal, only to find that when he pops the giant balloon that has been floating above the stage for his entire performance, absolutely nothing drops out. The necklace was supposed to be there, and now it isn't. The magician genuinely has no idea where it has gone. The diva is distraught. And Faulks? Well, he's tearing his hair from its roots. Because it looks as though someone has beaten him to the loot, and if he plans on fulfilling his assignment, he's going to have to figure out what on earth has happened.

Faulks wasn't alone in that. When I wrote the scene, I hadn't the faintest clue what had happened, either. Yes, I knew some close-up magic, and I liked to think that I was pretty good at sleight of hand, but I didn't know a thing about illusions. And so I found myself having to read all kinds of books and magazines and manuals, until I ended up learning far more than I needed to know. And one of the illusions I'd come to gain some understanding of was the one Victoria was presently undergoing.

The solution had everything to do with perspective, which is one of the reasons why the interior of the closet was completely black. And while I didn't know precisely how Masters intended to set about confounding his audience, I did know that the blades would be a fair distance away from Victoria's skin at all times. Actually, everyone in the theater knew that, but it was Masters' job to make us believe otherwise. And what I didn't want to happen, what I was positively afraid of, was that Victoria might panic. The illusion relied on the person inside the closet not moving in the slightest. That was something Masters' assistant, the one who was currently floating face down in his bath, would have been well practiced in. And yes, Victoria had been strapped in position to ensure that she didn't move too much, but what if she flinched or jerked her head forward? Couldn't the blades catch her then?

Thunk—Thunk—

The audience sucked in a sharp, collective breath and I snapped out of my thoughts to see that it was all quite academic. Masters had run the blades through Victoria and so far as I could tell, she was still in one piece.

"All set," Masters said, slapping the side of the closet. "You must be ready for that trip now, right? Could do with a little relaxation, I'm guessing."

Victoria blew a gust of air toward her fringe.

"Well, hold on, darling, we're almost . . . *there*."

Now perhaps if it hadn't been Victoria in the closet, and if I hadn't been so concerned for her welfare or so keenly attuned to Masters' behavior, I might not have registered the slight quaver in his voice, or the way in which he hesitated as he neared the end of his sentence. And if I hadn't been sitting in the front row, I almost certainly wouldn't have caught the way he frowned and gazed off to my right.

To most of the audience, his performance must have seemed flawless as he launched into the next part of his spiel, about how hot it was in Rio at this time of year and what a swell trip Victoria was sure to have, drinking cocktails and dancing the samba on the beach. But I had noticed, and so I looked to where he'd been looking, and I happened to see two men standing in the far aisle, one of whom was whispering into a two-way radio.

The two-way radio might have been enough to snag anybody's attention—this was in the middle of a show spectacular, and everybody had been warned to switch off their cellphones and pagers—but that wasn't why I continued to look. I continued to look because the men were identical.

They really were exactly the same. They had carroty hair, clipped close to the scalp, very pale skin dotted with freckles and prominent ears. They were strikingly thin, so much so that their Adam's apples seemed to protrude as though they'd each swallowed an egg, and they were dressed in the preppy style of Ivy League graduates, sporting blue knitted sweaters over blue checkered shirts, pale chinos and tasselled loafers. If it hadn't been for the way they'd interrupted Masters' rhythm, I might even have believed that they were a part of his act. It wouldn't have been the first time a magician had used twins to his advantage.

Back on stage, dry ice had encircled the cabinet and the music had increased in volume. Masters was holding a large black cape to his side, like a matador awaiting an invisible bull. Then he flicked the cape up onto his shoulders, pressed a finger to his lips and crept behind the rear of the closet.

And then we waited. And waited some more.

SEVEN

The scenario would have made for a cracking sociology experiment.

Question: How long will a theater audience wait if a performer vanishes in the middle of his act?

Answer: Approximately seven minutes.

I'm able to tell you this because once Masters had stepped behind the cabinet, I waited along with everyone else for him to emerge from the other side and complete his illusion. But he never did reappear, and as the dry ice began to thin, and as the jazzy show music looped and re-looped, and as the audience turned to one another and murmured uncertainly, it slowly dawned on us all that something was up.

Continuity aside, it was plain odd to have absolutely nothing happen for the first five minutes, and it was stranger still when the bald stagehand shuffled on to peer behind the closet, followed shortly afterward by the smartly dressed twins. But even then, I think most of us were holding our breath for some spectacular twist.

It never came, and we had to settle for one of the ginger-haired twins gesturing frantically to the wings until the stage curtain plummeted and a fit of whispers swept the crowd. The auditorium lights flashed on and a hasty announcement was made over the speaker system, apologizing for the cancelation of the show and asking us to exit the theater as quickly and as calmly as possible.

Some hope. We were bewildered, sure, but we were also intrigued—and I was worried about Victoria. A second announcement followed, more curt this time, and a team of security guards jogged down the aisles in their period cop uniforms to direct us outside.

I say "us," but I'm afraid I rather took matters into my own hands, and while everybody else was shuffling back toward the casino floor and speculating about what could have happened, I snuck up onto the stage and ducked beneath the heavy curtain.

As I pushed up from my knees and brushed stage dust from my palms, I noticed the identical twins and the black-clad stage-hand, huddled at the rear of the closet. I couldn't hear what they were saying and I couldn't see any sign of Josh. I'd half-expected to find him flat on his back with someone administering the kiss of life, but there was nothing to indicate that he was anywhere nearby.

I waved awkwardly at Victoria, who was still trapped in the cabinet, and was just in the process of approaching her when the twin with the two-way radio happened to catch sight of me.

"Sir, this is a restricted area and you need to leave along with everybody else. We can't have you back here."

He marched toward me and gestured over my shoulder toward the exit with his radio. Sure, he had the build of a class-room skeleton and the skin tone to match, but the edge in his voice told me he was used to having people do as he said.

"But that's my friend." I pointed to Victoria's face. She looked annoyed, which wasn't altogether surprising.

"Sir, we're dealing with a situation here and I'm asking you to make your way outside."

"Hold it," the second twin said, before either of us could continue. He looked from me to his brother and back again, then extended a bony finger and subjected me to a slow, watery stare. "This is the guy on the surveillance footage. You remember?"

I think I may have gulped, and I'm pretty sure the color drained from my face until I was nearly as pale as the twins themselves.

I certainly began to wonder if this was a situation Victoria could handle by herself.

"Look," I said, "maybe you're right and I should leave."

"This is the guy?" the first twin asked, ignoring me.

"I'm telling you. It's him."

Now, considering what had happened upstairs in Masters' suite, you'll understand that those words chilled me to the very core. You'll also appreciate that I wasn't spectacularly pleased when Victoria chipped in to conclude the introductions.

"His name's Charlie. And if it's not too much trouble, could somebody please release me and tell me what on earth is going on."

The twins peered at one another, adopting matching expressions that seemed to suggest they were running through the exact same thoughts. I got the distinct impression I wouldn't like where their thoughts were leading them, but before they reached a conclusion we were interrupted by an insistent knocking.

"Hello?" Victoria called from the cabinet. "Is anyone listening to me? I think I've been in here long enough now, don't you?"

The twins gazed at one another for a moment longer before approaching the closet. They stood in profile to me so that I could see their jug ears in all their glory, and they were just about to swing the doors open when I thought I'd better mention a minor detail.

"You'll need to remove the blades first."

"Excuse me?"

"The blades in the side of the closet. The ones poking through my friend. Often these illusions have to be undone in a certain order."

"Is that right?"

"So I understand."

While they hesitated, I stepped forward and, flattening my palm against the side of the closet, I very delicately removed one of the blades. Once it was clear that the blade was unbloodied, the stagehand followed suit and yanked at the blade on the opposite side. We all looked at Victoria. Her head didn't fall from her shoulders.

The twins hauled open the closet doors. I heard a hissing, shuffling noise, like shower water striking a tray, and then both twins leaped backward and cursed as a great volume of sand spilled out over their loafers.

I moved sideways and saw that Victoria's feet were buried up to the ankles in sand. I also discovered that the closet interior was no longer black. It was decorated with a beach mural featuring a pale blue sky, a turquoise sea and a yellow beach dotted with colorful parasols and figures in swimsuits. Victoria was still strapped in position, only now she wore a straw sunhat on her head and was holding a pink daiquiri glass with a cocktail umbrella poking out from it. Despite her props, she didn't appear to be in a holiday mood.

"Nice vacation?"

I won't describe the look I received, but suffice it to say that I unbuckled the straps and helped her out from the closet as swiftly as I could.

"What's happened? Where's Josh?" she asked, kicking sand from her stockinged feet.

"I think that's exactly what these gentlemen would like to know."

The twins snatched a look at one another and I found myself wondering if they ever spoke or took a decision without checking with each other first.

"You're saying he didn't plan this with you?"

Victoria scrunched up her face. "Plan what?"

Just for a change, they turned to consult one another. I could swear they almost blinked simultaneously.

"We barely know the guy," I explained. "My friend only met him this evening. He asked her to help out with his act. And now she's done that, and I think it's probably best if we just go."

I freed the daiquiri from Victoria's hand and passed it to the stagehand. He didn't look too chuffed about it, and he looked even less pleased when I plonked the floppy sunhat on his bald head. I didn't care. I grabbed Victoria's wrist and dragged her toward the curtain.

"Hold it. Nobody's going anywhere until we find Josh."

I'd been afraid one of the twins might say something like that. I wasn't crazy about the suggestion.

"But this has nothing to do with us."

"It has everything to do with you."

I steadied myself, then shook my head very slowly.

"You're mistaken. I don't know who you are and I don't altogether care. But we're going to leave now. And I'm afraid that's the end of the matter."

I parted the stage curtain and poked my head through, but before the rest of me could follow, I saw something that stopped me in my tracks—a string of security guards, arranged like a chorus line in their vintage uniforms. Somewhat disappointingly, they hadn't linked arms and they weren't high-kicking or singing a rousing show tune. They were standing with their feet shoulder-width apart and their hands behind their backs. One of them even patted a nightstick against his palm.

"Like I said, nobody's going anywhere until we find Josh."

I turned and offered the twins one of the colder looks from Victoria's collection. It seemed to lack the impact I might have hoped for.

"You asked who we are." The twin without the radio poked his thumb toward his brother. "We're the Fisher Twins."

Of course they were. The name suited them. It fit with their pale, fish-belly skin and bug-eyes. But from the way he'd said it, I got the impression the name was meant to mean something more.

"I'm sorry. Who?"

"We own this casino. We built it and we run it. We watch over everything that happens here. So understand that we know why it is that you're looking to leave in a hurry. And understand that we're not prepared to let that happen."

"Charlie?" Victoria said, from the corner of her mouth. "What have you done?"

I focused hard on what the twins had said. There was no

reason to doubt them, and short of disappearing in a puff of smoke, my only real chance of getting out of the scrape I'd landed myself in was to hand them the man responsible for the corpse I'd stumbled upon. Because it seemed to me now that Masters must have killed her. Why else would he have behaved the way he had?

"He's in the cabinet," I said.

"Say what?"

"Josh. He'll be in the cabinet."

I brushed past the twins and approached the cabinet in question, moving around to the back of it. I knocked on the rear panel with my good knuckles, trying to locate any hollow points. When that didn't work, I felt around the edges with my fingertips, hunting for a concealed hinge.

"But your friend was in the closet."

"Yeah, but there could be a rear section too. It's a perspective thing." I slapped my palm against the wood. "You can come out now, Masters. We know you're in there."

There was no response. I sighed and, moving around to the front, stepped inside the closet on top of the sand. I prodded at the rear of the beach mural, searching for a loose board or a catch.

"Where'd you get the drink?" I asked Victoria.

"The daiquiri? There was a cubby-hole near my shoulder. It had a sliding door. He told me to feel for it."

I looked to where Victoria was pointing and noticed an inlaid panel that had been painted to match the rest of the mural. It was around the size of a hardback book and I slid it aside and found a small cavity. There was nothing inside it.

"And the sunhat?"

"A panel above my head."

I checked up there too. The space was easy to access but it was completely empty.

"And the mural? Where did that come from?"

"The whole thing was covered by black roller blinds. He released them quite early on."

"And the sand?"

"I have no idea. He didn't warn me about it."

I turned to the stagehand. "Are there any trapdoors?"

He shifted uncomfortably, then glanced sideways at the twins. It seemed the habit was catching.

"You're saying he went through a trapdoor?" the twin with the radio said.

"I'm not saying anything. I don't even know if you have trapdoors. But if you do, it makes a lot of sense. He can't have just vanished. He's not that good a magician."

The twin pressed the radio antenna against his bottom lip as he considered my words.

"Okay. You need to come with us now."

"Come with you where?"

"Just get moving already."

It seemed like I was all out of options. Stepping down from the closet, I shook the sand from the bottom of my jeans, then squinted at Victoria.

"I'm really sorry about this. I'll see you later, okay?"

"Not so fast," the twin told me. "She's coming too. You're both going to run through every detail of your plan."

EIGHT

Plan? What plan? I didn't know of any plan besides the hasty getaway-themed one I'd been working on since I'd found the dead woman in Masters' bathroom.

Now, don't get me wrong, plans are mighty useful things and I have a lot of time for a well-developed scheme. But I hadn't the faintest idea what details our hosts were so intent on hearing. And I was pretty sure that wasn't something they'd be altogether thrilled about.

Speaking of not being altogether thrilled, I was becoming less and less enamored with the route we'd been following since we'd left the theater. To begin with, we'd been taken to a small dressing room so that Victoria could reclaim her handbag, and after that we'd been led through a door marked *Restricted Access* and down a flight of stairs into a basement level. The endless service corridors we were walking along featured bare concrete floors and whitewashed walls. Dusty pipes ran along the ceiling above our heads. Honestly, it was almost as if all the investment had been spent on the hotel tower and the casino floor.

The Fisher Twins marched in front of us and two male security guards followed from behind. The uniformed guards were Hispanic-looking, and they were of around the same height and build—their height being significant and their build rating somewhere beyond substantial. It occurred to me that Victoria and I must have looked out of place, as if we were on our way to some latterday Noah's Ark and hadn't got the memo about coming in pairs.

Eventually, we were instructed to wait outside an unremarkable white door. There was no sign telling us what to expect on the other side. I suppose I could have crossed my fingers (the healthy ones at least) and wished for something cozy and luxurious, but as the twins went in ahead of us and the security guards adopted an open-legged stance outside, it finally dawned on me that we were about to experience a piece of Vegas folklore that few tourists ever get to see. The back room.

The room was plainly decorated. There was a plastic table and four plastic chairs and a flat-screen television fitted to a bracket on the far wall. The remote for the television was on the tabletop. The ceiling was low and made up of square polystyrene tiles. Two spot bulbs pointed toward the back wall and cast the room in a dim yellow light. A grill above the door pumped cold air around, keeping the temperature about perfect for a morgue.

One of the side walls contained a rectangle of tinted glass. Through the glass I could see a second room that looked just like the one we were standing in, only lit more brightly. There was another television and another plastic table. Sitting at the table, squinting beneath the hard electric light, was a man I recognized.

I turned to Victoria and Victoria turned to me. We gave a fine impression of the Fisher Twins but it didn't clear up my confusion.

The man in question was the acne-scarred croupier from the high-stakes roulette-table. His head was bowed, his bony fists were bunched on the tabletop and he was fidgeting in his seat, jiggling his thighs and tapping his feet. On his pimpled neck, just above the open collar of his white uniform shirt, I could see a blue ink tattoo of a pair of dice. Each die showed a single dot. Snake eyes.

The croupier was nodding fast, almost like he had a nervous tic, and the skin of his neck was moving because of it, making it appear as though the dice were rattling against one another. He seemed to be murmuring continuously but his speech wasn't a monologue. A second man faced him from across the table.

The man was black-skinned and dressed in a blazer, shirt and tie. He was partially bald and the top of his bullet-shaped skull glistened under the low striplights like a bowling ball. A monk-ish band of cropped, silver-gray hair ran around his head just above his ears, and a goatee beard of the same shading ringed his mouth. His cheeks and his neck were flirting with the idea of becoming jowly, and he filled his blazer around the shoulders and upper arms in a way that suggested he used to be plenty mus-cular, and in another ten years might be plenty fat. I placed him in his mid to late fifties.

The black man smoothed the outline of his salt and pepper beard with the fingers of one hand. A cardboard file lay open on the table before him and he scribbled notes on a sheet of paper clipped to the file. From the speed of his writing, it seemed as though the croupier had a lot of talking to do.

I didn't think they could see us. In fact, I was pretty sure we were looking through a two-way mirror, which explained why the light in our room was so meager.

As we watched, the black man raised a palm and the croupier quit talking and slowly turned his head in our direction. His eyes didn't focus but I saw fear in his wavering pupils as he asked himself who might be watching over him. Before he could reach a conclusion, his interrogator finished his notes, closed his folder and exited the room.

It didn't take long for the man to appear in the doorway behind us. He nodded briefly to the Fisher Twins, and then he squinted through the dimness toward Victoria and me. When he was through gauging the threat we might pose, he kicked the door closed with a dismissive grunt and motioned to the chairs on the far side of the table.

"How about you folks sit down?"

"How about you tell us why we're here?" Victoria planted her fists on her hips. "We're guests of this hotel—not criminals."

I almost winced as she said it. True, I didn't welcome the label, but I had to admit it was somewhat apt.

"Let's just sit down and talk this through like adults." He pronounced "adults" without a hard "a." Like a dolt.

"Adults, you say?"

He lifted his shoulders. "It's a start, right?"

He tossed his cardboard folder onto the table without another word and took one of the plastic seats. I smiled crookedly at Victoria and followed suit. She delayed a moment longer before dragging back a chair of her own and sitting rigidly with her arms folded across her chest.

The black man opened the cardboard folder in front of him, carefully laid a fountain pen onto a fresh sheet of paper and exhaled heavily. He clearly paid attention to his grooming. The skin of his face and scalp was smooth and unblemished, and his beard was very neatly trimmed. His blazer was brown in color, his shirt a crisp Oxford blue, and his tie was yellow with blue diamonds. He smelled of grapefruit. Whether it was his cologne or his shower gel, I couldn't say.

"My name is Ricks." He opened his palms. "I work for Carson Associates."

"It's funny," I said. "People keep saying names as though we should know what they mean. The Fisher Twins. Carson Associates."

He smiled readily enough. "Carson Associates is a private security firm." He reached inside his jacket and removed a business card that he slid across the table toward us. The card was buff in color with a motif of a watchful eye in one corner. The name Terry Ricks was emboldened in the middle, above an italicised slogan: *Ever Watchful.* "We work alongside a couple other agencies here in Vegas, mainly on behalf of the casinos. My expertise runs to gambling irregularities."

"Gambling irregularities? You mean cheating?"

"You could say."

I palmed his card, acting as if we were two traveling salesmen about to do business. Alas, I didn't have a card of my own. Burglars don't tend to advertise—unless they want to get caught.

I must say I was more than a little confused by his introduction. A guy who specialized in gambling fraud didn't sound like the type of individual who should be tasked with investigating a murder-suicide.

"Are you planning to tell us what's going on here?" Victoria asked him.

"Well, ma'am, allow me to show you."

And with that he gathered up the remote control from the table and pointed it toward the television on the wall. We turned in our seats and peered at the screen through the gloom. A prick of light ballooned out from the center and I readied myself to be confronted with the evidence of my rather undignified escape from Josh Masters' suite.

To my surprise, I found myself watching color footage of the high-stakes roulette-table. I could see Victoria and Josh and a number of other players I recognized, including the elderly woman in the gold lamé jacket. I could also see the back of the croupier's head.

I watched for a good few minutes without the reason for the footage becoming any clearer. I saw Masters laying chips on the felt, and I saw him hand chips to Victoria. While she considered where to place them, Masters collected together a stack of blue one-hundred-dollar markers and slid them across to the croupier. The croupier traded them for the appropriate number of purple tokens. Then he spun the roulette wheel and sent the tiny white ball whizzing around its circumference until the ball settled in a number and Victoria jumped up and down in celebration. It was strange watching the scene unfold without any sound. The television was as silent as the rest of the room.

I scrutinized Ricks. "What are we supposed to be seeing here?"

He studied me coldly before pointing the remote at the television and prodding a button. The footage began to rewind. Ricks paused the recording just as Masters handed Victoria her chips, and then he started it playing again. I watched Victoria place her bet and Masters trade up his blue tokens. I still didn't get it.

"I still don't get it."

"Is that so?"

"Perhaps I'm being thick."

I glanced at the Fisher Twins. They were standing with their backs to the wall and their hands in their pockets. With their youthful, freckled faces, and their khaki trousers and knitted sweaters, they could have passed for the undernourished stars of a Gap commercial.

"What am I missing?"

One of the twins whistled and considered his nails. His brother exhaled sharply and shook his head. Ricks stroked his beard some more. After a long moment's contemplation, during which I could have produced a truly astonishing ECG read-out, Ricks delved inside his trouser pocket and removed something in his bunched fist. He set the item down onto the tabletop and lifted his hand away. A stack of five purple chips had appeared.

"Those are the casino chips Josh was betting," Victoria told him.

"Is that so?"

"I'm not color blind."

Ricks smiled benignly and contemplated us through hooded eyes. Then he extended his forefinger and thumb and lifted the chips from the table. As if from nowhere, a stack of three silver chips had appeared.

"How did you do that?"

"Aw, come on, lady. Enough with the act."

Victoria's fingers clenched the leather of her handbag as though she was administering a Vulcan death grip.

"I've had just about enough of this gangland nonsense," she said. "Now, either you tell us what's going on here or you let us go. If you plan on detaining us any longer, I'm going to have to insist that you call the police."

I gulped and held fast to the underside of my chair. The police? What the hell was she trying to do to me?

Ricks pouted and drummed his fingers on the table-edge. He tipped his chair back on its hind legs and casually tossed the purple chips to Victoria. She scrambled to catch them, batting them between her palms, but as soon as she managed to get a proper hold of them, her brow creased.

"What's this?"

"Bottle-top," Ricks explained. "A cap from a soda bottle, painted up to look like a stack of casino markers. Only the chip glued to the top is genuine." He pointed to the television. The screen was still frozen on the image of the croupier sliding Masters' purple chips back to him. "A player cashes up and the croupier hands him his chips—in this case a stack of purple five-hundred-dollar tokens in return for some hundred-dollar markers. The painted bottle-top looks genuine to a casual observer, but really it contains a stack of silver chips. One purple chip on top, three silver chips hidden underneath."

Victoria's mouth formed a perfect hole. "But why?"

Ricks exhaled and allowed his chair to tip forward again, as if he was deflating. "You really want to run with this routine?"

"The silver chips are worth more," I said, my voice catching in my throat. "Ten thousand dollars a piece."

"But . . . you're saying *Josh* was doing this?"

"Lady, we closed the table when you both quit. It's down a hundred eighty thousand dollars."

Victoria's eyes widened and her face became very nearly as pale as the wall. Maybe it was a good thing. Any paler and the Fisher Twins might have mistaken her for a close relative.

"But that can't be right."

"Oh, it's right. Reason we were watching is because he pulled a similar stunt yesterday evening."

"Well, that may be." She gathered herself and swallowed hard. "But I still don't see what this has to do with us."

Ricks pointed through the double glass at the croupier next door. The croupier was crouched forward with his face pressed against the table and his arms coiled around his head.

"It helps if you work a scam like this with a team. You need a guy on the inside, for one. It also helps if you have a distraction. A pretty girl who's mighty excited about winning, say."

"Oh good grief." Victoria cast her hand toward the twins. "We've already explained to these men that we'd never met Josh before tonight. We only arrived in Las Vegas this afternoon. You can contact our airline if you don't believe me."

Ricks inhaled very deeply through his nostrils. He stuck out his bottom lip and pointed the remote toward the television.

"The other thing that helps is if the cheating player can pass the chips off to another team member. That way, if he gets searched, he comes up clean."

Ricks jabbed the remote and I turned toward the television screen to see just what I'd feared he was driving at. By now, I'd entered the picture and I was talking with Victoria, a bottle of Budweiser in my bad hand. Josh interrupted us and pressed some chips into Victoria's palm, encouraging her to lay a bet.

Ricks slowed the footage, so that it advanced at half-speed. I watched as Victoria debated where to stake her chips and as Josh leaned over the table. I saw my recorded self edge close to him and my good hand slip inside his trouser pocket. My hand eased out and slid into my own pocket. Ricks freeze-framed the image.

"Sir, I'd appreciate it if you could stand up and empty your pockets onto the table."

NINE

I guess I've been lucky in life. There haven't been too many occasions when I've been backed into a corner. Sure, as a burglar, I've had some close calls. Times when I've had to hide and wait for a danger to pass, or scram to avoid getting caught. But usually I've had some control over the situation I've found myself in, and more often than not, it's worked out just fine. This time, I was struggling to see a way out of my dilemma.

"I'd rather not empty my pockets, if you don't mind."

"Oh, we mind."

"I'm an intensely private person."

"Believe me," Ricks said. "Nobody outside of this room will ever hear what happens inside of it."

I glanced through the side window to where the croupier was tapping his feet and clicking his teeth, then up at the Fisher Twins. The twins had their arms folded over their chests and they weren't saying a word. They hung back like a two-man jury, waiting to pass judgment, and I was beginning to find their silence menacing. Perhaps if there'd been just one of them, the effect would have been less powerful. Doubled up, it was making me sweat.

"Charlie," Victoria said, in a pointed tone. "These men are only interested in those silver chips. I'm quite sure they're not the least bit interested in anything else they might find on you. Right, gentlemen?"

Ricks rubbed the top of his skull some more. "That's a call we can make when your buddy turns out his pockets."

I held on for a short while longer but no solution presented itself. I stood up from my chair, feeling light in the head, and removed my wallet from my jeans and tossed it over to him, along with the key card to my hotel room. I added my passport and the plastic disposable gloves from my left pocket, and afterward I pulled out the lining of both pockets to contribute a haze of fluff and lint.

Ricks lifted my gloves, along with an eyebrow, as he inspected the space where I'd cut two fingers away. He shot a look toward my busted digits, then reached for my wallet and leafed through the various compartments in a fruitless search for chips. He slid out my driving license and checked it against my passport, then copied down my name, age and stated address. The address wouldn't be much good to him. The name might create some problems.

"Happy now?" I asked.

"And the jacket."

I eased my hands inside the front pockets of my jacket and flicked my fingers against the material.

"Inside pockets too."

"I don't carry anything in them. The jacket doesn't hang right if I do."

Ricks slapped my wallet down onto the table and wearily pushed himself upright, scraping the legs of his chair backward on the concrete floor. He didn't meet my eyes as he approached, as though he was embarrassed by my behavior.

At close quarters, he cut an intimidating figure. He was a good few inches taller and broader than me, and there was a calm assurance in the way he carried himself. He gave the impression that he'd handled some serious crooks in his time, and that so far as challenges went, I ranked a shade higher than an old lady diddling the penny slots. He beckoned with one hand for me to raise my arms.

"This is intolerable," Victoria told him. "Charlie's already told you that he doesn't have anything in his jacket. Here—do you want to check me too? You might as well see inside my bag if that's your attitude."

She popped the clasps on her handbag and shook its contents onto the tabletop. Everything fell out in a heap—her mobile phone, her make-up, a hairbrush, her room card, her purse and passport.

She tugged at Ricks' sleeve. I appreciated the gesture but it didn't work. Ricks merely snatched his arm free and backed me into the wall so that my head knocked against the television.

"Touch the ceiling," he snarled, and after a moment's hesitation, I found myself complying.

I really could touch the ceiling—it was that low. And just as I surprised myself with the revelation, Ricks reached inside my jacket and withdrew the sock full of chips.

I didn't dare look at Victoria as he returned to his chair, untied the sock and upended it above the table. My haul of purple and silver chips rained down. He threw up his hands in mock surprise, and then he set about organizing the chips into piles.

"He could have won those for all you know," Victoria said, surprising me with the lengths she was prepared to go to on my behalf. "He was playing poker earlier this evening."

"Sure thing."

Victoria flattened her palms on the tabletop and leaned toward Ricks. "You have absolutely no way of proving that those chips came from Josh Masters."

Ricks snorted and lifted the sock for her to see. He held it by the hem, between his forefinger and thumb, revealing the embroidered initials *J M*.

Victoria swallowed. "I'm sure there must be a perfectly reasonable explanation."

But there was no explanation, reasonable or otherwise. What could I say, after all? I couldn't tell them how I'd really come by the sock and the chips for fear of placing myself at the scene of a murder. And I couldn't think of any plausible stories I could weave. Sure, give me a few days, and I could probably have invented something in the same way I did for my books. But I didn't have a few days. I had seconds. And I'm sorry to say my brain wasn't capable of working that fast.

"Charlie?" Victoria prompted.

I contemplated the backs of my hands and let go of a faint breath. The silence in the room was almost too much for me to bear, but I had a feeling I might prefer it to whatever came next.

"So I was on it. What now?" I asked, chancing a sideways look at the twins.

They were standing shoulder to shoulder, as if conjoined. Their heads swiveled toward one another, naturally, and then the one on the right cleared his throat.

"Tell us where we can find Josh."

"I don't know that."

"Tell us where he is and we can come to an arrangement."

"I told you. I don't know."

"What about these chips?" Ricks asked. "Were you meeting him to hand them over?"

"They were my cut."

"Mighty generous."

"I drive a hard bargain."

One of the twins clucked his tongue, as if it was a metronome keeping time with his thinking. He stepped across to the table and gathered up the chips in his hands, tapping them together like a gambler pondering a large wager. It was hard to tell if he was angry or not. He seemed oddly calm. Almost too calm. He fixed on Ricks.

"Watch over them awhile. We'll go talk to the croup."

The twins left us and entered the room next door. I watched through the tinted glass as the croupier slunk down in his chair and clasped his shaking head in his hands. If he was afraid before, he seemed terrified now. It was peculiar. The twins looked as if they were dressed to negotiate a banking loan, not to reduce a casino cheat to jelly.

"What's their story?"

"How's that?" Ricks asked. He had occupied himself with the items Victoria had emptied out of her handbag. He undid her compact and checked beneath the circular foam pad, then unscrewed her lipstick and searched inside the lid. Victoria tutted loudly, but he ignored her.

"The Fisher Twins," I went on. "They look too young to own a casino."

"Internet."

"Excuse me?"

Ricks lifted Victoria's purse and prodded his finger inside the zipped compartments. When he failed to find anything of interest, he cast the purse aside and did the same with her handbag.

"Made it big in Silicon Valley. Forget millionaires. These guys have more money than Elvis."

Finally, Ricks grew bored of Victoria's handbag and his hand settled upon her passport. He flipped to the laminated back page and lifted his pen to begin jotting down her details. His eyebrows jerked up a fraction and a smile tugged at the corners of his mouth.

"Newbury, huh?"

Victoria lunged forward and snatched her passport from his hands. She began to re-fill her handbag.

"Used to know a Brit by the name of Newbury."

"Fascinating," Victoria said, gathering her lipstick and compact together.

"Alfred Newbury. He a relation of yours?"

"I very much doubt it."

"I guess I could check my records."

"I'm sure that whatever you choose to do with your time is no business of mine. Now, may I go?"

Ricks pursed his lips and shook his head. "Not my call."

"Listen," I told him. "Victoria wasn't involved in any of this. She didn't know what was going on."

"Tell it to them."

And with that, Ricks closed his cardboard folder, stood up from the table, gestured with his pen through the tinted glass window at the Fisher Twins, and left us alone in the room.

"I can't believe you," Victoria hissed, as soon as the door had clicked shut behind him. "We haven't even been here a day."

"Careful. This room's probably bugged."

She tensed her jaw and tightened her hands into fists. I could see her nails digging into the flesh of her palms.

"I'm so angry with you right now, Charlie. I can barely even look at you."

"If it's any consolation, I'm not having the best of evenings myself."

"It's no consolation whatsoever."

"I was afraid you might say that."

Gingerly, I slid back the chair alongside her and sat myself down. If there was anything to be thankful for, it was that I had a few moments to think. Unfortunately, I couldn't decide what I should be thinking about. The whereabouts of Josh Masters? The plight of his unfortunate assistant? The casino chips that I'd so recently forfeited?

As it turned out, I didn't focus on any of them, because I was distracted by what was happening next door. The croupier was pleading, red-faced, with spittle flying from his lips, but the twins appeared completely unmoved. I couldn't hear a word of what was being said, and I figured that was because the walls and the tinted glass had been soundproofed. I can't say it was an altogether comforting realization.

"You have much planned for the rest of the night?" I asked Victoria.

She groaned and pinched the bridge of her nose, as if she was suffering from a migraine.

"Oh, lighten up," I told her. "I've been in police cells a lot longer than this. And we've given them what they were after. They have their precious casino chips."

"They have *some* chips, Charlie. Not all. And since they seem to think we're both involved in a casino scam, I'd say they're not going to let us leave anytime soon."

"Sure they will. There's nothing more we can give them."

"I don't imagine they'll see it that way."

"Wanna bet?"

Let me just say, the glare I received was hands-down the most ferocious I've ever known.

"Trust me," I told her. "We'll be fine."

But of course we weren't fine. We were a long way from fine indeed. In fact, once I'd noticed that one of the twins had acquired a length of metal piping, and that he happened to be waving it in the croupier's face, I realized that I'd rarely been so far from fine in my entire life.

"Er, Victoria?"

"What?"

"I don't mean to alarm you, but have you seen what's happening next door?"

Victoria turned and let out a yelp. She flattened her hands on the glass partition.

On the other side of the glass, the twin prodded the croupier's chin with the metal pipe, tipping the man's head back and exposing his throat. He leaned close and breathed right in the croupier's face. The croupier gulped and clawed into his thighs with his fingertips. His lips trembled and he managed to stutter some words, but whatever he said didn't seem to go down very well.

The twin spun around and swung the pipe hard against the wall. Plaster debris showered his torso and face. He hefted the pipe and curled his lip as he assessed the damage. The damage was really quite terrifying.

"What's he doing?" Victoria asked. "Why is he swinging that pipe around?"

"I think it's safe to assume he's threatening him."

"You don't think he'd actually hit him, do you?"

"Of course not."

"Are you sure?"

"Absolutely. He's not the type."

"What about his brother?"

As we watched, the second twin stepped forward and seized the metal pipe.

"I'm not sure I can watch this, Charlie. Why doesn't he just tell them what they want to know?"

"He will."

"You think?"

"Well, yes. Unless he's a complete idiot."

"What if he doesn't actually know anything?"

"Then there's no reason for them to hit him, is there?"

I wasn't sure if I believed it or not. I felt a lot like a sports commentator trying to keep the home fans happy despite all the evidence suggesting that the visiting team were about to run amok.

"Oh God. What's the other one doing?"

I grimaced. "I believe he's holding the croupier's hand on the tabletop."

I didn't just believe it. I could see it too. The croupier appeared to be screaming—his mouth was wide open and the muscles of his neck stuck out like cords—but his scream didn't reach us.

Meanwhile, the twin with the pipe moved it up and down above the croupier's knuckles, like a woodsman lining up an axe blow.

"Charlie, tell me they're not going to do it."

"They won't, Vic. It's a bluff."

Some bluff. Without further ado, the twin whipped the pipe up above his head and brought it down hard on the back of the croupier's hand. There was a stunned pause and then blood misted on the mirror glass as the croupier bucked out of his chair, snatching his hand away from beneath the pipe and, it seemed to me, almost leaving his fingers behind.

Victoria screamed and buried her face in my chest just as the second twin lost his balance and clattered into the bloodied glass partition. His brother was grinning inanely, nostrils flared and eyes crazed. Specks of blood had mixed in with the freckles on his face, and when he wiped his lips with his sweater sleeve, a pinkish smear spread across his cheek.

"Oh God. Is he okay? Tell me he's okay."

"I hate to say this, Vic, but I really don't think that he is."

The croupier had formed himself into a ball in the far corner of the room. He was cowering there, crouched down around his hand as though trying to smother the pain. I wasn't sure how much of his hand remained, but I didn't think he'd be dealing blackjack anytime soon.

"I don't think I can stand much more of this."

"We'll be okay," I said, an unavoidable wobble in my voice. "They won't treat us like that."

I hoped it sounded more convincing to Victoria's ears than it did to my own. Because the moment the twins re-entered our room and stood panting in the doorway, any certainty I'd felt quickly evaporated.

The one with the pipe and the mad grin was short on breath but high on adrenaline. His knuckles were white around the shaft of the pipe and the end of the metal was clotted with what I sincerely wished was steak haché.

His brother was sweating profusely. He ran a damp hand through his ginger hair, kicking it up at the front as though he'd just applied pomade.

I was beginning to wonder what I should say when Victoria banged her fists onto the table and jumped in ahead of me.

"What the hell have you done to that poor man?"

The twins turned to one another. Smiles played around their lips, as if they were two unruly school pupils revelling in the dressing down they were about to receive.

"Lady, we can't have dealers cheating our tables. We paid that guy a fair wage. Benefits. Medical care. And that's how he repays us?"

"Medical care? You've ruined his hand."

"Guy knew the consequences of his actions. Just as you should too."

He lifted the pipe and waved it between us, as though he was playing a game of Eeny, Meeny, Miny, Mo. I found myself covering the knuckles of my bad hand beneath the table. Sure, my arthritis was a problem, and even with my medication it could hurt like merry hell, but that would be nothing compared to the damage the pipe would do. Screw dealing blackjack. My days of burglary would be behind me forever, and a long future of typing novels with only my left hand lay ahead.

"Listen," I began. "You have all of the chips that I took. If you let us go, we won't be any trouble to you. We'll check out of your hotel, and we won't set foot in your casino again. Come to mention it, we'll leave Las Vegas altogether."

"Not so fast," the twin with the pipe said. "Maybe we don't want you to leave in a hurry."

"Yeah," his brother added, pointlessly.

"Maybe we think that you owe us."

I sneaked a look at Victoria. "Like I've told you, my friend really had nothing to do with any of this."

"Save it. And listen to what we have to say."

I did as I was asked and listened to what they had to say. And when they were through talking, my eyes very nearly popped out of my head.

"You can't be serious," I said.

"We're always serious."

"But this is ludicrous."

"I guess that depends on your perspective."

Well, from my perspective, it was verging on insane. What we'd been told, you see, was that there were two options available to us. The first was to hand them Josh Masters. If we did that, we'd be excused. If we refused, we could opt to repay every last cent our "team" had stolen. We had twenty-four hours to comply. Oh, and if we failed, some less than sketchy allusions had been made to a one-way trip into the Nevada desert, of the kind you couldn't ordinarily book through one of the tourist booths stationed along the Strip.

"I don't know what to tell you," I said, shaking my head.

"Neither one of us has any idea where Josh is right now. And we don't have that kind of money."

"Then you have a problem."

Victoria threw up her hands and made a choking noise. "Am I to understand that you're actually threatening to kill us?"

"I guess you could view it that way."

"But that's abhorrent. It's illegal."

"So is stealing from our tables. You can do a long stretch in Nevada State because of it. What we're doing here is offering you an alternative."

"You're talking about murdering us."

"Only if you don't repay the money you stole."

"Plus interest," added the twin with the pipe.

They shared a look.

"Did I forget to mention the interest?"

"I guess you hadn't got around to it just yet." He jerked the pipe at me. "Call the debt an even two hundred."

"What the hell is this?" I asked. "The old bad twin, bad twin routine? I thought the gangster theme in your casino was just that."

The twin with the radio smiled flatly. "Funny guy. I like that. And we can be reasonable. Take the sixty thou you had in chips. We'll set it against the two hundred."

"We're not bartering over a used car here," Victoria told him. "I'd rather you called the police."

"No," I snapped.

"Charlie, they're threatening to kill us."

Yes, I thought, but if the police become involved, they'll want to take a look for Masters up in his suite. And then they'll find the same thing I found. And then they'll check the security tapes from the hotel corridor. And I'll be in all kinds of trouble.

Come to mention it, every minute we spent in the interrogation room was a minute longer for somebody to find the redhead's body. So yes, I admit, I wasn't exactly cock-a-hoop about the ultimatum we'd been given, but a period of twenty-four hours in which to track down Josh Masters seemed a hell of a lot more appealing than taking my chances as a murder suspect. And besides, who was to say the police weren't in cahoots with the Fisher Twins? I mean, Vegas was meant to have cleaned up its act, but from what we'd just experienced, I wasn't convinced we could take that chance.

"Charlie, I'm not the least bit comfortable with this," Victoria said, in a stern voice.

"I get that, Vic. But I'm asking you to trust me. Just pretend I'm asking for a small extension on a deadline."

"Yes, but that phrase really means something on this occasion, doesn't it?"

"Enough already." The twin with the pipe consulted his watch. "It's nine forty-five. You can have until ten o'clock tomorrow night."

"What about the croupier?" I asked. "He must have some of your money too."

The twin snatched a look through the mirror glass, a neutral expression on his face. "No money. Masters was due to pay him his cut after his show. The croup says he has no idea where Josh has gotten to either."

"And you believe him?"

The twin raised the bloody end of the pipe before his eyes. He turned it slowly, as if he was mesmerized. "Guess he would have told us if he could have."

"But that leaves us with a hundred and forty thousand dollars to find."

"That, or your buddy the magic man. And don't even think about running. We have eyes at the airport."

"And we'll need your passports," added the other twin.

"Oh yeah," his brother said. "Hand us your passports already."

TEN

I don't recall a great deal about our journey back to my hotel room, but one thing I do remember is that we didn't talk. I was busy thinking and Victoria was busy fuming and that kept us occupied until I closed the door behind us and collapsed onto my bed with a groan.

"Get up." Victoria kicked my foot. "And start packing. We have to get out of here."

"You heard those nutters," I said, into the mattress. "They have 'eyes' at the airport."

"They can't watch every departure gate."

"Maybe they can."

"So we'll hire a car and drive somewhere else. We'll find an airport where they don't have 'eyes.'"

I turned over on the bed and rubbed my face with my hand. "I think it was just an expression, about the airport. What they mean is, they'll be watching us. And besides, they have our passports."

"Passports don't matter. We can get to a British Embassy and wait for new ones."

"And meantime they'll file a police report connecting us to a casino theft. Showing up at an embassy would be like handing ourselves in."

"Not necessarily."

"Yes, necessarily."

I rolled off the bed and dropped to my knees. My holdall was right beside me and I unzipped it and started to root around inside. I hadn't unpacked just yet, so my holdall was stuffed with my clothes and possessions—my laptop, my framed first edition of *The Maltese Falcon*, my writing notebooks and pens. And somewhere, way down toward the bottom, my spectacles case.

Aha. My fingers tightened around the dimpled plastic shell and I pulled it from my bag.

"Aha," I said, and went to show Victoria.

But Victoria had moved from where she'd been standing. She was over by the desk with the telephone on it. The telephone receiver was hooked under her chin. Her fingers were prodding numbers.

"Who are you calling?"

"The police."

"Oh no, you don't." I raced across and pressed down on the cradle, cutting her connection.

"Charlie, let go."

"Not until you put the phone down and listen to me."

I reached for the receiver but Victoria snatched it away. Her skin had taken on a grayish tone and she was visibly shaken. Whether from anger or fear, I wasn't entirely sure.

"We have to call the police, Charlie. Those psychopaths have threatened to kill us."

"Yes, and I got the impression they meant it. But we can't get the police involved."

"Whyever not?"

I sighed and pressed the flat of my hand against my forehead. "Take a seat," I told her. "I need to tell you something."

"Charlie?"

"Please just sit down." I motioned toward the corner of my bed. "I'm pretty sure you're not going to like what I have to say."

For once, I was absolutely right. Victoria didn't like it one little bit. She didn't like me very much either, but I have to say I was prepared for that. After all, it's hard to explain to your best friend how you ignored their advice and lost a small fortune at poker, or why petty jealousy led you to steal a man's wallet. It's harder still to admit that you broke into that same man's room and raided his safe out of pure spite, and it's even more difficult to put into words what compelled you to rob him of sixty thousand dollars of casino chips. But all of that pales into insignificance when you're faced with confessing how you stumbled upon a dead woman and left her just where she lay (or happened to be floating) without alerting anyone to her plight.

Every one of the excuses I'd come up with for the benefit of my own conscience sounded utterly ludicrous when I heard myself speaking them aloud, and long before Victoria said anything in response, I already knew there was no way of justifying my behavior.

That didn't make the things she had to say any easier to hear. And on that basis, I'd rather not repeat them in print. True, I might be a coward and a reprobate, but I'd much prefer to skip the details of just what a lowlife she took me to be, and jump ahead to the part where she began to run out of steam and throw her hands into the air and sum up her thoughts by saying, "What on earth were you thinking? I can't believe you stole his wallet in the first place."

"I'm a thief, Vic. It's what I do."

"But this was meant to be a holiday. Your words."

"What can I say? I'm a workaholic."

"Charlie. Be serious for once. Please."

"I can't be serious. If I'm serious, I'll have to admit what a git I've been."

"You have been a git. And you've placed us in real danger."

Technically, I didn't think it was fair of Vic to put all the blame on me. I mean, if she hadn't gravitated toward Josh in the first place, none of this would have happened. Then again, since I wasn't a complete numbskull, I wasn't going to voice that particular theory.

Victoria glanced at her watch. "It's almost half-past ten already. I feel shattered, and I'm angry and I'm scared. And now I really don't know what we should do."

"There's only one thing to do. I need to break back into Josh's suite."

Victoria leaned back on the bed and crossed her legs at the knee. "Well, that's a terrible idea."

"Of course it's a terrible idea. Unfortunately, it's also essential."

"I fail to see why."

"Well, for starters, Josh might be there. But even if he isn't, I might find something in his room that could tell us where he's gone. The quickest way to satisfy the Fisher Twins is to find Josh."

Tiny frown lines appeared between Victoria's eyebrows. "He's hardly likely to have left directions."

"Maybe not. But it's worth checking."

"Is it? Wouldn't it be a lot more sensible to work out how we can prove that we weren't involved with him in the first place?"

"Feel free to try. My take is that it's not something the Fisher Twins are likely to entertain."

"Because of the chips you had in your pocket."

I squirmed a little. "That, and the fact I happened to confess to being a part of the scam."

"But you weren't a part of the scam."

"Christ, no. I already told you that. I only said it because it seemed like the best way to get us out of that room."

"You'll forgive me for wanting to make sure."

I bunched my hands into fists and pressed them against my chin. "Vic, I steal things, and I've always admitted as much, but I'm nowhere near stupid enough to try to steal casino chips under a bunch of security cameras on a casino floor."

Victoria placed her head onto her shoulder. "Let's not get into an argument about how stupid you are, okay?"

I paused and moved across to the window at the front of the room. Neon throbbed through the net curtains and I pulled them aside and peered out. I'd paid extra for a view of the Strip and it was alight in all its tawdry glory. Pinks and yellows and greens and whites. Car headlamps and brake-lights. I could glimpse a slither of the illuminated Colosseum Theater outside

Caesars Palace. A billboard out front told me that Elton John was in town. I didn't imagine we'd be watching his show any-time soon.

"I have to get going," I said.

"But what if the twins have already sent someone to Josh's room?"

"Then I won't go in."

"But what if you do go in, and then they turn up and find you with the dead woman?"

"Then I'm in trouble. And the longer I stay here running through the variables with you, the greater the risk becomes that something like that might happen."

"You're certain she was dead?"

"That, or she's the first aquatic human being in history. And she's strangely underwhelmed by her status."

Victoria snatched at her handbag and began to search through it. When she didn't find what she was looking for, she huffed and she sighed, and then she upended her bag above my bed and shook its contents out for the second time that day. She moved her make-up and purse around, but she still didn't appear satis-fied. She checked inside her purse, then let her shoulders fall.

"Damn it."

"What?"

"I can't find the key card to my room."

"Maybe it got lost when you emptied your handbag down-stairs."

Victoria stamped her foot and squealed, and then she paced across to the double doors that connected our suites.

"Will you open this door for me?"

I batted my eyelids. "But it's locked."

"Oh, grow up."

I didn't grow up, but I did crouch down before the snap lock on the doors and open my spectacles case. From within the case, I selected a likely pick and screwdriver and a little over a jiffy later, the door popped open. I swung it back on its hinges and waved Victoria through. She brushed by me without acknowledging my prowess, tossed her bag onto her bed, lifted her right foot into the air and heaved off her shoe.

"Are you going to take a nap?" I asked.

"No, I'm bloody not." She reached for her other shoe. "I'm changing into something more comfortable. And then I'm coming with you. You might be the buffoon who got us into this mess, but I'll be damned if I'm going to stand idly by while you run around making it worse."

ELEVEN

Up on Floor 40, with Victoria dressed in jogging trousers, a sweater and training shoes, and with me gripping a wire coat hanger behind my back, we emerged from the service stairs and crept along the corridor toward Masters' hotel suite.

I'd acquired the coat hanger from Victoria's luggage. The hangers in the hotel closet were no good. They were wooden and fixed to the rail, and I needed something that could bend. I suppose I could have suggested using the under-wire from one of Victoria's bras but I somehow doubted she'd be likely to dignify that particular request.

I would have felt a lot more comfortable if Victoria had been walking alongside me, but she'd taken to following from behind on tiptoes, as if she was in rehearsals for the role of Burglar #2 in a light-hearted play. By the time we reached the door of Suite H, I wouldn't have been surprised to find that she was wearing a black eye-mask.

"Why don't you go ahead and check around the corner," I said.

"What do I do if I see someone coming?"

"You could tell me. That'd be dandy."

"But how do I tell you without making it obvious that I'm warning you not to break in?"

"Obvious doesn't matter. The warning is the key part. Go ahead. See if the coast is clear."

As Victoria tippytoed to the end of the corridor, I began to unwind the coat hanger and straighten it out as best I could without breaking it. Once I was satisfied with my handiwork, the wire formed a shape like a capital "L," only with a hook at the top.

"What's that?"

"Christ." I reached for my heart. Victoria was standing right next to me. "You almost gave me a stroke."

"Oops," she said. "But what have you done to my coat hanger?"

"I'm going to use it to open this door."

"Why not use one of your picks?"

"This is quicker."

"If you say so."

"I do." I peered over Victoria's shoulder. "I take it we're clear."

"I couldn't see anyone coming."

"Right-ho." I crouched down toward the base of the door and fed the hook of the coat hanger underneath.

"Shouldn't we knock first?"

"Ssshh."

"I'm just saying, in your books you always have Faulks knock on a door before he breaks in."

I took a breath. "We don't want to knock if Masters is inside. And keep your voice down, will you?"

I focused my attention on the hook, feeding it under the door with all the care and precision of a medic performing keyhole surgery. Of course, that would be a really cracking analogy, if only the door had a keyhole in the first place. But, as I've already mentioned, the hotel employed a card entry system, which was why I'd resorted to such a makeshift approach.

Using a coat hanger was damn frustrating. The idea was to hook the door handle from the inside, then tug down on the wire, thus turning the handle and opening the door. Problem was, the procedure was fiddly at the best of times, and it was only made harder with two of my fingers out of commission. Oh, and I had to try not to make too much noise for fear of alerting anyone

who happened to be inside the suite. Already, I was becoming annoyed, and that was making me reckless. The wire was scratching
around far more than I would have liked.

"You're making a bit of a racket," Victoria told me.

I scowled up at her from where I was lying with my back on
the floor.

"Just trying to help," she said.

I gritted my teeth and did my best to visualize where the hook
had ended up.

Victoria pressed her ear against the door, saying, "You're close."

"Higher or lower?"

"Higher, I think."

"There?"

"No, lower."

"There?"

"Lower still."

Christ, this was beginning to sound all too familiar.

"How about there?"

I heard a clink of metal and saw the door handle flicker. Holding my tongue between my teeth, I very steadily pulled down on
the wire. The handle turned, and turned and . . . the door popped
open just as the hook slipped free and scratched loudly down
the reverse of the door.

I pushed the door inward and rolled in out of the corridor.
Victoria followed me and closed the door behind us.

"Phew," she whispered.

"Indeed."

"It's dark in here."

"We'll come to that."

I set my trusty coat hanger down on the kitchen counter and
reached inside my pocket, removing a pair of plastic gloves. I held
the gloves out to Victoria and returned to my pocket for my doc-
tored gloves.

"Do I have to?" she asked.

"This is a crime scene, Vic."

"It's a hotel room."

"Just put them on."

"I don't know, Charlie. It makes me feel odd."

"And breaking in didn't?"

"*You* broke in."

"Oh, I see. Like that, is it?"

"I'm just saying."

"Put the damn gloves on."

Victoria held off for a moment longer, then sighed and slipped her fingers inside the sheer plastic. I followed suit. It took me a little more time than I might have liked, but once I was done, I flexed my healthy fingers before my eyes.

"Looks like Masters has been here already," I said.

"Really? How can you tell?"

I pointed toward the wall behind the door. "When I was here earlier, there was a key card in the plastic slot and the lights were on."

"Oh."

"No key card now."

"So I gathered. Do you have a torch?"

"I have a penlight. But I can do a lot better than that."

Stepping through the kitchen, I stumbled down the steps that led into the sunken lounge. I was halfway toward the large picture windows and the sodium glare beyond when I sensed that Victoria hadn't followed me.

"What are you waiting for?" I hissed.

"I'd rather stay here for now, if that's okay."

I grumbled to myself and marched on into the bedroom. The thick curtains hadn't been drawn but it was dim inside all the same, and the bathroom door was in darkness. In the movie soundtrack in my head, an ominous note sounded, as though warning me not to approach the door. Unlike the teen starlets of most horror movies, I didn't need the reminder. I was a long way from ecstatic to be in the vicinity of the bathroom again, and I'd be happy to leave it behind just as soon as I could.

With that thought at the very front of my mind, I threw back the closet doors and crouched down to the room safe. I withdrew my penlight from my jacket and, in the startling glare of the beam, I punched in the code I'd been so proud of—50-50—and the word OPEN scrolled across the electronic screen. Masters' wallet was just where I'd left it, and so was his key card. I stuffed his wallet inside my pocket and hurried back through the suite to slip the card into the receptacle on the wall, bathing the place in light.

"Wow, impressive," Victoria said.

"Thanks."

"I was talking about the suite." She shoved past me and approached the black leather couch, running her gloved hands over its surface. "This place is huge."

"I've seen bigger."

"What, in this hotel?"

I slapped my forehead with my palm. "Just how many rooms do you think I've broken into?"

Victoria moved across to the window and took in the distant mountain view. She shivered.

"Do you really think Josh has been back here?" she asked.

"Seems that way. If he came up here the moment he vanished, he would have had a head start. And if he was planning to go on the run, he might have wanted to grab some of his stuff. More importantly, he didn't know I'd taken the chips from the safe. It's a lot of money to leave behind."

She turned and scanned the room. "Have you noticed anything missing? It's so tidy in here. Unless it was very different earlier on, it doesn't look like he had too many personal effects."

"It doesn't look any different."

She gave me a dubious look. "There's not much to search."

"Still worth checking."

"And how do you suggest we go about it?"

"There's no particular technique, Vic. Just be orderly. We don't want the place to look like it's been ransacked."

"Gotcha. But how do I know what's important?"

"You'll just know."

She kicked at her heel and clenched her hands. "Can I search in here?"

"Sure."

"I'm just a bit uncomfortable about being near the bathroom."

"I'll handle it."

"And you don't think anyone will turn up?"

"Hope not."

"What do we do if somebody does?"

I tried not to sound too irritable as I said, "I wouldn't recommend going out through the window. We are forty floors up."

"I'm serious."

"Me too. It'd be one hell of a drop."

"Charlie."

"Just focus on the search," I told her. "If you start worrying about anything else, you'll freak yourself out."

"I'm already freaked out. I'm no good at this sort of thing."

"It's your first time, Vic. Cut yourself some slack. I was a complete wreck on my first break-in."

"I'm hardly planning on making a career out of it."

"Funny. I used to say the same thing myself."

I left her to gawp at that one, and duped myself into returning to the bedroom. The bathroom door was still closed and the closet doors and the safe were still open, just as I'd left them. Victoria was right—other than his neatly arranged clothes, Masters really didn't have many possessions. It made me wonder if he had a more permanent home elsewhere in the city, and whether his suite was simply a base between shows. It was certainly something to bear in mind.

I began with the closet, searching to the back of every drawer and beneath every T-shirt, sock and pair of underpants. I felt inside the pockets of the trousers and leather jackets hanging from the rail, but all I found was stale air. It was the same with the bedside cabinet nearest to me. The alarm clock, the spiral notepad and pen, the covered water glass and the paperback book hadn't moved in the slightest, and when I opened the drawer of the cabinet all I found was a red Gideon Bible. The only thing inside the Bible was the Scriptures.

I crawled across the bed and pulled open the drawer of the other bedside cabinet. The first thing I found was a small wooden box containing a man's antique wristwatch. The watch had a brown leather strap, gold-plated casing and a white analog face. The glass was worn and scratched, so that it was almost opaque in places, and the gold casing was discolored with age. The hands weren't moving. I wound the tiny mechanism and watched the second hand twitch into life. On balance, I doubted that it was worth the kind of money that could get the Fisher Twins off our backs, but it was certainly not to be sniffed at. I checked over my shoulder to be sure that Victoria wasn't watching, and then I slipped the watch on to my right wrist. It felt a good deal heavier than the cheap digital watch I wore on my left arm, though I believed I could get used to the sensation.

The drawer was also filled with scores of loose business cards. There were cards from television executives, agents and promotion scouts; entertainment lawyers, corporate attorneys and tax advisers; limo drivers, call girls and casino hosts. But if any of the cards were significant, I had no way of telling.

Beneath the cards I found a small velvet bag filled with sponge balls of the kind that magicians can make appear as if from nowhere. I also found a tube of Superglue, pinched in the middle, and a hobby craft set containing several very fine paintbrushes and a whole spectrum of miniature acrylic paint pots.

I got off the bed and hunted beneath the bed box. Nothing doing. I was just about to get up off my knees and check how Victoria was getting on when I heard the mattress springs compress and found that she'd sat down next to the cabinet with the Bible inside it.

"Any luck?" she asked.

"Not so far. You?"

She showed me her gloved hand and began to count off her findings on her fingers and thumb.

"One hotel stationery set and pen—nothing out of the ordinary. One hotel guest information folder—no markings. One answering machine—no messages. One fax machine and printer—

nada. Two decks of Fifty-Fifty casino cards—all cards present and correct. One deck of MGM Grand Casino cards—ditto."

"You counted all of the playing cards?"

"I was being thorough."

"No kidding. Go on."

She drew an audible breath. "The kitchen cupboards and drawers contain the usual crockery and cutlery. The fridge is stocked just like the mini-bar in our rooms and everything matches the contents card, except that he has six bottles of Mountain Dew and all of the bottle caps are missing."

"Aha," I said, and tossed the hobby craft set onto the bedcovers. "I think it's safe to assume that Ricks was right and Josh really did make that dummy chip-holder."

Victoria reached for the craft set. She opened the cardboard flap at one end and eased out the plastic tray containing the paints and brushes.

"There are a couple of pots missing," she told me.

"Purple and lilac, by any chance?"

"There's no purple or lilac here." She put the craft set back together again and resealed the box. "Did you find anything else?"

"Nothing of use."

"Terrific."

Victoria transferred her attention to the bedside cabinet and picked up the paperback book beside the water glass. Now that I gave the book my attention, I could see that it was a biography of Harry Houdini. The jacket featured a bold image of a young Houdini wearing a hospital straitjacket, suspended upside down from a high crane, with the upturned faces of a huge crowd focused upon him. His name blazed out from above his feet in a stylized yellow font, like an old vaudeville show poster. Victoria turned the book in her hands and read the flap copy.

"There is another room we could check," she said, trying to act casual.

I glanced toward the bathroom door and a shudder ran through me.

"I don't think that's a good idea."

"It didn't sound to me as though you spent very long in there."

"I guess I was a little distracted by the corpse doing breast-stroke in the Jacuzzi tub."

"There could be something in there, though. Imagine if she was a suicide. There might be a note."

"Unlikely."

"But possible." She turned to the front of the Houdini biography and fanned the first few pages.

"Take it," I told her.

"Excuse me?"

"The book. If you like it, you should take it."

Victoria set the book down onto the bedside cabinet. She raised her nose in the air, looking very prim all of a sudden. "No, thank you."

"But it's something you'd like to read?" I pressed. "It interests you?"

"Perhaps if I saw it in a bookshop."

"So take it."

"I'm not going to just take it, Charlie."

I propped my elbows on the bed and my chin on my fingers. "Why not?"

"Because."

"Because it's stealing? Look, it doesn't seem as if Josh will be returning for it in a hurry. And unless it happens to be overdue from the Nevada State Library, I'd say it's a win-win situation for you."

"It's not mine."

I frowned. "You do remember we accessed this room illegally?"

"For good reason."

"Listen, breaking in somewhere and not taking something, it's kind of pointless. And it's just a book, Vic. You could try selling it secondhand and you wouldn't get anything for it."

Victoria showed me a lot of eyeball. "Are you going into that bathroom?"

"I'd rather not."

"Because of the dead body?"

"Don't make out like it's a minor thing. Trust me, I've seen people who've been killed, and it's a long way from pleasant."

She smiled glumly. "You do have a rather unfortunate talent for stumbling across corpses."

"Tell me about it."

"In fact, I wouldn't be surprised if some of your Faulks novels have fewer killings in them than you've experienced in the last couple of years."

"Well, it's an interesting point. And something I'll give a good deal of thought to. Assuming we're still alive by this time tomorrow night."

Getting up from my knees, I moved around to Victoria's side of the bed, picked up the Houdini biography and scanned the flap copy for myself. Victoria looked from me, to the bathroom door, and back again.

"What if I go in there?" she asked.

"I'd advise against it."

"But would you let me?"

"Be my guest. Just don't expect me to watch."

After a moment's hesitation, Victoria removed a strand of hair from her eyes, rose to her feet and walked around to the bathroom door. She circled her head on her shoulders, cleared her throat, and reached for the handle. It seemed as though she was all set to go through with it when she lowered her hand.

"Shouldn't there be a smell?"

"You mean from the body?"

"Uh huh."

"I imagine it depends how long it's been there. I didn't notice one earlier, but maybe when you open the door . . ."

She swallowed. "I see."

"Sure you want to go through with it?"

She closed her eyes and squeezed her fists tight shut.

"Come on, Victoria," she said, in a quiet voice. "You can do this, girl."

I suppose I should have been mesmerized by her little pep talk, and to some extent I was, because it did make me wonder if she would do something similar before calling my editor to plead for a slightly less measly advance. But the truth was I'd long since learned to seize upon an opportunity when it presented itself, and so while her eyes were shut I stuffed the Houdini biography down under the waistband of my trousers. I just had it secured and happened to be jerking my hand away from my groin when Victoria's eyes snapped open. She gave me a somewhat perturbed look, then faced the door, pushed down on the handle and stepped briskly into the bathroom.

I covered my eyes with my hand, afraid of her reaction when she saw the dead woman for the first time.

"Oh God," she gasped.

I braced myself, wondering if she might faint and whether I'd be able to spring across the bed to catch her before her head struck the floor.

"Charlie." She gulped. "I really think you'd better see this."

"Nuh uh. I'm through looking at corpses."

"But that's exactly my point. The bath's empty, Charlie. There's nobody here."

TWELVE

Victoria was absolutely right. The bath was empty. No water.
No floating corpse. Not even a ring of bath scum or a wayward
hair caught up in the plughole.

I checked behind the bathroom door. The robe and the pink
leotard were no longer hung up on the floor. They weren't on the
hook behind the door, either. They'd vanished along with the
body.

I returned to the bath and stared down into it, looking, I imagine, altogether gormless. There was nothing to suggest that the
redhead had ever been there. Perhaps she never had. Perhaps all
those years of writing mystery novels had finally caught up with
me and I'd invented the entire episode. I'd been aware for some
time that my imagination could play tricks on me when I was
writing a book. When I was sleeping, say, characters would fill
my dreams and behave in ways that contradicted everything I'd
written. And sometimes it could feel as though I was in danger
of falling over a mental precipice into a world where I'd be inca-
pable of telling fact from fiction. Is that what had happened? No,
surely not. For one thing, I hadn't written a word in over a fort-
night, and the Faulks novel I'd been working on didn't feature a
single redhead. And I'd stuck my fingers in the cold bathwater.
All right, I hadn't actually touched the dead woman, but she'd
definitely been there. And now she no longer was.

"This is spooky," Victoria said, from over my shoulder.

"You're telling me."

"I don't like it."

"I'm not crazy about it myself."

"Josh must have taken her."

I nodded. "Maybe he worked out some way of disposing of the body. It's tough enough to run from casino debts, let alone a murder rap."

"You really think he killed her?"

"It's beginning to make complete sense." I sat down on the toilet and idly pinched my bottom lip. "I was having trouble understanding why he fled in the middle of his act if he was only worried about the chips he'd stolen. I mean, yes, it's a lot of money, and the Fisher Twins were bound to be pretty steamed up about it, but I bet he makes a small fortune from his act. I wouldn't be surprised if they pay him close to what he stole every month—maybe even every week. So they could have straightened things out. There's no way they would have wanted him to disappear on them like he did, because now they have a stage that's completely out of commission, plus a heap of rumors swirling around the hotel."

Victoria rested her head against the doorframe and crossed her legs at the ankle.

"Charlie, do you think the scam he pulled on the roulette table could have been a cover? What I mean is, if he could make people think he went on the run because of the chips he stole, they might never ask themselves what happened to his assistant."

I dropped my hands into my lap. "They'd probably just assume she ran with him."

"That's what I was thinking."

"But didn't Ricks say he pulled the same scam last night as well?"

"He did mention something along those lines."

"So the girl could have been in the bath for over a day," I said. "Which means he might not have even drowned her. It could be he just dumped her in the water to stop the smell getting too bad."

"That's disgusting."

"You're telling me."

Victoria folded her arms across her chest and contemplated the bath. "Although, I suppose the other possibility is that he planned the murder ahead of time. It could be he killed her today, but that he stole some chips last night to lay the groundwork for a smokescreen."

I reached for the toilet roll dispenser and tugged off a few strips of paper, scrunching them in my hand as I considered the theory, turning my thoughts to the chips I'd found in his room safe.

"You could be onto something. He's a magician, after all. His whole act is based on diverting people's attention from what he's up to."

Victoria peered at me. "Should we go to the Fisher Twins with this?"

I tossed the balled-up toilet paper into the wastepaper bin.

"With what? We don't have a body." I shook my head. "Listen, there might be some security camera footage of him carrying the girl away. He can't have hidden her here because we've been right through this suite and we haven't seen her. I'm guessing he might have used the service stairs to avoid the concierge, just like we did on the way up. But even if he's been caught on camera, there might be no way of telling from the footage that she's dead. And the twins have no reason to believe me."

Victoria pressed her lips together and made a humming noise. "And even if they did believe you, it places you at the scene of a murder."

"Yup. And I don't like that at all. If the redhead's body is ever found, it might be possible to prove that she was killed before we arrived in Vegas."

"But if she was killed not long before you broke in . . ."

"Then I could be in real trouble."

"Quite the predicament." She sighed. "So what's next?"

I was about to offer Victoria my considered response to her question, when we were interrupted by a noise I really didn't welcome—a fast knocking on the front door of the suite.

I froze, and gawped at Victoria, and she did much the same

thing to me. The atmosphere in the bathroom became charged all of a sudden and my scalp prickled, as though a fork of lightning was about to strike. We waited in silence for what was beginning to feel like an unbearable amount of time, and then the knock sounded again.

Victoria paled and shook her head at me. I didn't know what she was shaking her head for, but it didn't seem good. Meanwhile, I was thinking how dumb we'd been not to hang a *Do Not Disturb* sign on the outside of the door. At least that way, if our visitor was a maid aiming to carry out the turn-down service, she'd be deterred. But what kind of hotel offers a turn-down service at a quarter to eleven at night?

I didn't have long to pursue the thought before the knocking came again, much louder this time. It was accompanied by a male voice. The voice was high in tone, and kind of squeaky, almost as though our visitor had been sucking on helium.

"Josh? Josh—open up!" the voice piped. "We need to talk."

At long last, I sprang into action and jumped up from the toilet seat, grabbing Victoria by the hand and dragging her out through the bedroom.

"Josh? Caitlin?" The squeaky voice and the knocking came again. "Open up already."

"What do we do?" Victoria hissed.

"Wait here," I mouthed, and hurried to the door on my toes.

Very carefully, I set my eye to the peephole and peeped outside. But I couldn't see anything other than a fish-bowl view of the door to Suite G across the way.

Bang—bang—bang.

Somebody was definitely knocking, and the force of it damn near broke my nose. I didn't think it could be hotel staff, or else they'd be standing directly in front of the door and they'd be a lot more polite.

And right then a nasty thought occurred to me and I got a sick feeling in the pit of my stomach. How many movies had I seen over the years where pairs of crooks, or even cops, stand with their backs against a corridor wall, pistols drawn, waiting for a hapless homeowner to snap back a door latch?

The knocking came again, and I *still* couldn't see them. It seemed to me that my guess had to be right. Whoever was out there was flanking the door. The Hispanic security guards had done the same thing down in the basement, but I'd be truly astonished if the squeaky voice belonged to either of them. I was just debating what on earth I should do when I heard a second voice.

"Maybe I go find janitor." The voice was male and the speech deliberate, laced with an East European accent. "Maybe I give them some money."

"Good idea," the soprano replied. "Give 'em twenty bucks and tell 'em to spring the lock on this door."

That was all I needed to know. Our bashful guests were planning to get inside, come what may, and it wouldn't do for them to find us.

Backing away from the peephole, I fumbled in my jacket for my spectacles case, meanwhile hustling Victoria beyond the glass dining-table to the double doors that connected with the neighboring suite. Victoria groaned when she saw what I had in mind but I didn't have time to reassure her. I armed myself with one of my more reliable picks and a short-bladed screwdriver and then I crouched down and addressed the spring lock.

I guess it helped that I'd duped the same variety of lock on the communicating doors to Victoria's suite downstairs, but even I was surprised by my speed. I'd barely had time to hang my tongue out of the side of my mouth before I heard the muted tinkle of the internal pins lifting up and the snick of the bolt withdrawing.

I steadied my gloved hand and eased the door open a fraction. The room was in darkness. I reached inside my jacket for my penlight and shone the beam through the crack. I poked my head through after it and swept the torch quickly around—one pass, like a lighthouse. There was nobody to be seen. I edged the door fully open, gripped Victoria around the wrist and dragged her in behind me, closing the door softly after us.

The knocking sounded again. I scurried through the blackness toward the front door of the suite and pressed my ear to the wood.

"Come on, Josh," the squeaky voice whined. "You know you're going to have to talk to us. Why don't you just let us inside?"

I put my eye to the peephole but all I saw was more corridor. I cursed and shone the torch beam against the wall. There was no key card in the plastic receptacle. I mouthed a silent prayer of thanks, and then I turned and cast my torch into the darkness. The penlight revealed a mirror image of Masters' suite. We'd entered the room just behind the dining-table, and Victoria was standing over it with her palms flattened against the glass surface and her head bowed. Leaving her to her own devices, I raced past the black leather sofa and the flat-screen television to the bedroom.

I made sure there was no one sleeping in the bed, and since I didn't want to be accused of failing to learn from my mistakes, I checked the bathroom too. There was nobody inside it, alive or dead, but there were two wash bags beside the sink and several items of underwear, male and female, scattered on the floor amid some damp towels. The shower looked as if it had been used in the not too distant past, and the hairdryer was unhooked from its bracket and resting on the toilet cistern.

On my way out from the bedroom, I opened the closet and sorted through the clothes hanging from the rail until I found a hotel robe. Then I rushed back through the sitting room, the beam from my penlight slashing Victoria's face. She appeared stricken, rooted to the spot. I held myself back from approaching her and hurriedly undressed behind the breakfast bar. Once I was down to just my boxer shorts, I ripped away my plastic gloves and climbed into the robe. I was just knotting the tie cord and ruffling my hair when I heard more knocking coming from outside Masters' suite. It seemed like a good moment to stick my head out into the corridor and ask what all the fuss was about, so I yanked down on the door handle and did just that.

"What's all this fuss about?"

It wasn't until I'd delivered my line and added a yawn for good measure that I chanced a look at Masters' tenacious visitor.

At first, I didn't see him. I blinked, trying to adjust my vision to the light in the corridor. I glanced to my left and to my right, and then I gazed down and finally understood why I hadn't spotted him through the peephole. He hadn't been hiding with his back to the wall—he was no more than four feet tall.

I did a double-take—I couldn't help it—but he definitely wasn't resting on his knees. He was a little person, or vertically challenged, or however you care to say it. It was a hell of a surprise, let me tell you, but when he turned his neckless head and began to speak, the high pitch of his voice made a whole lot more sense.

"Hey, I'm sorry," he said, his larynx sounding constricted. "I'm just calling on my friend."

"Well, he obviously isn't there," I growled.

The little guy gazed up at me uncertainly, and for the first time in my life I felt like a giant among men. His face was sort of squished, and his complexion was ruddy. He had a very large and prominent nose (at least for a chap his size) that looked as if it had been broken and re-set badly in his youth, and his front teeth were gapped and crooked. His dark hair was thick and bristly, grown long over his stubby ears, and his eyebrows were creeping toward one another above the bridge of his nose. It was hard to gauge how old he was with any accuracy, but once I'd factored in the bright yellow sneakers, faded jeans and Death Metal T-shirt he had on, I would have put him somewhere in his mid-thirties.

I looked at my watch—the cheap digital one, not the antique I'd swiped from next door.

I said, "I saw a man leave that suite half an hour ago. I've just arrived from a transatlantic flight and I was trying to sleep before you started hammering on his door."

"You're sure it was Josh?"

I sighed, heavily, and spoke through my teeth. "I saw a gentleman leave that room. He was an American. He said goodnight to me. He was wearing a brown leather jacket."

"That sounds like Josh. Anyone with him? A girl with red hair, say?"

"Look, I'm sorry, but I'm tired and I need to get some sleep. Can I suggest you telephone him, or leave a message at the concierge desk—and that you stop banging on his damn door."

"Er, sure. I'll do that. Thanks."

I offered him a stern look, willing him to make his exit, but before I managed to send him on his way his companion came back around the corner. I suppose the good news was that I didn't feel like a giant any more. In fact, I tend to think that if Goldilocks had happened upon the three of us, she might have been so kind as to say that I was just right. Because just as the man alongside me could be said to be a little on the short side, so his companion could be said to be a trifle tall.

I can't tell you how high the guest corridors are in the Fifty-Fifty, but I can tell you that this guy's head was skimming the ceiling. If I'd been so bold as to lift his pint-sized buddy up onto my shoulders, I dare say the two of them could have held a conversation eye-to-eye. But it wasn't simply his considerable height that made the man memorable—it was also his physique. He was wearing sports clothes—a pair of huge white gym shoes, dark blue jogging pants and a pale blue vest top—and his biceps and triceps and pecs looked like an advertisement for anabolic steroids. He had the appearance of a basketball player crossed with a wrestler crossed with a male model, and if I really had been woken from a deep slumber to find him and his knee-high pal outside my hotel room, I probably would have thought that I was having a very strange dream indeed.

The man-mountain was carrying a key card in his meat-slab hand. He barely frowned when he saw me, displaying all the concern a bull might show a fly, and then he held the card out to the little guy as if he was handing a ticket stub to a child.

"Oh swell. Did Josh give you his card?" The little guy squealed the line insistently, in the most awkward of prompts. Even so, his friend didn't pick up on it in the most seamless fashion imaginable.

"Huh?"

"I said," added the little guy, motioning at me with a nod of his head, "did Josh give you his card so we could wait in his room."

"Oh. Yes. That is right," the man replied, in his awkward Euro-English. "Josh give me his card so we could wait in his room."

"Well, that's great." The little guy showed me just how many teeth were crammed inside his gums. "Say, thanks for your help. We'll just go ahead and wait inside."

"And you'll keep the noise down?"

"Sure thing." He waved a doll-like hand. "Don't even worry about it."

THIRTEEN

"Have they gone?" Victoria whispered.

"Sounds that way."

"They weren't inside for very long."

I separated my ear from the glass tumbler I'd been holding against the communicating doors to Masters' suite and checked my digital watch with a pulse of torchlight.

"Just under five minutes."

"What do you think they were up to?"

"Mischief, I imagine. But it wouldn't hurt to check."

Setting the glass down, I took my pick and my screwdriver from my spectacles case. Turning the lock for a second time was simple, and I didn't bother asking Victoria to shine the penlight over my shoulder. I worked by touch alone, and I doubt I'd have been any faster with a key.

The lights were still on in Masters' suite and his key card was still in the receptacle by the door, but it hadn't seemed to tweak the curiosity of the little man and the gym giant. So far as I could tell, they hadn't been concerned by the unwound coat hanger I'd left on the kitchen counter, either. Who knows, maybe the little man hadn't been tall enough to spot it, and perhaps his gym buddy had been too distracted by the wonders of a room that looked to have been built to his exact proportions. Either way, I was grateful that they hadn't stayed for too long, and after snatching up the coat hanger, I conducted a quick search.

So far as I could tell, only one thing had altered. A note had been left on the desk over by the picture windows. The message had been written in blue ink on a sheet of hotel stationery and it had been printed in a rushed, slanted hand.

CALL MAURICE, OK? HE'S KIND OF PISSED.

I knew just how Maurice felt, but sadly, I had no idea who he was. I guessed Josh did though, because no contact details had been added to the note.

I asked myself which one of the men had left the message, and I had an inkling it was the little guy. He'd taken the lead role out in the corridor, so it made sense that he would have penned the message. I also thought the use of capital letters could be significant—perhaps he wrote that way to make up for his height.

Since I didn't have my gloves on any longer, I used the tie-cord of the robe I was wearing to carry the note across to Victoria. She was standing on the threshold of the rooms, one foot in each suite, as though she was unsure which space she felt more uncomfortable in. She scanned the note, and shrugged and frowned in much the same way as I had, and then I returned the note to the desk and nudged Victoria back into the darkened suite. I gently closed the communicating door and allowed the snap lock to engage. The blackness seemed complete all of a sudden.

"So who's Maurice?" Victoria asked, as I fumbled for her hand and pressed the coat hanger into it.

"No idea."

"One of the twins, maybe?"

"I doubt it. Masters already knows they're looking for him, and why would anyone mention just one of them in a note?"

"Neither one of them looked like a Maurice to me."

"They're both identical, Vic."

Through the darkness, I heard the distinct note of a raspberry.

I felt my way over to the kitchen area to put on my clothes and had ditched the robe and was zipping the fly on my trousers before Victoria spoke again.

"Charlie, was one of those men really a . . . you know?"

"Short individual? Why would I make something like that up?"

"You wouldn't. It's just a bit surprising."

I buttoned my shirt and put on my jacket, then reached for my socks and began to hop around as I pulled them on.

"It's reassuring in a way," I told her. "It's good to know that crooks come in all shapes and sizes."

"You think they were crooks?"

"They didn't exactly have permission to be next door."

"Maybe they really are Josh's friends."

"Yeah, his crook friends."

I ducked behind the breakfast bar to tie my shoes. While I was crouched there, I collected the Houdini biography from the floor and slipped it back down into my trousers. I straightened and flattened my hair, then gathered together my surgical gloves and blew air into them.

"Are you putting your gloves back on?"

"Yup."

"Can I ask why?"

"Because we're not done yet."

"But I thought we were just hiding in here?"

"We were. But you know what they say about gift horses."

"Leave them alone and get away while you still can?"

I snapped the plastic of my left glove against my palm. "Relax. This won't take long."

"It's funny. You wouldn't believe how many times a man has said those words to me after slipping a pair of surgical gloves on."

I clicked on my penlight and shone the beam at Victoria's face. The room was blue-black around her.

"Humor in the face of danger? If I didn't know better, I'd think you were a natural at all this."

Victoria covered her eyes with her spread fingers. "A momentary slip. Can you hurry up?"

"Funny," I said. "Women very rarely say those words to me."

I breezed past Victoria toward the bedroom and returned the robe to the closet, then started to feel my way through the clothes that were hanging from the rail, checking the pockets. I didn't find anything useful, so I dropped to my knees and parted a few skirts until I located the room safe. I shone my penlight on the keypad and summoned some inspiration. I began with 111, then 1111, then 999 . . .

"Why bother?" Victoria asked, from just over my shoulder.

"We need the money."

"Not if we find Josh."

"Finding him isn't going to be easy. It looks like he's running from a murder. We don't know where he went. We don't know the city."

"But we have this Maurice clue. We have this . . . little fellow, and his muscular friend."

I softened my tone. "I really think we need to focus on our second option, Vic. At least for a little while."

"But you'll never be able to steal the kind of money we need."

"Maybe not directly."

The safe wasn't opening. The codes I was punching in were having no effect whatsoever. I aimed the torch beam at the credit-card reader beside the keypad and growled to myself.

"Can't you pick it?"

"If I had some of the kit I keep in my bag downstairs, then yes. But not with the gear I have on me."

I reached out a finger and began to punch in some new codes. 911, 1234, 9876 . . .

"Charlie, what did you mean when you said you might not be able to steal the money we need directly?"

"Oh," I replied, shooting for carefree. "I figure I can at least steal a good stake."

"A stake? For what?"

2222, 3333, 4444 . . .

"Oh no," Victoria said, cracking me on the back of the head. "That's a terrible idea."

"You haven't let me explain."

"I don't need to. You think you can win the money. At poker."

Her voice was laced with skepticism. I didn't like the way it sounded.

"I'm better than you think. Honestly."

"You lost a fortune earlier tonight."

"I made an error of judgment. I know what to do differently now."

"Too right. Don't sit down in the first place."

I rocked back on my heels and rested on my buttocks, then wrapped my arms around my knees and hugged them to my chest. There was a question I'd been thinking about posing, and now seemed as bad a time as any other.

"How much money do you have in your bank account?"

Victoria cracked me on the back of the head again. "I can't believe you're asking me that."

"I'll pay you back, you know."

Victoria paced to the far side of the room. I heard her flick the finger of one hand into her gloved palm. Maybe she was picturing my forehead where her palm happened to be.

"It's nowhere near enough. And I can't get at it anyway. It's Saturday night, Charlie. Sunday tomorrow."

"You can pull something out though, can't you?"

"The maximum I can withdraw is two hundred and fifty pounds a day."

"Close to four hundred and sixty dollars. What about credit cards? I don't have any."

It might have been dark, but I had a fair idea of the expression on Victoria's face, and was glad that I couldn't see it.

"I have one," she said, in a terse voice. "But my credit limit isn't as big as you might like."

"But it's a start, right?"

"A pretty measly start. And set against the money we'd need? Frankly, it's ludicrous."

"Which is why I was trying to get inside this safe. Plus some others. If I can steal a big enough stake, I could maybe get us somewhere."

Victoria glanced toward the illuminated display on the bedside clock. "In twenty-two and a half hours?"

"Hey, if you have any better suggestions, I'm willing to listen."

We looked at one another in the dark and I felt the room grow even blacker around Victoria. Eventually, she crossed her arms and let go of a sharp breath.

"Blackjack," she said, as though she was tossing the idea carelessly aside.

"Sorry?"

"Statistically, you have a better chance of winning. The house edge is reduced."

"But if I can find a no-limit poker game . . ."

"You could lose all your money again."

I hummed, and for good measure, I hawed. "To tell you the truth, Vic, I'm not all that great at blackjack."

I waited for her to tell me the same could be said of my poker, but instead she dropped onto the bed alongside me and stared at her hands in her lap. She didn't say anything for a long moment, and I punched another code into the keypad. Same result. I was beginning to think it was time to check the suitcases and bedside drawers.

"Here's what we'll do," she said finally. "*I'll* play blackjack. I'll start with our stake money and see how things go for the first few hours. And meanwhile, you can do what you do best."

"This is no time for me to hammer out a quick novel."

"Idiot." I received another crack on the head. "We'll go to a different casino. I can't imagine the Fisher Twins will let us play here. And while I play, you can . . . you know."

"Steal things?"

"If you want to be crass about it."

I turned and reached for Victoria's curled fingers. There was no response, almost as though she hadn't fully engaged with what she was suggesting. As though she'd switched off.

"Are you okay with this? The gambling and the stealing?"

Victoria didn't speak. I was about to ask what had come over her when she slid off the bed onto her knees and extended a finger toward the keypad. She punched in four digits, and a moment later, the safe whirred and clunked and the word OPEN appeared.

"Fifty-fifty," she said, as the door sprang back. "Pretty good, eh?"

I groaned and gave myself an imaginary crack on the head for being such a dunce. Then I shone my penlight inside the safe. The contents weren't anything to write a love song about. I found an MP3 player, a digital camera, a gold necklace and a curled bundle of dollar notes. I reached for the notes and counted them off. One hundred and ninety dollars. I passed them to Victoria, who juggled them like a hot coal, and then I rested a finger against my chin and considered my next move.

The electrical equipment and the necklace were valuable, sure, but I didn't have the time to track down a likely pawnbroker or a dive bar where I might sell them on. We needed cash or casino chips, and we needed them fast. In the hour it might take me to shift the valuables, I could break into another two hotel rooms, with the chance of finding just what we were after.

With my mind made up, I closed the door to the safe and re-entered the code so that everything (aside from the money) was locked away, and then I took a quick peek around the rest of the bedroom and the bathroom before telling Victoria that we were done.

"We can leave?"

"Absolutely. In fact, I'd positively recommend it."

"Well, that's a relief."

I smoothed the bedcovers where Victoria had been perched, and then I straightened the clothes in the closet and shut the closet doors. I shone my penlight around the room to make sure we hadn't left anything behind, and then I shone the light in Victoria's face.

"I do wish you'd stop doing that," she said, squinting.

"Where's the coat hanger?"

"Oh. I might have left it in the other room."

She was right about that. I found the coat hanger on the glass dining-table. I eased it up inside the sleeve of my jacket, and then I led Victoria to the front door and put my eye to the peephole. Assuming my diminutive friend wasn't waiting on the other side, all looked to be clear, so I hauled back the door and waved Victoria through.

We were making our way down the service stairs before I paused between levels, reached inside my trousers and removed an item that made Victoria's eyes boggle.

"For you," I said, handing her the Houdini biography.

"Oh Charlie, I really wish you hadn't."

"Well, I had." I shrugged. "And unless you want to put it back, it's yours now."

"And when exactly am I supposed to find the time to read this?"

"When we're out of this mess. Or maybe before. Houdini was the king of escaping sticky situations, right? Perhaps you'll pick up a few tips."

FOURTEEN

We returned to our rooms, and while I set about changing into some unremarkable black trousers, ditching my jacket and arming myself with a few choice pieces of equipment, Victoria slipped into something a little less comfortable.

"Tra la!"

I glanced up from my holdall to find her performing a dinky curtsey in the doorway between our suites. Gone were the loose-fitting clothes that she'd selected as burglar-chic, replaced by a midnight-blue cocktail dress, a matching clutch purse and a pair of high heels. She also appeared to have acquired a plunging neckline and a nicely proportioned pair of legs, though I refrained from saying as much.

"How do I look?" She clasped her hands together, lowered her eyelids and worked an expression that beat the hell out of bashful.

"You look fine."

"Just fine?"

I stepped into a pair of polished black shoes and ducked down to tie my laces, hiding my face. "What did you expect me to say?"

"Oh, never mind." She slapped her hands against her thighs. "So, are you going to show me the Strip?"

The Strip hit me like a blow to the face. The night air was warm, spiked with engine fumes and the odor of suncream on burned skin. It was late already, just gone midnight, but the sidewalks were awash with light—a mixture of garish neon, colored marquee bulbs, flashing video screens, car headlamps and traffic signals. I swayed at the ankles, dizzied by the unexpected heat and the glare. Terrific, I thought. As if my body clock wasn't messed up enough with jetlag, now I was adding perpetual twilight to the mix.

Vehicle traffic on the multi-lane Strip was constant. High-end sports cars, bling SUVs, stretch limos and blacked-out Hummers competed for tarmac and attention, their paintwork glimmering like liquid beneath the lights. Crammed Deuce buses groped for the curb outside the hotel, and low-slung taxis weaved between lanes. A flat-bed truck crawled along, towing a double-height advertising hoarding that featured a bikini-clad goddess and a slogan for some variety of strip club. I tried not to gawp, but I didn't try all that hard.

"Look." I pointed out the shapely beauty with the words *Girls, Girls, Girls!* scrawled above her raised derrière. "We have twenty-two hours left. You want to catch a show?"

"Pig," Victoria shouted, above the noise. "Don't these people know what time it is?"

"Look on the bright side. At least they're not in their hotel rooms."

Just as I finished speaking, we were jostled by a group of college girls drinking alcoholic slushies from novelty glasses shaped like the Statue of Liberty. The girls were pursued by a line of frat boys in pressed khakis, smelling of cologne, with plastic beer kegs strapped to their chests. They barged between us, and I stumbled into a suit and tie conventioneer slurring cellphone greetings to his wife, then apologized and stepped aside just as an old lady in a motorized wheelchair very nearly amputated my toes.

"Come on." I reached out and grabbed Victoria's hand. "Let's get moving."

I led her south toward the toxic-pink glow of the Flamingo Casino Hotel, forcing our way through revellers and around palm trees and concession stands and yellow fire hydrants, darting beneath the upraised arms of drunken co-eds and skirting the crowds of people waiting for the pedestrian lights to change so that they could experience the pleasures of Caesars Palace. In the shadows, dusty men and women wearing colored bibs riffled flyers and pressed cards offering call girl services into unsuspecting hands. The spent cards littered the sidewalk like sordid confetti.

We passed over a cross street on a skybridge and were almost parallel with the elegant façade of the Bellagio, nearing the illuminated Eiffel Tower outside Paris-Las Vegas, when I dragged Victoria up the curving pavement toward the entrance of Space Station One.

We'd just missed the final performance of the casino's big low-roller draw—a simulation of a space-shuttle launch. The shuttle was juddering back down a crane-like structure that extended way up into the night sky, and dry ice billowed out from the fiery hole in the ground from which it had emerged. Based on the disgruntled mumblings of the few onlookers, I wasn't altogether sorry we'd missed the spectacle. And judging from the crowds of revellers across the street, singing along to Elvis Presley's "Viva Las Vegas," it certainly wasn't as popular as the Bellagio fountains.

The main entrance to Space Station One was a hangar-like structure that protruded outward in a glossy white arc, like the front end of the Starship *Enterprise*. Colored laser beams trawled the perforated metal walkway in front of the doors, and dry ice snaked around our ankles. Oversized robots that already looked a decade behind the times moved their arms and heads in a jerky fashion, while casino staff in tired alien outfits and latex masks posed for photographs with middle-aged housewives and Japanese pre-teens.

The revolving casino doors twirled around to a sound effect straight out of *Doctor Who*, and one of the robots offered us a computerized greeting in a voice I recognized from my old ZX Spectrum.

"Welcome to Space Station One, earthlings."

I wondered if it said the same thing on the way back out.

The interior was like nothing I'd ever seen, and yet at the same time it was eerily familiar. It was as though every sci-fi movie that had ever been made had been cut up, swallowed down and spewed out onto the space before us. Key characters, scenes and props were everywhere, ranging from *Star Wars* through to *Alien*, *E.T.* to *Buck Rogers*, *Blade Runner* to *Independence Day*. Most curious of all was how many guests were walking around in costume. The croupiers and pit bosses were all dressed in white, NASA-style jumpsuits, but among the everyday folk at their tables I could see several Flash Gordons, numerous Darth Vaders, two Spocks, a handful of Princess Leias and at least one Chewbacca.

"Now I know what hell looks like," Victoria grumbled.

"Bet you're glad you got dressed up."

"To tell you the truth, I feel a little under-dressed. What on earth possessed you to bring us here?"

"The geek quota."

"Excuse me?"

"It's a well-known fact that sci-fi fans are nocturnal. So I figured if we came here, I'd have a better chance of finding empty hotel rooms."

"Not too empty, I hope." Victoria scanned the tables in front of us. "It's hardly the classiest venue. Do you think you'll find much cash?"

"Hope so. But hey, look at it this way—at least our stake money won't be sneered at."

I directed Victoria toward an ATM that was positioned alongside a bank of *Battlestar Galactica* slot machines. We withdrew as much cash as we possibly could, and after adding a little extra that Victoria had been carrying in her purse and the bundle of notes I'd taken from the room safe in the Fifty-Fifty, we approached a nearby blackjack table.

Victoria took a seat on a raised metal stool beside a pair of Stormtroopers. The croupier was a young guy, mid-twenties at most, with a blond crew cut and a glint in his eye that went along with the name on his staff badge. *Randy*.

"Welcome to Deep Space, ma'am. Table minimum is twenty-five Earth bucks."

Victoria laid three hundred dollars on the plush gray felt. While she waited to receive her chips, she popped the clasps on her handbag and reached inside. I glimpsed the cover of the Houdini biography, which made me smile, and then something metal caught the light. Victoria pulled out a signet ring made from polished silver and slipped it onto her finger.

"This belonged to my father," she said, to her new friends around the table. "A lucky charm."

The Stormtrooper nearest to Victoria raised his bottled beer at the news. His beer had a drinking straw poking out of it.

"Sure could use some luck tonight," he said, and lowered his masked face toward the straw.

"Amen," his friend added, and slapped his gloved fingers against his buddy's armor plating.

"Well, let's see what I can do," Victoria told them.

As it happened, she couldn't do all that much. She drew a five and a seven on her first hand, while Randy had a Jack of Spades face up. Victoria hit, playing the odds, but she caught a ten and bust out. Randy turned over his hole card. The Queen of Diamonds. The Stormtroopers lost too.

"You might want to take the ring off," I advised Victoria. "Maybe your dad's take on gambling is stopping it from working."

Victoria swiveled on her stool and hoicked her eyebrows toward the aluminum foil mock-up of Apollo 11 suspended above our heads. "Don't you have something to take care of?"

"Just offering a little moral support."

"I think I can cope without it."

I leaned toward her ear. "Well, be careful. I'm beginning to suspect that your two friends here work for the dark side of the Force."

Victoria introduced me to the back of her head and pushed another twenty-five-dollar chip into the betting circle on the gray felt. The Stormtroopers followed suit. I only hoped they weren't gambling on duty—I'd heard the Galactic Empire took a dim view of such behavior.

The casino floor was every bit as confusing as I'd come to expect, though it was quieter than the Fifty-Fifty and the tables were more spaced out (if you'll excuse the pun). Sure, the aliens and astronauts milling around made the entire place seem utterly surreal, but at least the information signs were in American English rather than Klingon. One of them even told me where the food hall was located, and after following a path that seemed to take me via every conceivable gaming-table and gambling machine in the known universe (and beyond), I eventually found myself on a downward escalator that led me to the Officers' Mess.

It didn't look like the type of canteen you might find on a spaceship. In point of fact, it was just like every other food hall on the Strip, offering the usual pizza and pasta, Chinese food, hamburgers and fries, and coffees and pastries. I didn't mind. Truth was, I was simply hoping to find a route into the service corridors that might eventually lead me to the main hotel kitchens, and after locating a likely door to the side of the pizza outlet, I'm pleased to report that I found just that.

FIFTEEN

I had on a dark red, collarless tunic with polished brass buttons and a plastic name badge. The badge told me that the tunic belonged to a gentleman by the name of *Gerry*, who'd been considerate enough to leave it on a hook in a staff cloakroom not too far from the hotel kitchen. Fortunately for me, it didn't seem as though Gerry was particularly well-known, because when I stepped inside the kitchen and tried my best to look as though I knew exactly where I was going and precisely what I was doing, nobody stopped me to ask why the hell I was wearing Gerry's uniform.

Nobody asked me where I was taking the room service trolley I'd acquired, either. The trolley was draped with a white linen cloth and it was stocked with a coffee pot, a wine cooler with a bottle of white wine inside it, a carafe of iced water and the customary crockery, cutlery and napkins. Underneath the table was a small warming oven where the hot meals were to be found.

I wheeled the trolley into a service elevator, dragged the wire cage across and pressed the button for Floor 8. There was a mirror inside the elevator and I took a moment to straighten my tunic and clear a spot of dirt from my black trousers. Ask any con man and he'll tell you how effective the right costume can be. Go for something like a security guard's outfit, and you have instant authority. Opt for a janitor's get-up, and you can go almost anyplace you please. And while Gerry's tunic was a couple of sizes too big and a little loose around the hips, it certainly helped to create the illusion that I belonged.

As an added bonus, I'd found a pair of white cotton gloves in the pockets of the tunic. The gloves would be just as effective as my plastic disposables, and since they complemented the uniform, they'd be an awful lot less conspicuous. So as the elevator climbed, I used one of the serrated table knives to saw away fingers three and four on the right-hand glove, and then I slipped the little beauties on.

At Floor 8, the elevator pinged, the doors parted and I wheeled the trolley out into the guest corridors, searching for a likely suite. I'd selected the eighth floor for good reason. My theory was that the lowest floors contained the most basic rooms and the guests with the least disposable income. By going just a little higher, I figured I'd improve my chances of finding cash without running the risks associated with a concierge desk, or having to contend with the class of wealthier guest who might be inclined to deposit their valuables in the hotel's main safe storage facility.

Obviously, any door that had a *Privacy Please* sign hanging from it was one to avoid. There were quite a few doors featuring privacy signs, as it happened, not to mention one or two with dirty food trolleys outside, and it took me a good few minutes to select a possible candidate. Suite 844 seemed to fit my criteria, and so I rested my trolley against the wall, straightened my shoulders and knocked on the door. No answer. I checked the corridor around me, and once I was sure the coast was clear, I reached inside the sleeve of Gerry's tunic and removed my coat hanger.

Now, either my technique was improving or the door handles inside Space Station One were unusually large, because I had the thing hooked in close to no time at all, and then I yanked the wire down, poked the door open and scrambled inside.

And a few minutes later I scrambled back out.

Turned out there was a flaw in my plan. True, there was nobody inside the room, but there was nobody checked into it either. Just my luck. I'd eaten into something like forty minutes already, and I'd drawn a complete blank. Worse still, I had no way of improving my odds. All I could do was try elsewhere until I found a suite that happened to be empty of people but not of their possessions. And I had to hurry up about it, too.

I hauled the trolley on down the corridor, passing two men in lounge suits and a woman in a bulging, XL *Star Trek* uniform. I kept going until I was out of earshot of anyone who might already have heard my routine and within sight of another possible target.

Suite 858.

Ah, I have such fond memories of the place. Not only did my coat hanger key work even quicker than before, but the first thing I spied upon wheeling my trolley inside was an open suitcase on the nearest of the twin beds.

I closed the door to the corridor behind me and immediately swung the beam from my penlight around the darkened bathroom and the rest of the suite. Once I was sure that I was alone, I gripped my penlight in my teeth, cracked the knuckles on my left hand and approached the suitcase.

The suitcase was filled with women's clothes. There were another two suitcases down on the floor and the same was true of them. If I had a shoe fetish, there would have been plenty to excite me, and if I'd had the desire to dress in women's underwear, I could have quite readily satisfied the urge. But so far as money or casino chips or gold bullion were concerned, there wasn't anything to get giddy about.

There was, however, still the room safe to consider, and it would have been remiss of me not to seek it out. A built-in closet with louvred doors was positioned alongside the first of the beds, and I slid the left-hand door open and shone my penlight over a clothes rail, a hotel laundry bag, an ironing board and a fold-out suitcase stand. I tried the right-hand side. More empty hanging rail. Oh, and the safe. It was on a shelf above the rail, at around eye-level.

This particular safe didn't have a credit-card reader but it did have a numbered keypad. The exterior had been fashioned from a cream, hardwearing plastic, with a sculpted handle built in, and it had one feature that especially pleased me—a small enamel badge bearing the manufacturer's name. The lozenge-shaped badge was held in place by two screws, and I had no trouble removing them with one of my screwdrivers while I held my penlight between my teeth.

Behind the badge was a modest hole. The hole in question functions as a back-up, of sorts, because it allows a qualified locksmith to open the safe without the code. Mind you, it also permits a trained monkey to do much the same thing.

The hole, you see, grants access to an electric motor that drives the components that do the physical locking and unlocking. And clearly, if you can operate the motor quite independently of any code, why, then Robert's your mother's brother, and you have an easy way in.

Now, you might imagine that independently driving the motor requires some pretty complicated kit. And you'd be wrong. It takes a paperclip, a 9-volt battery and two short lengths of electrical wire.

Naturally, I always carry a paperclip—it's a dim thief indeed who doesn't arm himself with the most universal picking tool known to man. But my spectacles case can only carry so many items, and until I'd returned to my room earlier at the Fifty-Fifty, it hadn't been stocked with the 9-volt battery and the electrical wire. Now that it was, I gleefully removed the ingredients for my classic safe-cracking recipe and set to work.

First, I unbent the paperclip and poked one end inside the hole. I jiggled it toward the reverse of the keypad, where the motor wiring was located, until it wouldn't budge any farther, then I attached one strand of electrical wire to the negative terminal on the battery and another strand to the positive terminal. I connected both ends to the paperclip, running a charge through to the motor wiring on the safe. And you know what? A wonderful

four-letter word flashed up on the digital display above the keypad, the motor buzzed and the door popped open.

I stood on tiptoes and flashed my penlight inside. There's not
much you can fit inside a hotel safe and it certainly wasn't stuffed
with casino chips. Thankfully, there was some cash, and I pulled
it out and counted it. Four hundred and twenty dollars. Given
my predicament, it wasn't to be sniffed at, so I gratefully slipped
the bundle into my pocket. Alongside the notes was a bottle of
perfume, which I suppose *was* to be sniffed at, though I didn't
bother to sample the odor for fear it might make me sneeze. Next
to the perfume were two passports. I reached for them and had a
quick peek. It was sheer curiosity that made me look, though it
never hurts to check these things.

It hurt on this occasion. The passports belonged to two British women from Bolton. They'd been born within a year of one
another, and their dates of birth put them somewhere in their
early forties. And while passport photos are terrible things and
very rarely flattering, these photos didn't make the women appear
altogether wealthy.

I felt a pang of guilt. How often, I asked myself, did the
women get to take a holiday like the one they were currently
enjoying, and would the robbery I was committing ruin it for
them?

Now I really wished I hadn't looked at their passports. Stealing from my compatriots was one thing, but being able to picture the expression on their faces when they opened their safe
was quite another. I tightened my fingers around the cash in my
pocket, unsure what to do. Ordinarily, I liked to think of myself
as a gentleman thief, a pretty classy kind of crook. But what I
was involved in right now was petty theft, and they call it petty
for a reason.

Then again, I wasn't sure I could afford to be all that decent.
Victoria needed stake money if we were to have even the slight-
est chance of raising the cash the Fisher Twins were demanding.
And anyway, I told myself, the women were bound to have

travel insurance. Hell, they might even finesse their claim and compensate themselves for any money they'd lost at the casino tables.

Before I could tussle with the rights and very wrongs of my actions any longer, I left the money in my pocket and put the passports back where I'd found them. Then I reached up and grabbed the final item from the very back of the safe. A packet of cigarettes.

Boy, this was going to be harder than I'd thought. I checked the time on my watch. Then I checked the time on Josh Masters' watch. They both agreed. It was three days, six hours and thirty-four minutes since my last cigarette.

For some reason, the exact merits of which still escape me, on my final day in Paris, I'd had the very dumb idea of kicking my smoking habit. And during a haze of early optimism, I'd had the even dumber idea of mentioning it to Victoria. Unsurprisingly, Victoria had made me promise to follow through, and while I'd slipped a number of times since, if there was one good thing to say about the peril I was facing in Las Vegas (and believe me, there really was only *one* good thing), it was that it had at least distracted me from my cravings. I guess that should come as no surprise. Finding a dead woman in the middle of a break-in, and then having your life threatened unless you can somehow pull together an inordinate sum of cash in just over twenty-four hours, tends to focus the mind somewhat. But now cigarettes were in front of me again. And I wanted one. Badly.

One lousy cigarette. Was that really so much to ask? It might calm my nerves, make me feel more alert. And that had to be a good thing. Right?

I got as far as locating an ashtray on the television cabinet before I finally got a hold of myself. Yes, it was a smoking room, but if the two women returned soon after I'd left, then in all likelihood they'd smell the fresh smoke. If they had any sense, they'd check their safe and they'd find that their money had gone. And then they'd report the theft, and my night of larceny would need to be cut very short indeed. I'd have to whisk Victoria off to a new hotel, and find a new way to access the guest rooms, and all the while it would be getting later and more people would be going to bed. And, well, those were enough reasons for me to show a little willpower and hold off from lighting up in the middle of a damn heist. So I did, although I have to confess that I also pocketed a free box of smokes.

Re-locking the safe was easy enough. I simply closed the door and ran another charge through the paper clip until the word OPEN flashed up. Open? Well yes, that was an odd quirk of the technique, but the safe was locked solid. And even better, the code hadn't been altered in the slightest. So whenever the women decided to check on their belongings, the same code they'd used to lock the safe would be fully capable of opening it again. Admittedly, once they discovered that their cash had gone walkabout, it might not strike them as the greatest consolation, but hey, at least it was something.

I slid the closet door across and made sure that I'd put the suitcases back where I'd found them, and then I dragged my trolley out into the corridor. The corridor was empty again, and after the darkness of the hotel room, it seemed startlingly bright.

Out of curiosity, I lifted the tablecloth on the trolley and opened up the warming oven I'd been wheeling around. There were two plates inside, both covered with metal warmers. I used my gloved fingers to take a peek at what was on offer. Meatloaf and mashed potatoes, or spaghetti bolognese. I prodded the spaghetti with my finger. I was beginning to feel a little hungry, but I thought it would stay warm for a little while yet.

Up ahead, another door seemed to be calling to me, and I pushed the trolley close before applying the brake and knocking confidently. When nobody responded, I slid my coat hanger out from where I'd hidden it beneath the tablecloth and dropped to my knees. I was just about to feed the coat hanger under the door when all of a sudden the damn thing swung open and I almost rolled forward into the room.

Ten hairy toes confronted me. I looked up and discovered

that the toes belonged to an overweight type in Daffy Duck boxer shorts and a wife-beater vest. I whipped the coat hanger behind my back and scrambled to my feet.

"Whaddaya want?" he asked.

The man was chewing on a chicken drumstick, with a bucket of wings tucked under his arm. Grease shimmered around his lips, and his cheeks and forehead were flushed. Tufts of dark chest hair poked out from around his vest, and his belly protruded from below the hem, weighed down like a balloon (a pink, hairy balloon) filled with motor oil.

"R-r-room service?" I stammered, and nodded toward the trolley.

The man dropped his drumstick into his bucket and wiped his mouth with the back of his hand. He jabbed a slick finger toward my back.

"What gives with the wire?"

"Just some litter I found." I shrugged. "Don't want anyone tripping."

He studied me with glassy eyes.

"You know, I'm pretty sure I have the wrong room." I gazed beyond him toward the number on his door.

"What do you got on the table?"

"Er, it's meatloaf and pasta with meat sauce. But I'm sure this is the wrong room."

The man looked toward the trolley, then back at me. He licked his lips.

"Nah. That's us, all right."

My eyes fairly bugged out of my head. "Um, are you sure, sir?"

"Sure I'm sure. Bring it in."

He backed up and held his door open with a stubbed toe. I peered inside at the mess of clothes and bedcovers on the floor. The widescreen television on the facing wall was screening a NASCAR motor race.

"What are you waiting for? You want it to get cold?"

He didn't know the half of it, and I didn't feel as though I had any alternative. I let off the brake and wheeled the trolley into his room, and a few minutes later I shuffled back out with a dud receipt and a dollar tip for my trouble. The guy had just swiped my cover, not to mention my evening meal, and I had to ask myself: could things get any worse?

SIXTEEN

Things were certainly about to get worse for the two women from Bolton. Now that my trolley was gone, I had to find a new excuse to be knocking on doors, and their suitcases struck me as the neatest solution. Letting myself back into their room, I gathered up the two cases from the floor and emptied their contents into the closet. Then I tossed my coat hanger inside one of the cases and made good my escape.

My escape was mighty timely. As I turned the corner at the end of the corridor, I walked into a haze of perfume, hair spray and coarse northern language. It seemed the women's passport images hadn't been as unkind as I might have believed, at least not when they were steaming drunk and leaning heavily on one another for balance.

Luckily for me, there was nothing the least bit noteworthy about their suitcases. Looking at the women now, I was surprised that they hadn't favored bright pink plastic or fake Burberry prints. Not that I was complaining. Their drunkenness and my uniform seemed to combine to render me invisible, and when they lurched right, I swerved left and passed without comment.

I headed straight for the service elevator. I had high hopes that the folks on Floor 12 would be far more honorable than the deviant who'd nabbed my trolley, and I also hoped that they stayed out a little later than the Bolton Babes. Time was moving on, nudging toward one-thirty in the morning, and every break-in I attempted was beginning to carry more risk. Before too long,

I'd have to call it quits and make my way to the casino floor to see how Victoria was faring. And at some point, we'd need to sleep. Yes, we'd been in the States for close to a week already, and we were working to a pressing deadline, but I still hadn't adjusted to the time difference completely, and Vegas had added another few hours to the burden. In Europe, dawn had been and gone, and I was feeling badly fatigued. My eyes ached and my limbs were weary, and all the nicotine patches in the world couldn't make up for a well-timed doze.

I tell you, just thinking about it made my head loll, and the laundry carts outside the service elevator suddenly looked mighty appealing. If it hadn't been for the risk that I might wake in the middle of a fast-spin cycle in an industrial washing machine, I could very well have climbed inside and closed my eyes for a short while. But ever the professional, I resisted, and meanwhile I allowed my good friend the service elevator to save my legs the trouble of climbing four flights of stairs.

The guest corridors on Floor 12 looked just like the ones down on Floor 8, and I only wished the same rooms would be empty too. Yes, there were a bunch of *Privacy Please* signs, and they definitely helped, but so far as the other doors went, it still felt as though I was playing a large game of Russian roulette.

I passed beyond the guest elevators before slowing to look for opportunities. There was a store cupboard on my right and I poked my head inside, but since I didn't plan on making my fortune by hawking vacuum cleaners, there wasn't anything to delay me. Farther along the corridor were a couple of doors with signs hanging from them requesting a room service breakfast, and they were followed by three doors featuring no signs whatsoever.

I paused outside the middle door and tried listening for any noise—a toilet gurgling or a television blaring or a fat man inhaling chicken wings—but I couldn't hear a thing. Dropping the empty suitcases beside my feet, I freed a crick in my neck and flexed my fingers and finally used my good knuckles in the way God had intended. And when nobody came to answer my call,

I removed the coat hanger from my suitcase and used my fingers in the way I had intended, until I was inside yet another darkened hotel room where I had no right to be.

I cast my penlight around the space and discovered that the room looked just like the ones downstairs. The bathroom was on my left as I entered, and while it was by no means as plush as the bathrooms at the Fifty-Fifty, it was perfectly respectable. There was the usual toilet and sink and shower and tub, and mercifully, there was no trace whatsoever of a floating corpse.

Beyond the bathroom was the bed-sitting area. This particular suite only had one bed, though admittedly it was king-sized. Facing the bed was the customary flat-screen television, and the mini-bar, and an easy chair positioned close to a desk. The curtains hadn't been drawn but a gauzy net hung over the window glass and I set the suitcases down on the floor and used an electric control panel on the wall to draw the net aside. The view wasn't anything to write home about. The window looked out onto another hotel window that belonged to the Paris-Las Vegas resort across the street. And since this isn't a Hitchcock movie and I don't run into murder scenes quite as often as Victoria would have you believe, there was no beautiful blonde being throttled in front of me. There was just a blank window, no light, like a hundred others around it.

I turned, and the beam of my penlight settled on a briefcase on the desk. The briefcase was upholstered in a supple black leather and it featured a pair of three-dial rotary combination locks. I sat in the easy chair and rested the briefcase on my knees and tried the double latches. No joy. Undeterred, I rolled the dials until every single one was set to the number nine and then I killed my penlight so that I could focus on my sense of touch.

I applied sideways tension to the left-hand latch and pressed my gloved index finger down hard over the first dial, rolling it slowly upward. Spinning the dial in the other direction was no good, because every number would seem to click and tense up. But by rotating upward, and by being careful about it, I could feel the dial stiffen and the latch twitch when I hit upon the correct number. Once I had it, I repeated the process on the next two dials. The technique was one I'd practiced many times in the past and it took barely a minute until I was done.

I reached for my flash and read the code—545. I turned the second pair of dials to the same sequence, tweaked both latches, and hey presto (as Josh Masters wouldn't have said), the little beauty opened.

Sadly for me, it wasn't stuffed with casino markers. Instead, there were a good deal of business papers and a wide selection of cheap pens, as well as a pocket calculator and a BlackBerry device. I unhitched the strap shelf in the lid of the case and took a peek. I found notepads and highlighter pens and a Dictaphone. Oh, and a laptop. The laptop was one of those dreary, gray machines that weighed about the same as a truck and was a smidgen less aerodynamic. It was worth perhaps a couple of hundred dollars in the dark recesses of a parking garage, but I wasn't inclined to sell it. I was, however, happy to open it up and see if it had any battery power.

No, I wasn't planning on writing the opening section of the short story Victoria had mentioned. All I wanted was to connect to the Internet, and to my surprise and delight, it turned out that the owner of the laptop had already paid to access the hotel's Wi-Fi service. It wouldn't save me any cash, because naturally I'd been intending to charge my web time to one of the credit cards in Josh's wallet, but it did save me a precious few minutes setting up an account. The laptop had one of those archaic red nipples instead of a track pad, and I moved the screen arrow to the address bar in the web browser before calling up YouTube.

I wasn't sure what to search for exactly, but in the end I tried the following collection of words: *Josh Masters Vegas Show Vanishing Holiday Cabinet*. Right away, I scored a bunch of hits for the self-same magician, and top of the list was the very thing I'd been looking for. Setting the speaker volume to low, I clicked Play on the video clip.

The footage had been shot from the rear of the Fifty-Fifty theater and it was poorly focused and unsteady, and quite obviously illegal. The back of somebody's head blocked the bottom left of the screen, at least until the camera zoomed into the stage, and I could barely hear the music, let alone what Masters was saying into his microphone bud. Even so, the routine was recognizable as the one Victoria had been involved in, the only difference being that Masters' flame-haired assistant was on stage too.

Dressed in a short, gossamer-thin, babydoll negligée, she wore very high heels and showed an awful lot of leg. Something glittered in her hair—a tiara, perhaps—but it was nowhere near as bright as her stage smile. She fixed the audience with her teeth as she gestured toward the open cabinet, waving her hands at the blackened interior.

I increased the volume on the laptop but I still couldn't hear what Masters was saying. Not that it mattered. I was fairly certain that his patter wouldn't change much between performances and I was far more interested in what the redhead was up to. Currently, she was lowering a hula-hoop down over the cabinet, presumably to show that there was nothing attached to it. And now she had hold of a long white ribbon, and was prancing around and around the cabinet with the ribbon floating behind her, binding the cabinet in such a way that any attempt to open the doors would cause the ribbon to tear. The low res video gave her movements a mechanical quality, as though she was a clockwork ballerina in a musical jewelry box.

As Masters kept up his monologue, the redhead raised a finger to her pursed lips and bunched her shoulders theatrically before tiptoeing in an exaggerated fashion around to the back of the cabinet. It was only a matter of seconds before Masters caught up with her disappearance and went in search of his girl. When he couldn't find her, he scratched his head and tapped his feet, acting completely bamboozled. He even interrogated the front row of the audience without success.

He shrugged and spun the cabinet around in a half-turn to check the reverse. No sign of her. Then he turned the cabinet frontwards, revealing the redhead's mischievous face poking out through the circular porthole in the double doors.

The moment he saw her, Masters clicked his fingers as if she'd outwitted him one time too many, and then he smiled wickedly and danced across to the wings, returning to center-stage with a pair of steel blades. He slapped the blades together and held them above his head. He contemplated his reflection in the mirrored surface and he kissed the cold steel. Then he turned quite abruptly, spun the cabinet around so that the redhead's face was hidden from view, and rammed both blades through the side.

The audience gulped and turned to face one another, but before my mystery cameraman had fainted in his seat, Masters twirled the cabinet back around to a crescendo of music that made the laptop thrum. I peered hard at the screen and waited for the stage-lights to dip until I could see that the redhead was still grinning through the circular hole in the front of the cabinet.

The audience howled with laughter, to Masters' evident disgust. He stamped his foot and shook his head, wagging his finger at this pesky young upstart. She wiggled her nose and rolled her eyes, goading the master magician until he could take no more.

Masters turned back to the crowd, sneering and snarling like an utter ham, and then he rubbed his hands with glee before bending down to the stage and lifting a large black cape for all to see. He turned the cape in his hands, showing us the front and the reverse. He wafted it before his beautiful assistant. Then he snapped his wrists and flicked the cape up into the air, allowing it to fall down over the cabinet. Quickly now, he twirled the cabinet around and around on its castors at a dizzying pace, and while the audience were suitably distracted, he stepped behind.

I watched closely, waiting for Masters to re-emerge, but to my genuine surprise, he wasn't the one to do so. The cabinet had barely quit spinning when the redhead skipped out, sporting a rather eye-catching bikini and straw sunhat, and sipping gamely from the pink daiquiri in her hand. Before the audience had even begun to applaud, she whipped the black cape away to reveal Josh Masters trapped in her stead. Playfully, cheekily, she snapped the white ribbon with a long, outstretched finger, withdrew the steel blades, and finally threw open the wooden doors to reveal the colorful beach mural. And then good old Josh leaped out, his jeans, white T-shirt and leather jacket replaced with Bermuda shorts and a floral Hawaiian shirt, golden sand spilling from around his feet, and that million-dollar grin fixed smack in the middle of his stupid, fake-tanned face.

The video clip stopped just as Masters and the girl took their bow. I rewound the footage, trying to see how they'd done it, but it was hopeless. Even if it might have been possible to catch a glimpse of the secrets behind the trick, the images available to me were far too grainy to help. But I had at least learned something—I hadn't been completely nuts to think there was a hidden way in and out of the cabinet.

Now obviously, Josh hadn't got as far as discussing any of that with Victoria, or she would have told me about it. After all, I didn't believe she was a paid-up member of the Magic Circle, and I liked to think she would have trusted me with the information even if she was. And besides, it was quite clear that Josh had reworked the cabinet trick to make it a lot less ambitious with Victoria involved.

The thing that really puzzled me was whether Josh had always planned to vanish during his show. On balance, I didn't buy it, because it would have been a hell of a lot simpler to walk away from his dressing room before he got up on stage. It seemed to me that the appearance of the Fisher Twins was what had caused him to run, and the only question that remained was: where had he gone?

Well, that wasn't the *only* question, but it was the most pertinent one from my point of view, and it was certainly something to ponder. And ponder it was just what I intended to do, once I'd slipped the laptop away and finished the task at hand.

Before closing the laptop, I called up the browser history. The history showed the YouTube video I'd just watched, and to be prudent, I thought I'd better delete it. Perhaps there was a way to delete just that one record, but since I didn't know how to set about it, I ended up wiping the entire history instead. Mind you, I didn't think the owner of the laptop would be inclined to complain, since the majority of his links related to the kind of material he could have watched on the flat-screen television, if only he'd been prepared to opt for the pay-per-view channels.

With the evidence of my web activity deleted, I powered down the laptop and returned it to the briefcase. Then I closed the briefcase and spun the dials at random and set the case back down on the desk.

There was a suitcase next to the bed and it was half-full of clothes. The clothes belonged to a man (or a seriously butch female). I sorted through Y-fronts and ankle-length socks, khaki trousers and pastel polo-shirts, round-neck sweaters and hand-kerchiefs. There was a charging device that most probably fitted the BlackBerry or the laptop, and a battery-operated razor and a pack of travel tissues.

Leaving the suitcase as I'd found it, I approached the closet on the other side of the bed. I slid the louvred door to one side and passed my torch beam over a couple of creased business shirts hanging from the rail before focusing in on the safe.

The safe was the same make and model as the one on Floor 8, and it was every bit as susceptible to the same approach. Armed with my tools, I opened the thing up and had a good look inside. And almost immediately I was prepared to forgive the guy his porn habit because the only thing in the safe was a brown, pad-ded envelope, and the only thing inside the padded envelope was good old-fashioned cash. The bundle of crisp notes had been secured together with a bulldog clip, and since the note on top happened to be a fifty, and the bundle was at least an inch thick, I had a very good feeling about it.

Of course, time was getting on, and despite the sudden urge I had to count how much money I'd just found, the most impor-tant thing was for me to get out of the room while the getting was still good. So I tossed the padded envelope down onto the cabinet beside the bed, gripped my penlight in my teeth and set about securing the safe. Before very long, I was done with the battery and the paperclip, and after screwing the manufacturer's badge back into position, I put my gear away in my spectacles case and fairly glided across the room to gather up my empty suitcases. I was just in the process of unzipping one of them to place the padded envelope inside when I heard a sudden noise of the kind that members of my profession are inclined to heed.

The noise was the high, wheezy snigger of a man's laugh, and the raucous counterpoint of a woman's cackle, and it was coming from just outside in the corridor. Now, on any other night I'd have taken house odds that they couldn't possibly be heading for the one room I happened to be inside. But somehow, given everything that had already befallen me in Vegas, I just knew that they were. I knew before I heard a thud against the door, and before I heard the bark of the woman's laugh again, and before I heard the sound of a key card being slid home. And I sure as hell knew before the door burst open and the man tumbled inside and fell hard onto the floor, because I'd long since grabbed my suitcases, ducked inside the closet and slid the louvred door closed behind me.

SEVENTEEN

The lights came on, bright and startling, and I watched through the slatted bars in the closet as a skinny man crawled on his hands and knees toward the foot of the bed. He hauled himself up onto the mattress, rolled onto his side and laughed a high, giddy laugh. He was dressed in a cheap brown suit with a tie that had been loosened off at the collar and a yellowing shirt with the top button undone. His left foot was missing a shoe and there was a ragged, wet graze on the side of his face that looked as though he had fallen on gravel.

"Sit up, Harry," drawled a brassy, full-bodied voice.

The voice wasn't the only thing that was full-bodied. So was the woman who tottered into view. She was a brunette, with coils of thick hair that fell down from a severe center parting and framed a face that reminded me of a moderately famous television wrestler. She had an ample waist and an even more ample bosom, barely contained by a blouse that appeared to have been styled on the coat of a Dalmatian. Her stockings were fishnet, her skirt was unseasonably short, and if any doubts lingered as to what her profession happened to be, it wouldn't be long before she dispelled them.

"You don't look like a Harry," she growled, and snatched at the man's tie to hoist him upright. "That really your name?"

He swayed and gurgled before slumping forward into her voluminous chest.

"Hey." She yanked his head back by the roots of his hair. "Money first, doll."

Harry didn't seem capable of reaching inside his pocket, so she took it upon herself to assist. Evidently, she wasn't a practitioner of the light-fingered approach I'd favored with Josh Masters. I'd seen cops frisk suspects with more care, and she was equally brazen about counting his money. Not a single note found its way back to his wallet, and I watched with some amazement as she removed a high-heeled shoe and poked the bundle of dollars down toward the toe.

I glanced at the envelope full of cash on the bedside cabinet. So far, it had gone unnoticed, and I just hoped things would stay that way.

"Now take off your pants."

The man fumbled listlessly at his belt buckle, blowing bubbles from his lips.

"You want me to do it?"

"Yessss . . . ma'am," he slurred.

"So lay back, why don't you?"

She pushed him so hard that he almost went clean through the bed and wound up on Floor 11. Loosening his belt, she then unzipped his fly, braced her foot against the end of the mattress and heaved at his trousers. Once she had his underwear down as far as his shins, she hitched up her skirt and straddled his chest, pinning his lean arms with her knees while she unbuttoned her blouse.

I suppose I could go on, but titillating you with details of their coupling really isn't my style. For starters, it's tricky for a hack like myself not to sound like a pervert when describing a big sex scene (and believe me, they really couldn't get much bigger than the one I was being compelled to witness). But there are plenty of other pitfalls too. Do you try for a romantic vibe, and risk using a whole bunch of clichéd metaphors? Do you aim for graphic realism, at the cost of alienating readers of a more chaste disposition? Or do you opt for summing it all up in a few neat lines, and run the danger of sounding like a medical textbook?

I've never been able to settle on a particular technique, and as a result, I tend to avoid writing love scenes in my mystery novels. As I recall, the very most that Michael Faulks has ever experienced is a smoldering look, followed by a snappy stage direction and a sudden break in the text. Like this.

Now granted, the carnal intricacies that an educated reader such as yourself might impose on that white space are anyone's to guess, but I've always thought it must be seriously frustrating for poor Faulks. Until now. Because let me tell you, if there was any way that I could have blanked out the sights and sounds of the beguiling coitus I was forced to endure, I would have gladly done whatever it took.

True, to begin with I watched with an avid, if somewhat mortified, curiosity. But as their thrusting and grunting and groaning and clutching dragged on, my interest soon began to wane. Sadly, they showed no sign of following suit. I had a feeling that had a lot to do with how drunk the skinny guy happened to be, and I suspected his partner's engagement list wasn't as full as perhaps she would have liked. During a particularly loud and energetic phase I took the opportunity to sit down on one of the suitcases and rest my head against the wall. I'd heard of people feeling like a spare part in a threesome, but this was plain ridiculous.

I closed my eyes and did my best to block the lovebirds out. To begin with, I focused on how I might extricate myself from the closet and grab the envelope full of cash, soon concluding that it would be a hell of a lot simpler if the closet was gimmicked like the cabinet in Masters' show. That got me thinking of Josh again—of his performance and his disappearance and his possible next moves. I asked myself where he could have gone, and if there was a clue to his whereabouts that I'd missed, and then I thought of the redhead in his bath, of the way she'd smiled and joked on the Internet video, and of how she wouldn't be doing that again in a hurry. I thought of Victoria sharing the stage with a murderer, and of our interrogation by Terry Ricks of Carson

Associates, and of the borderline psychotic behavior of the Fisher Twins, and of the oddball partnership of the high-pitched little chap and the Eastern European giant. I asked myself whether they'd been involved in the murder and the gambling scam, and the gambling angle got me wondering how Victoria was doing at blackjack. For all I knew, she might have enjoyed a run of good fortune that would balance out all of my bum luck. She might even have won enough to pay off the Fisher Twins and enable us to leave Vegas in one piece, in which case I'd owe her much more than a dumb short story.

Maybe, I thought, I'd wind up writing her a story based on some of the things that had happened to us. Maybe I'd use my exact predicament in the closet, or maybe I'd do something with the illusionist angle. My Faulks novel with the magician in it had received some favorable write-ups when it first came out, so perhaps there was more mileage to be had from the character. I could picture myself crowded over my laptop writing about him again, and as so often in the past, the version of me doing the typing appeared to have a cigarette in his hand. Damn. I shouldn't have thought about cigarettes. Now I couldn't get my mind off the pack in my pocket. I could feel the edge of the carton poking into my thigh. Would it be so bad to try and smoke one? The way Dirty Harry and his gal were carrying on, they might not even notice. Then again, maybe the cigarettes were my way out. Perhaps I could wait for them to conclude their lovemaking and emerge from the closet to offer them a smoke?

I smirked in the darkness, readjusted my weight on the suitcase and checked the time on my digital watch. Almost 2 a.m. I thought of the watch on my other wrist, and to be honest I felt pretty good that I'd stolen it from Josh. It was a nice timepiece, and maybe it held some sentimental value for him, and maybe I didn't altogether care if he never saw it again.

Thinking of the watch made me think of Josh's wallet. I felt plenty smug about that too. Without his credit cards, he might find it harder to run. Was there anything else in his wallet that could make things difficult for him? Well, there was the signed color photograph, and the key card, and the torn napkin with the telephone number scrawled on it.

Hang on a minute. *The torn napkin with the telephone number scrawled on it.* The note the little guy had left in Masters' room had told him to call someone called Maurice. Could the number on the napkin belong to the same person? And if it did, how long would it be until I could do anything about it?

I felt for Masters' wallet inside my pocket, but there was really no sense in removing the napkin because I couldn't risk being heard by either of my naked playmates over on the bed. The bed. Hmm. That made me think of my own bed back at the Fifty-Fifty. The mattress was well-sprung, the cotton sheets were luxurious, the feather pillows were plump and soft and inviting . . .

Boy, was I tired. So tired, in fact, that my head was beginning to loll and my thoughts were becoming vague and confused. My eyes fairly burned with fatigue and my lids were drooping. I blinked once. I blinked twice. I blinked three times and finally allowed my eyes to rest for just a few pleasant seconds.

Curious visions began to form in my mind. I saw Josh lying dead in a bath tub filled with casino chips. I saw the redhead dancing nude on the theater stage while the Fisher Twins were locked inside the magic cabinet. I saw the tiny man smoking a cigarette inside a hotel room safe that his giant pal carried under his arm. I saw Victoria writing a story on my laptop while Terry Ricks made notes from behind a two-way mirror.

And before very long, I was no longer conscious of what I was seeing, because I'd been just dumb enough to fall fast asleep.

EIGHTEEN

I awoke into a haze of darkness and silence. At first, I couldn't remember where I was staying, or even which city I happened to be in. Then my brain slowly registered that there was a wall behind my head instead of a pillow, and a suitcase beneath my buttocks rather than a mattress, and as realization gradually dawned, I felt a painful contraction in my chest, and my skin began to tingle.

Grabbing for the clothes rail above me, I heaved myself upright. I pressed my forehead against the louvred doors of the closet and cupped my hands around my eyes. With the lights turned off and the curtains drawn, it was like staring into the depths of a cave, but after a short while I was able to make out a hump under the bedcovers. There was a digital clock on the television across the way, and it cast the form on the bed in a greenish glow. I wasn't sure if it was one person or two. I couldn't tell if they were fast asleep, or if they were simply lying very still, waiting for me to make my move.

The time on the television read a quarter to six in the morning. So I'd slept for more than three hours, cooped up in a closet with a set of burglary tools in my pocket, sitting upon a suitcase that didn't belong to me, wearing a stolen tunic and carrying another man's wallet. Talk about dumb. I mean, talk about flat-out stupid. What the hell had I been thinking? Was I so eager to get caught that I was prepared to lock myself up and just wait to be found?

If I could have smacked myself over the head without making the slightest sound, I would have done it without delay. I simply couldn't believe the jeopardy I'd placed myself in, and it only got worse when I considered the time pressures I was working under. Because who knew how long ago Harry and his girl had concluded their lovemaking? It could be that I would have had the chance to escape many hours earlier, and that I'd be walking around as a free man, if only I'd had the sense and the self-control necessary to stay awake.

The form on the bed grunted and snorted and kicked out a leg from under the bedcovers. Judging by its lean hairiness, I was pretty sure it didn't belong to the tubby hooker. I guessed that made sense. After all, she wouldn't have been likely to hang around once she'd fulfilled her side of the bargain, not least because of the cash she'd taken from Harry's wallet and pushed down inside her shoe.

I eased up from the suitcase and straightened my knees. My feet buzzed with pins and needles, but that was the least of my concerns. My most pressing conundrum was how to slide back the closet door without making too much noise. Did I go for quick and sudden, or slow and steady? I chose slow and steady, easing the door aside and just praying that the mechanism wouldn't squeal. I tested the gap with my hands. I'm kind of a slim fellow, and as I hadn't eaten all that many hamburgers since I'd arrived in the States, I was able to suck in my belly and edge out through the space between door and wall.

As soon as I was free, I pursed my lips and let go of a soundless whistle. I even wiped the back of my gloved hand across my brow. For once, it seemed that things were turning in my favor. In fact, it seemed that things were going altogether swimmingly. Or rather, they were, until the moment I reached a tentative hand out toward the money-filled envelope that I'd so conveniently left on the bedside cabinet.

Funny. It didn't appear to be there.

I frowned, as if that might help, and then I used both hands to feel around the top of the cabinet. Still nothing. It occurred to me that perhaps the envelope had fallen down onto the floor during all the bedroom gymnastics, so I dropped to my knees and passed my hands over the carpet. I didn't find anything with my first sweep, or my second. On my third sweep, my busted knuckles struck the cabinet.

I snatched my hand away and bit hard on my bottom lip to stop myself from yelping. Harry stirred and groaned and pulled the covers tight around his shoulders. He farted. I tried not to let my pain or his stench get the better of me, and meanwhile I reached inside my jacket with the fingers of my good hand until they touched upon my penlight. I pointed the lens down against the floor, then twisted the dimpled shaft so that the bulb came on. Using my palm to shield the light, I tilted the lens and angled the glow across the carpet. All I saw was more carpet. I checked around the side of the cabinet and under the bed. I even skimmed the light across the top of the cabinet. The envelope was gone.

I didn't believe Harry had tidied the envelope away. He'd been too drunk earlier and he was too comatose now. So it seemed to me there was only one place the envelope could be—it must have vacated the scene along with Harry's date.

Could I blame her for taking it? Not really. Did I blame her for taking it all the same? Hell, yes.

I was the one who'd faced the risks and deployed the necessary skills to open Harry's safe. I was the one who'd chanced upon the envelope and the cash. And what's more, I really needed the damn money. Without it, I had two empty suitcases, a staff uniform and a little over four hundred dollars to my name. So it seemed to me singularly unjust that a woman of low morals should have stooped a shade further and added thievery to her criminal repertoire. And if she'd been there just then, I'd have given her a piece of my mind, and perhaps even a kick in the shin to boot. But she wasn't there. She was long gone. And she made me a good example.

I inched backward toward the door. Given how things stood, it seemed way too ambitious to attempt to remove the suitcases from the closet and take them with me. So as it happened, I was leaving with even less than I'd had when I'd first broken in. And I guess that explains why, despite all my years of training, and my dedication to the noble art of inconspicuous access and egress, I felt compelled to bang the door closed behind me as I left. Because hell, I may not have been capable of ripping the poor sap off, but at least I could introduce him to what I sincerely hoped would be the mother of all hangovers.

NINETEEN

I returned Gerry's tunic to the exact same peg in the exact same cloakroom from where I'd acquired it, pulled my shirt out of the waistband of my trousers and made my way back to the casino floor. It turned out that Victoria hadn't moved from the blackjack table where I'd last seen her, but she appeared to have aged quite dramatically. The skin around her eyes was swollen, as though she'd been stung by a swarm of insects, and her eyes appeared bleary and unfocused. Her face was pale, her lips were cracked, and she looked so drawn that I wouldn't have been altogether surprised to learn that her glass of cranberry juice had been laced with Rohypnol. I could only imagine how desperately she must have wanted to sleep, so I knew right away that I wouldn't be mentioning my accidental nap.

"Hey, Big Spender." I pointed toward her surprisingly respectable pile of chips. "You're doing pretty well."

"I'm winning, if that's what you mean."

"How much?"

Victoria shrugged and ran her thumbnail up a stack of red markers. "Something in the region of nine thousand dollars."

"That's terrific."

She didn't look as though she believed it. Don't get me wrong, if she'd simply walked in off the street and made that kind of money, I'm sure she'd have been delighted. But the fact was she knew as well as I did that it left us considerably short of where we needed to be.

"Come on," I told her. "Imagine if you'd lost everything."

She barely smiled as she tossed two chips into the betting circle on the felt. Her dealer had changed—Randy had morphed into Estelle. According to Estelle's name badge, she hailed from Fort Lauderdale, Florida, and if it wasn't for her ill-fitting spacesuit, she would have made an ideal extra on an episode of *The Golden Girls*. Her hair was dyed a virulent chestnut brown, and it was cut short and feathered around her temples. She had on a pair of gold-rimmed, half-moon spectacles, secured around her neck with a gold chain. There was more gold on her wrists and her fingers, and when she slipped Victoria's cards from the shoe and turned them over, I couldn't help but notice her plum-colored nails.

"What happened to the Stormtroopers?" I asked Victoria, as she studied the pair of eights she'd been dealt.

"They left. Hours ago. Where have you been?"

I watched as Victoria slid two more chips forward and opted to split the eights.

"Working," I said, and shot a look toward Estelle, who stared fixedly at Victoria's cards.

"You were gone a long time."

"I was working hard."

"And?"

I patted my nose. "And maybe we should discuss this in private."

Estelle did her best to act invisible, meanwhile dealing Victoria a Ten of Diamonds and a King of Spades. She flipped her hole card over, showing a four and a nine. She hit and bust out with a Jack of Hearts, then reached for her chip tray and paid Victoria her winnings.

"Is it good news?" Victoria asked, with a yawn.

"It's not great news."

"Then perhaps I'll just stay here."

"I can give you a little more cash, if you like."

Victoria held out her hand and I dropped the four hundred and twenty dollars I'd cadged into her palm. She hesitated. Her expression darkened and her eyebrows knitted together as though I'd confounded her.

"You really weren't kidding about the little part."

"I encountered some difficulties."

"But you've been gone for hours, Charlie."

"And you're beginning to repeat yourself."

Victoria considered the cash for a long moment, then shook her head and pressed the notes back into my hand.

"You might as well hold onto it," she said. "If we get really desperate, at least we'll have something left."

"You think?"

"I do."

"Maybe you're right." I slipped the money into my back pocket. "Feel free to take a break. I won't be able to work for a good few hours now. Too many people asleep."

Victoria laughed half-heartedly. "They should come down here and breathe some of the oxygen being pumped out of those vents. A few lungfuls and you begin to forget what time it is. Not that there are any clocks, of course."

"You look pretty wiped out, Vic."

"You hear that, Estelle? He wants me to quit." Victoria doubled her bet and gestured for Estelle to lay the next card on the felt.

"Some people quit when they're winning," Estelle observed.

"Sure," Victoria replied. "But how are you going to get along without my stimulating conversation?"

Estelle's eyes twinkled, and she worked a sly grin as she dealt Victoria's cards. She tapped the top card with one of her plum fingernails.

"Blackjack, hon."

"See?" Victoria said, gesturing to the Jack and the Ace of Spades on the felt in front of her. "Can't quit when I'm running this hot. And besides," she added, nodding toward a near-deserted bar on the far side of the room, "I have no idea what our friend would do if I left."

I glanced in the direction Victoria had indicated and felt my breath catch in my throat. Staring clean back at me from over the rows of twinkling slots was Terry Ricks. He was sitting on a galvanized metal stool, legs parted, with his elbow resting on the glass screen of one of the video poker machines that had been sunk into the bar counter. He still had on his brown blazer and blue shirt, though he'd ditched the yellow tie and his top button was undone. His pressed brown trousers had ridden up on his thighs, and I could see that he sported pale yellow socks to complement the absent tie.

While my jaw grazed the table felt, Ricks raised a bottle of spring water in a wordless toast. He reached for some bar nuts, tossed one into his mouth and cracked it between his shark-grin teeth, then smoothed the silver-gray hairs of his beard with his finger and thumb.

"What's he doing here?"

"What does it look like?"

"It looks like he's making a nuisance of himself."

"I get the impression that's something he's very good at."

I felt Ricks' eyes on me again, and turned to find him winking as he threw another nut into his mouth. He chewed and swallowed without averting his gaze, almost as if watching us was entirely beyond his control. I found that hard to believe. Even supposing he'd finished his shift, Space Station One was an unlikely venue for him to come to, to wind down. It was dead of all atmosphere, the casino floor empty aside from the hardiest of gamblers, the most determined of boozers and the loneliest of night owls.

A skeleton staff crewed the tables, while in the background a team of cleaners and janitors did their best to refresh the area for another day. Carpets were being shampooed and machine dried; flower arrangements perked up; table felts vacuumed; litterbins emptied.

I edged closer to Victoria and spoke from the corner of my mouth. "Maybe we should go back to our hotel for a few hours and get some rest. Let Ricks bother someone else for a while."

"Oh, I don't know," Victoria said. "I quite like it. It's almost like having a guardian angel watching over me."

I slumped onto the metal stool alongside her and helped myself to some of the cranberry juice she was drinking. Even the juice tasted stale. Pushing her glass away, I scanned the area for a cocktail waitress but couldn't see one anywhere close.

"Can I borrow your phone?"

Victoria sighed rather dramatically and snatched open her bag. She held her mobile out to me, but when I reached for it, she didn't let go.

"I don't know why you can't get one of your own," she told me.

"What, and risk having someone call me in the middle of a job? I don't think so."

"Who are you going to call?"

"Tell you in a minute."

I pulled Josh's wallet from my pocket and was just using my thumb to edge out the napkin with the telephone number scrawled on it when Estelle interrupted me.

"I'm sorry, sir, but you can't use a cellphone at our tables."

I pulled a face. It was a pretty unflattering kind of face. "Even when it's so quiet?"

She blinked from behind her half-moon spectacles, completely unmoved. "House rules."

"Then I guess I'll go breathe some real air." I checked on Ricks' position and comforted myself with the knowledge that he hadn't moved. Victoria caught me looking and I rested my hand on her shoulder. "Don't worry about him. You'll still be here when I get back, right?"

She shrugged. "I may try my luck at the roulette-table. But you won't be long, will you?"

"Absolutely not. I'll be five minutes, maximum."

TWENTY

The bland morning light wasn't kind to Las Vegas. What had appeared glamorous and spectacular in the dark, now seemed cheap and badly staged, like the backdrop to some improbable B-movie. Take the shuttle outside Space Station One. The nose cone was pitted with dents and nicks, the paint on the launch tower was flaking, and the bare bulbs strung along the metal structure looked like ugly glass cysts. If that was bad, then the robots beside the entrance doors were even worse. I'd owned toasters that were more technologically advanced.

On the opposite side of the Strip, along from the cranes and construction towers that dotted the evolving skyline, and beneath the chain of tourist helicopters flying toward the Grand Canyon, the Bellagio fountains were undergoing maintenance. A man in a wetsuit yanked at one of the fountainheads while a second man in a rubber boat fished litter from the lake. While they worked, a section of the fountains and lights were being tested. I watched the water loop and whirl and dip. The effect wasn't nearly so spectacular without Sinatra's "Luck Be A Lady" blaring out of the speaker system.

Flipping open Victoria's mobile telephone, I punched in the number from the napkin in Masters' wallet. The display on the telephone told me it was twenty past six in the morning, which was hardly the most civil of times to place a call—but I didn't care. If Tom-Thumb-gone-bad and his oversized companion were prepared to break into Josh's room to leave a note telling him to ring a gentleman called Maurice, I figured the man in question would be willing to have his beauty sleep interrupted. Of course, the fact that I couldn't tell him where Josh had run to might darken his mood just a fraction, but I was prepared to run that risk.

The phone rang twice before my call was answered. There was a pause, and I was just readying myself to speak when a recorded message cut in.

Thank you for calling Hawaiian Airways. Please press one to speak to a booking agent, press two for flight inquiries, press three for . . .

I closed the phone and stuffed the napkin back inside Josh's wallet. So it wasn't the number for the mysterious Maurice, though at least I finally had some idea of where Josh had disappeared to. Hawaii. Not somewhere I'd ever been, and not somewhere I'd been planning to vacation anytime soon, but I imagine it had its charms, particularly if you were looking for a place to hide out and avoid having your limbs remodeled with a metal pipe.

Discovering that the telephone number belonged to an airline booking service didn't do a great deal to improve my mental health. On the one hand, it seemed very possible that Josh had flown so far away from Nevada that I wouldn't have a hope of handing him to the Fisher Twins in what remained of my twenty-four hours. And on the other side of what was turning into a seriously bleak equation, my badly fatigued literary agent was preparing to take her chances at roulette. I hadn't had the energy, let alone the desire, to ask Victoria how she intended to play. It could be she was aiming to bet small sums on red or black, with the idea of building toward our target figure. Or it could be she was planning to gamble it all on a single, straight-up bet. If she did, and she happened to win, the payout would answer all our prayers and buy us a speedboat besides. And if she lost—well, I really didn't want to think about what we'd do if she lost.

All things considered, it struck me as an ideal moment to smoke a cigarette. A little nicotine, some fresh desert air, perhaps as much as a minute to relax and try to shut out the prospect of being shot in the back of the head somewhere in the middle of the barren Mojave . . . It didn't seem too much to ask, so I headed around the side of the casino toward the main entrance of the hotel, where the valets and doormen and bell staff looked as if they'd just started in for the day. They had on cotton polo-shirts and khaki shorts, and they fairly bounced on the toes of their smart white sneakers as they hailed cabs and stacked suitcases and ushered guests in and out of the hotel foyer.

The cab passengers themselves were a different story. Bedraggled women in skimpy outfits; middle-management types in creased suits; honeymoon couples still reeling from their Drive-Thru vows; all of them wearing dazed smiles and blinking in the early sun as if their retinas might burn.

I cracked the seal on my precious cigarette packet, flipped back the cardboard lid and inhaled the new-box smell. I slipped a filter between my lips, and just the weight of it caused me to groan and close my eyes in satisfaction.

One of the bell staff obliged me with a light in return for a dollar tip and I might go so far as to say it was the best dollar I've spent in my entire life. From the instant I inhaled, I could have wept at how perfect the cigarette tasted, at how full the smoke felt in my mouth, at how wonderful it was to experience the familiar warmth spreading out through my chest.

Two draws later, and I felt so light-headed I could have believed the cigarettes packed a mildly illegal punch. It didn't help when I saw a group of men pacing across the asphalt toward the revolving glass doors in matching Elvis costumes. They had the side-burn wigs and the gaudy plastic shades, the fake medallions and the powder-blue jumpsuits; they even had the platform shoes. The formation they walked in went from slim through to fat, with the belly of the last guy bulging against his jumpsuit as though he was pregnant with Tom Jones.

My, but cigarettes were wonderful things, and as if to prove as much, I was about to catch one heck of a break. I put it entirely down to the smokes. After all, if I hadn't been standing at that exact spot, inhaling that exact cigarette, I might never have seen the yellow Ford Crown Victoria taxi pull up and deposit two Nordic blondes with very fine legs. And if those same legs hadn't belonged to those same blondes, my attention might never have lingered on the cab they were vacating. And, well, if none of those things had happened, I almost certainly wouldn't have seen the advertisement on the cab roof.

The advertisement was pasted to a triangular pod, and it was colorful and arresting in the way that any decent ad should be. The main image featured a troop of performers lined up as if they were standing on water, with fountains bursting and fireworks exploding from behind them. The troop included showgirls and clowns, acrobats and trapeze artists, jugglers and sword swallowers, elephants and tigers and snow-white stallions. Above them all, in a bold aqua font, were the words: *The World-Famous Fate of Atlantis, at the Atlantis-Las Vegas Casino Resort.*

It was a busy poster, made even more crowded by a couple of "sensational" quotes from the local rags, and it might have caught my eye regardless. But the reason I stared particularly hard, and even went so far as to approach the taxi to get a closer look, was that I recognized two of the performers. One was the trapeze artist in the skin-tight Lycra, hanging upside down from a horizontal bar with a waif-like girl suspended from his wrists. The other was the clown at the front of the troop, who looked no taller than a child. And although the trapeze artist was the wrong way up, and the clown wore white face paint with a blue rubber nose, they sure looked like the unlikely couple who'd come calling for Josh.

It would have been nice to have studied the poster for a little longer, but all of a sudden I heard a door thud closed and the burst of a throaty carburetor as the cab pulled sharply away. I suppose I could have run after it, or yelled at the driver to stop, but the truth is the taxi was gone before it even occurred to me.

There were at least a dozen more cabs waiting in line to be called upon, but none of them featured the same advertisement. I walked among them just to make sure, feeling as though I should perhaps shake my head and acknowledge that I'd experienced some variety of hallucination. A large part of me wanted to believe that my lack of sleep, combined with that first cigarette, had somehow made me see something that wasn't really there. But the reality was that I finally had a lead to follow up. And if only I could pull my wits and my guts together, I thought I might be so bold as to do just that.

TWENTY-ONE

The watery theme of the Atlantis-Las Vegas was painfully apt, since the resort-casino had fallen into administration twice in the last five years, and gags about it "going under" or "sinking without trace' still lingered. If the casino's latest owners had possessed the funds to remodel the place, I'm sure they would have done just that. But apparently they didn't, and evidently they hadn't, and the Enchanting Lost City Beneath the Waves (as the publicists would have you remember it) went on struggling to stay afloat, not helped by its position at the very end of the Strip, way beyond the comic book Manhattan skyline of New York-New York, the castle turrets of the Excalibur and the burnished exterior of the Mandalay Bay party casino.

Even from the outside, the Atlantis looked and felt like a downmarket option; inside, that impression wasn't helped by the stench of chlorine from all the fountains and ponds, not to mention the giant water slides that weaved through the ceiling space above the casino floor.

There's a theory I was beginning to subscribe to that says you can judge the success of a Vegas casino by the cocktail waitresses who work there. True enough, while the drinks at the Fifty-Fifty had been served by women who looked as though they modeled in their spare time, and Space Station One undoubtedly had its fair share of beauty pageant winners, the Atlantis was staffed by mere mortals, of the kind I would have felt comfortable talking to if it wasn't for the outfits they were required to wear. Skimpy is an understatement—you'd see less flesh at a burlesque review.

I guess just before seven o'clock in the morning wasn't the fairest time to gauge the success of the place, but from the looks of how empty the casino happened to be, I didn't think it would be long before it went bust yet again. Not that the lack of people concerned me. After all, it made finding the theater an awful lot simpler.

Alas, the theater was closed, which I supposed was understandable, considering how few people would be likely to queue before breakfast to buy tickets for a water-themed circus review. The main doors to the Oasis Stage were roped off, the concession stand was in darkness, and the ticket counter was secured behind a metal grill. The lock on the grill was worth no more than thirty seconds of my time, but I wasn't intending to pick it. I was far more interested in the framed show posters displayed on the walls surrounding me.

The posters were enlarged versions of the advertisement I'd seen on the roof of the taxi cab, and I was certain by now that I'd tracked down the two men I'd seen outside Josh's room. It wasn't simply that the trapeze artist and the clown looked like the men I'd spoken with, it was also that their roles in the show made complete sense to me. A trapeze artist would need exactly the kind of physique belonging to the tall, muscular Eastern European, and I guessed his little pal had traded on his size to carve out a career in showbiz. As I peered into his eyes, staring out from behind his clown make-up, they erased any doubts that might have remained. The only problem now was finding them.

Sure, it was possible that they lived in the hotel, but it would be helpful if I could narrow it down a little further than that. There was a television screen above the ticket counter, screening footage of show highlights and information about performance times. I didn't relish the prospect of waiting until the next show. Even supposing I could somehow access a backstage area, there was no guarantee they'd talk to me, and my deadline would be looming.

I picked up a flyer and turned it in my hands. No solution jumped out at me, but I read over it a second time, paying attention to the detail. Some of the stars of the show were mentioned, and it seemed the trapeze artist went by the name of Kojar and that his female partner was called Kitty. The lowly clown didn't merit a name check, which was bad news for him as well as for me.

I scanned the rest of the flyer, and was almost done with the thing completely, when my eyes snagged on something at the bottom of the reverse side. I looked closer. Yep, there it was. Amid the show credits, in a tiny, light-blue font, I could just read the words: *Producer Maurice Mills.*

Now okay, it was a long shot, but I'd never met a chap called Maurice in my entire life, and I didn't believe it was a common American name. Yes, there were likely to be more than a few men called Maurice in the Las Vegas metropolitan area, but how many men called Maurice could there be who happened to be connected to a seven-foot gymnast and a four-foot clown? Who also happened to be a part of the Las Vegas showbusiness fraternity, to which Josh Masters belonged? Who also happened to represent my only tangible lead?

Granted, it was tenuous, but I couldn't afford to doubt myself, because once that happened, I'd start to worry about how little time was left, and whether Victoria was mad that I hadn't returned to her yet, and if Ricks was giving her a hard time. And since I didn't want to do any of that, it was far simpler to move forward without second-guessing myself.

Moving forward meant finding Maurice Mills, and I'd written enough mystery fiction in my time to know that finding Maurice Mills meant asking questions.

I started with a nearby cocktail waitress, doing my best to talk to her eyes rather than her cleavage. At first she played dumb, and then I discovered that she wasn't just playing at it, and so I tried one of her colleagues who was working the keno pit.

This second waitress was a mousy brunette who shook her head when I pointed at the flyer and mentioned Maurice's name, but she did it a little too fast for my liking. As in all the best private-eye novels, I tried asking again, only this time with the assistance of a twenty-dollar bill. Miraculously, her response changed, and she directed me toward a male dealer on a nearby blackjack table.

After playing two hands, and leaving another twenty-buck tip, a pit boss was summoned to talk with me. The pit boss had a hairless scalp and a barrel chest and an attitude that told me to get right to the point. I explained who I was and who I was looking for, and I dropped the name Josh Masters along with some more of the cash I'd stolen from the Bolton Babes, and without another word he approached a telephone behind a small podium.

Five minutes went by, and then a startlingly attractive woman in a fitted business suit came and shook me by the hand before escorting me out of the casino and ushering me into a waiting town car with tinted windows. I didn't catch the address she gave the driver and I didn't have an opportunity to thank her. The car pulled away before I'd even fastened my seat belt—and it wasn't until the Strip was far behind us and we were racing along the bleached expressway that I started to wonder if I'd made a terrible mistake.

TWENTY-TWO

The town car stopped outside a squat, Spanish-style villa in a modern gated community. The villa had terracotta roof tiles, white-washed walls and a double garage with a soft-top sports car out front. The lawn grass was lush and finely trimmed, and two palm trees leaned on one another at the entrance to the paved driveway, like a pair of amorous drunks.

I stepped out of the car onto asphalt that was cleaner than most carpets, and approached the front door of the house. There was no sound whatsoever—no birdsong, no insect calls, no traffic noise. I pressed a muted doorbell, and turned to see the town car pulling off along the street, its engine so subdued it might have been running on air.

The woman who answered the door had a doughy, Asian face. Her eyes were dark, worn buttons and the skin around them was pinched and wrinkled like the fabric on an old chesterfield. She wore a button-down tunic that was white in color, over matching cotton trousers. Her feet were bare, and very small, like the feet of a child. Her toenails were painted a startling lime green.

She beckoned me inside without a word and led me across a floor of white marble tiles and on through a pair of double glass doors into a stark living area. The room was furnished with more of the white marble tiles, a white marble fireplace and brilliant white walls. Two slim-line sofas, upholstered in white leather, faced each other from across the fireplace, and a white coffee-table was positioned between them. I was beginning to suspect that Maurice Mills was a fan of the color white, and that was before my speechless guide led me through a set of patio doors toward a decked pool area that featured a collection of white marble sculptures.

I could see prancing horses, stalking tigers and leaping dolphins. It might have made a little more sense if the tigers had been emerging from behind some shrubbery, or the dolphins jumping out of the pool, but there were no plants to be seen and the sculptures were all positioned on the pale-gray decking. The combination of the white marble animals, white perimeter walls and sparkling blue water was beginning to make me wish I'd worn sunglasses.

Fortunately, my host appeared to be wearing sunglasses that were sizeable enough to share. They had very large, very round lenses, and were deep black in color, so that they gave him the appearance of a fly. His fair hair was shaved close to the scalp and I could see a squiggle of purple veins at his temple. His left earlobe featured a matte black stud, and his bottom lip was pierced with a silver ring about the size of a dime. He was dressed in a white silk robe and white pajama pants. The robe was open at his neck, exposing a pale chest that looked as if it had been waxed smooth.

He was reclining on a white, padded sunlounger, with his right knee in the air and a tall glass of milk in his hand. A white telephone handset and a white iPod were on the deck beside him, and a spare sunlounger was positioned close by, with a rolled white towel upon it.

"Mr. Mills?"

He studied me for a long moment without saying anything.

"My name is Charlie Howard. I understand that you're looking for Josh Masters."

So far as I could tell, he didn't react. But then again, his eyes were unreadable from behind his sunglasses.

"I'm looking for Josh too," I went on. "I met some of your . . . associates. They were trying to find him."

Still nothing.

"Listen, I spoke to them just before they broke into Masters' hotel suite."

Mills leaned his head to one side and used the tip of his tongue to jostle his lip piercing. He slid a finger up and down his chilled milk glass.

"You're mistaken," he said, with the barest hint of a lisp.

"I don't think so. It was a big guy and a little guy, from your show at the Atlantis. They cadged a room card from a maid, and left Josh a note telling him to call you in a hurry. I know it for a fact, because I broke into his hotel room just after them."

Maurice moved his lip ring around some more, but he didn't speak. Usually, I would have waited him out, or at least given it a shot. But I don't know, maybe Vegas was getting to me. Or maybe it was the sensation of time running out. Either way, I decided to lay my cards on the table.

"I'm a burglar, Mr. Mills. A pro. Breaking into places is what I do for a living."

My words carried so little impact that I might as well have told him I was a Bible salesman. I shifted my weight between my feet, and turned to my side, so that the morning sun wasn't in my eyes. I glanced at the freeform pool. The water looked cool and inviting, though my host didn't seem inclined to ask me if I'd brought my swimsuit along.

"I see you're wearing Josh's wristwatch," he said.

"Excuse me?"

"The man's timepiece. You have it on your wrist."

I nudged my shirtsleeve back and contemplated the face of the watch I'd stolen. The hands weren't moving—the mechanism seemed to have stalled shortly after 3 a.m. If this was one of my mystery novels, the stopped watch would be a major clue. But the only significant thing to have happened at three in the morning was that I'd been brainless enough to fall asleep in a closet. And the only thing the stopped watch indicated was that I might very well have stolen a dud timepiece.

"He gave it to me."

"He gave it to you?" Maurice stuck out his bottom lip, giving his piercing some air. The back of his lip looked swollen and inflamed, the skin a sickly greenish-yellow. "I don't think so."

"No?"

"Is he dead?"

I let my wrist drop, along with my jaw. "What makes you say that?"

"You have the man's favorite timepiece. He can't be found."

"He vanished in the middle of his show. He ran away."

"Where?"

I felt my eyes narrow as I tried to gauge how much I should say. I could have done with another cigarette while I considered the matter. My brain felt sluggish and my thinking delayed. Another jolt of nicotine would sharpen me up. Then again, pausing for a cigarette was unlikely to lend my words any more credence.

"Hawaii."

"Hawaii?"

"I think so. But I don't know for certain. That's why I came to speak with you."

Maurice raised his glass of milk to his mouth, and I watched his throat bob as the liquid went down. He was studying me from over the rim of the glass, though I didn't know what he hoped to see. Once he was done, he sucked on his bottom lip, clearing the milk from his piercing.

I noticed that I was fussing with Masters' wristwatch, smoothing my fingers over the pitted face. I tucked my hands under my armpits to break the habit.

"Sit down," he said. "Speak to me."

I moved across to the spare recliner and sat on it sideways. I propped my elbow on my knee and shaded my eyes with my hand. My host swiveled his head until I could see two tiny images of myself in the lenses of his sunglasses. A white marble stallion appeared to be vaulting my left ear.

The sensation of having him consider me from behind the glasses was unsettling, and for some unknown reason, I was just dumb enough to ponder whether he ran casting couch sessions with wannabe showgirls that began in a similar fashion.

"Tell me how you know Josh. The truth."

Talk about your starter for ten. Yes, I've heard it said that honesty is the best policy, and I suppose that's absolutely right—if you're a complete bonehead. But there was no way I could tell Maurice the truth if I wanted him to trust me. The only way I might mean anything to him was if he believed I was somehow important to Josh. Josh was clearly important to him, and I needed to close the circle.

At the same time, Maurice didn't strike me as the type of individual who made his living through entirely legal means. To the outside world he functioned as a show producer, but I had a pretty thorough appreciation for the value of a good cover profession. Maurice hadn't flinched when I'd told him what I liked to get up to in my less-than-law-abiding moments, so it seemed fair to assume that he had a somewhat relaxed sense of right and wrong.

"The truth is we worked a scam together."

"Casino scam?"

"There were three of us, plus the croupier. It was a roulette wheeze."

"Sounds kind of smalltime."

"We were starting out with something simple," I replied, meanwhile thinking that if he pictured Masters' take in those terms, he definitely wouldn't be impressed with the perilous state of my finances. "Getting to know one another, before moving on to something more serious."

"Huh. And this more serious work—was that riding on you, or Josh?"

Christ, what exactly had Josh been up to? Mixing writing with thievery was one thing, but combining high-profile stage magic with a criminal career seemed mighty ambitious.

"Er, it was his job."

"Yeah, doing what?"

"He didn't say exactly." I let the words hang in the air while I thought about where to take things next. On balance, I couldn't see any harm in adding, "I got the impression you were involved."

"You did, huh?"

"He mentioned your name."

"But no details."

"I was all set to hear them when he pulled his disappearing act."

His eyebrows scaled his forehead. "So you figured you'd break into his hotel room."

"Well now, you can't blame me for that. Your circus freaks had the same idea."

Maurice set his milk down and reached for his lip piercing, pinching the silver ring between his fingers. I began to suspect it was a recent addition to his face—something he was still getting used to. His tongue must have been getting used to it as well. That would explain the slight lisp.

"I still don't buy him gifting you his watch."

I let my shoulders fall. "I stole it. When I broke into his room."

"Just like that."

I thought back to the croupier who'd been involved in Josh's roulette fix.

"He never paid me my share of the roulette take. When he ran, I figured he owed me."

"You speak to Caitlin about it?"

"Caitlin?"

"Yeah, Caitlin. His assistant."

"The redhead, you mean?"

"That's her."

"No. I was beginning to think she must have run away with him too."

Maurice shook his head. "Wipe that. She'd never leave Vegas."

"No?"

"Girl needs to perform. You catch her act?"

"A little. She seems good."

He threw up his hands, as though I'd just uttered the understatement of the century. "Girl has stadium talent. Word is she's been working on something new—something folks here would go nuts over. Kind of act I could build an entire show around at the Atlantis."

Not any more he couldn't.

"So why don't you?" I asked. "With Josh gone, she'll be looking for work."

Maurice jerked his head back, as though stunned by the suggestion.

"She'll never leave the Fifty-Fifty. Leastways, not while her asshole brothers still own the joint."

Oh, terrific. That really did cap it all. Because assuming my ears weren't deceiving me, it sounded as if the extravagantly talented Caitlin, whose buoyant cadaver you may just remember my bumbling across and abandoning in the early stages of this particular tale, was none other than the close blood relation of the terrible twins who were lately threatening to kill me. Could that really be right? I didn't have an awful lot to go on, other than Maurice's say-so. Although, now I came to think of it, the girl's flame-red hair wasn't all that far removed from the fair ginger locks of the Fisher Twins.

Hmm, so that was hearsay and genetics going against me, and just willful denial on my side. Still, it's refreshing to know that things can always get worse, and the revelation didn't change my reasons for being there. I needed Maurice to tell me something that might give me the vaguest hope of contacting Josh, or failing that, raising close to one hundred and forty thousand dollars in cash.

"Was I right?" I asked. "About you being involved in Josh's other job?"

Maurice nudged his sunglasses up on the bridge of his nose. "Maybe you should move on. Quit asking questions."

I lowered my eyes and contemplated his bare feet. His toenails were painted a luscious black. I wondered if perhaps he split the cost of varnish with his silent housekeeper with the lime-green toes.

"I need a lot of money," I told him. "Quickly."

"Is that right? And you figured your take would cover what you need?"

"I wouldn't have been wasting my time otherwise."

"And Josh was cool with that?"

I let go of a lungful of dry morning air. "We didn't get into specifics. Hell, he hadn't even told me what the job entailed. But he knew my reputation. He knew the kind of fee I'd have expected."

"So you're good at what you do?"

It seemed wise to ignore the more recent entries on my résumé.

"I'm very good."

"Tell me about it."

I looked at him as though he'd scrawled a tough algebra problem on a nearby blackboard.

"Come on, is it locks?" he asked. "Josh was good with locks. You've seen his handcuff act, and the crate escape in his show, right?"

"Locks are my speciality."

"Safes?"

"I'm pretty handy with those too."

"Alarm systems? Movement sensors?"

"It depends how advanced we're getting." I raised a hand. "Listen, I'm sorry, but it's beginning to feel as if I'm in therapy here. I seem to be the one doing all the sharing. I appreciate you talking to me, I really do, but if you can't help me out, I might as well leave."

I stood to do just that, and looked down over Maurice.

He worried his lip piercing some more, weighing my words. I was beginning to think I'd screwed up, that maybe I'd pushed things too far, but just as I was about to turn and make my way back through the house, he tugged his robe together and found his feet.

"What's up with your hand?" he asked, and grabbed my forearm, turning my palm upward so that he could study my taped fingers. "You trap it in a vault, or is this a memento from the Fisher Twins?"

"Basketball," I told him.

He dropped my hand, along with the corners of his mouth, stepped back and assessed me from head to toe. I guess it's fair to say that he wasn't looking at somebody who appeared capable of pulling off a slam dunk.

"No shit?"

"I caught the ball wrong. But don't worry, I can still work." I circled my index finger and thumb, snapping them together like a crab's claw.

"If you say so." He ran a hand over his shaved scalp. "Listen, why don't you come on inside? Let's talk some more."

TWENTY-THREE

So much for talking. Maurice had me wait in the white living room while he placed a telephone call elsewhere in the house. There wasn't anything other than white to look at. I had no television or magazines to distract me from my thoughts, and since my thoughts were mostly unwelcome, it didn't help my nerves a great deal.

After sitting and playing with my thumbs for a time, I turned my attention to the wristwatch I'd stolen. I was impressed that Maurice had spotted it, but then again, it was fairly distinctive. It was smaller than a modern wristwatch, though not as small as a woman's timepiece.

I slipped the watch from my wrist and wound the mechanism backward until I felt resistance, and then I raised it to my ear and listened to it tick. The second hand seemed to be moving again, sweeping past the black roman numerals on the pearlescent dial. I checked the time on my digital watch and set the wristwatch to match. Then I buffed the face on my shirt and slipped it back on. Messing with the watch was probably a bad idea. It just reminded me of how much time I was losing.

Another ten minutes went by before I heard engine noise outside the house, followed by the soft percussion of car doors closing. Footsteps and a two-tone doorbell beckoned Maurice back to the room. He was still wearing his white silk robe and pajama pants, not to mention his wrap-around sunglasses. True, it was light and airy inside his home, but it wasn't *that* light.

He opened the door and the identity of his guests left me suitably underwhelmed—Kojar the lofty trapeze artist and his gap-toothed, knee-high pal.

"This guy," the diminutive one squeaked, and pointed a stubbed finger at me. "Yeah, we seen him all right."

He had on the same bright yellow sneakers and crumpled jeans as he'd worn the previous night. His T-shirt was black again, but it featured a different rock motif—a human skull with flames burning through the eye-sockets. He cupped his chin and tapped his yellow sneaker against the floor.

"So you're a housebreaker, huh, guy?" he piped.

"I prefer 'gentleman thief.'"

"And last night, that wasn't your room?"

"My, you do catch on quick."

Kojar rested a plate-sized hand on his miniature friend, as if to hold him back. "You find Josh?" he asked, in his stilted Euro-English.

"I'm still looking for him."

His companion crossed his stubby arms. "Yeah, how come?"

"I've been through all this with Maurice," I said. "And I'm pretty sure he must have told you some of it on the telephone."

"Maybe I wanna hear it myself."

"Likely as not you do. What's your name, anyway?"

His eyes darkened beneath his uni-brow, but he didn't answer me.

"Christ, his name's Salvatore," Maurice cut in. "Sal to you and me. He's from New Jersey. And this here is Kojar. He's from Croatia."

Kojar squared his shoulders and lifted his chin, as though he was standing on the top step of a medal platform waiting to hear his national anthem. He had on a blue tracksuit with white piping along the arms and legs, and he wore flip-flops on his huge feet. His big toe alone was enough to intimidate me.

I looked at Maurice. More accurately, I looked at his blackened sunglasses.

"You said you wanted to talk."

"In my office."

I followed the three of them along a white hallway into a smaller white room. There was a white gloss desk positioned in front of a circular window that looked out over the corner of the pool. The walls were hung with framed show posters, including the advertisement I'd seen for the revue of the Fate of Atlantis.

The three men gathered around a glass table in the middle of the room. In the center of the table was a white cardboard model of a building complex—the kind of thing an architect might put together to give a client a better understanding of how a project could turn out. The complex was made up of three separate tower blocks, joined together by a much lower building that appeared to be around three stories in height. Surrounding the base of the complex were a number of white cardboard trees, a line of miniature white cars and a scattering of tiny white people.

To my right, Sal was on tiptoes, pressing his nose close to the structure. I thought about giving him a boost onto the table in case he wanted to stomp around the cardboard world like he was Godzilla.

"So, er, what is this?" I asked.

Maurice raised his hands and flipped his sunglasses up to rest on his scalp. It was the first time I'd seen his eyes. They were blue-green in color and strikingly alert, like the eyes of a jungle predator.

He watched me closely for quite some time, and I began to wonder if perhaps the cardboard model was about to split in two so that a dummy missile could emerge from a concealed silo in one of the towers. And sure, while it wouldn't have completely shocked me to learn that Maurice was the owner of a snow-white feline, I somehow didn't picture him as a megalomaniac with a cunning plan for world domination.

"So what, is this the model for a new casino?"

Maurice eyed me with suspicion, as though I'd made an impossible leap of logic.

"Well, is it?"

He held my gaze for a few beats more, as if he was debating

whether to share one of the foremost secrets of the ages. Then he waved his hands above the model in a circular fashion, as though summoning a mystic force.

"This is Magic Land."

Oh boy. Just as I thought things couldn't get any weirder . . .

"Magic Land?"

"The name, it may change," Kojar offered, with a pragmatic heft of his shoulders.

"Huh. So your big secret is that you want to build a casino with a magic theme. Which I guess is where this all ties in with Josh."

Maurice withdrew a slim white baton from the sleeve of his robe. He pointed it toward the rear quarter of the squat central building.

"Magic Land is a casino entirely dedicated to the art of magic. It will house a museum devoted to the greatest illusionists of all time." He moved the pointer to the opposite side of the structure, where a circular appendage seemed to bulge out like a white cardboard hernia. "It has a state-of-the-art, two-thousand-seat auditorium. The magician who headlines at this theater, in this casino, will have the greatest magic show of all time."

Maurice raised his baton in the air and pressed it against his lip ring. He gazed at me hawkishly, as though I couldn't possibly fail to comprehend the significance of it all.

"*Right.* But what are you saying exactly? Did Masters run away because he didn't want the Fisher Twins to know he was planning to quit?"

Sal thumped his fist down onto the glass table. "Enough with the questions. Just let Maurice explain."

"I'm trying, believe me."

Maurice tapped his baton against his lip piercing. He wanted to be careful. The move had all the makings of a nasty accident.

"You've heard of juice, right?"

"Fruit juice?"

He exhaled and closed his eyes. "In Vegas," he began, in a studied tone, "if you have juice, you have influence. Juice is power."

"Oh, okay."

"The guys who made this town, they brought the juice. Guys like Bugsy Siegel, Meyer Lansky, Benny Binion. Serious guys."

I think he meant mobster guys. I was tempted to ask if I should take notes and if there was likely to be a mid-term exam, but somehow I sensed that now wasn't the time.

"If you want to build a new casino in Vegas," Maurice went on, "you need juice."

"And a heck of a lot of money, I'm guessing."

"Money, sure. But plenty of people want to invest in Vegas. Finding money is the easy part."

Kojar and Sal nodded along. Funny. Getting hold of cash wasn't proving that easy for me.

"And the hard part?"

"Clearance. To build a Strip casino from scratch in this town, a major casino like Magic Land, requires a whole lot of clearance."

"And to get clearance you need juice?"

"That's the deal."

"So how do you get this juice?"

"There are ways," Sal cut in.

"I may need a little more detail than that."

Maurice knocked his baton against the edge of the table. "The traditional route? You need to be part of a network. People you can rely on, folks you can call on. Maybe you need some muscle. You'll always need green." He shrugged. "Have all of that behind you, and you have a reputation. You have juice."

"You're talking about the Mafia."

The three men flinched, and Kojar shot an instinctive look out through the circular window, as if he feared that a mob sharpshooter with a sniper rifle and a listening device was on the other side of the pool.

Maurice waved a hand at me. "Cool it on that talk."

"Why? Is saying the 'M' word in Vegas like mentioning the title of the Scottish play in a theater?"

Maurice looked at me blankly. Evidently, he'd never produced a Shakespearian tragedy.

"We don't talk about it no more," Sal explained. "We're trying to make Vegas a respectable town."

"Tell that to the Fisher Twins. They threatened to have me killed."

Maurice nodded. "They have the juice to do that."

"Well, how did they get it? They don't look like gangsters. Even the guys dressed as gangsters in their casino don't look like gangsters."

"That's what we wanted to talk to you about."

I was all set to hear more when we were interrupted by a strange buzzing noise, accompanied by an odd little ditty. The tune sounded electronic, like the chirping of some deranged, robotic bird. I frowned in confusion, but the noise grew steadily louder, the chirruping repeating itself over and over. Then I realized that everyone was staring in my direction, and shortly afterward it occurred to me that the noise was coming from my back pocket.

Victoria's mobile.

I reached for the stupid contraption, opened it and grimaced at the illuminated screen. *Withheld Number*. I didn't think that now was the time to function as Victoria's answering service, so I pressed the button with the tiny red handset on it and cut the connection. The screen went dark and the handset quit buzzing and tweeting.

"Sorry about that," I said, and pocketed the phone. "You were saying?"

Maurice looked down at Sal, then up at Kojar, then back at me. He placed his hands in the pockets on the front of his robe. I really wished he'd pull the material across his chest and cover himself up—I'd just about had it with being winked at by his left nipple.

"The Fisher Twins have a juice list."

"A juice list?" I repeated.

Maurice nodded. So did Sal and Kojar.

"And what exactly does a juice list do?"

"It contains every dirty little secret about anybody with a role

to play in Vegas. It tells you the politicians who take kickbacks
and the lawmakers who cheat on their wives. It tells you who's
dirty on the State Gaming Commission, who you can bribe to
obtain your casino license, which folks in city planning might
crack under pressure, which newspaper hacks have a soft spot
you can exploit."

"I see. And how did they come to have this list?"

"Private investigators, mostly. They hired a whole team before
they moved into town. They identified key people and had their
investigators dig information on them until they found dirt."

I thought of Terry Ricks, watching over Victoria back at
Space Station One. He'd struck me as a capable and resourceful
man—the type who might excel in an intelligence-gathering role.
It wouldn't have surprised me to learn that he'd been involved in
work of that nature.

Maurice smiled a lazy smile, and quite suddenly his eyes
looked entirely benign. "The Fisher Twins are smart. They knew
the kind of money they could make here, but it's tough for an
outsider to get a foothold. They needed to rig the odds."

"So they developed a blackmail dossier."

"Uh huh."

"And if you want to build Magic Land, you need a list just
like it."

"We need a list *exactly* like it."

Maurice loaded weight onto his words, watching me quite
calmly. Kojar and Sal watched me too. I felt a surge of electricity
in my fingertips (even the dud ones) and ran my tongue over my
lips. My lips felt a good deal drier than my armpits.

"Josh was meant to get you the list," I said.

Maurice nodded.

"And he hasn't delivered, or Sal and Kojar wouldn't have
been looking for him last night."

He nodded again. "You mentioned he wanted you involved in
a job."

"Right. And you think he wanted me to steal this juice list?"

Sal was fussing with the cardboard model, pinching one of

the miniature trees between his finger and thumb. Kojar was rocking on the balls of his feet, like he was practicing his balance. Maurice removed his hand from the pockets of his robe and fiddled with his lip piercing.

"You want in?"

"That depends. How much does it pay?"

"How much do you need?"

I turned my response over for a few moments. There was only one sum of money that would make any difference to me, so it seemed senseless to try for anything else.

"One hundred and forty thousand dollars."

A nerve twitched in Maurice's cheek. "Okay," he said, at length. "Let's talk details."

TWENTY-FOUR

Eight-thirty in the morning, and people had long since gravitated back toward the gray felt jungle in Space Station One. The croupiers and cocktail waitresses appeared fresh-faced and alert, the carpets were vacuumed, the slots gleaming, the air newly perfumed and low on cigarette smoke. Even the table limits had been re-set, and tourists destined for home were pausing to stake their last remaining chips before wheeling suitcases away.

I couldn't find Victoria. She wasn't playing blackjack and she wasn't trying her luck at roulette. I scanned the keno pit and the sports book and the slots. I even checked the food hall and the winding queue for the breakfast buffet and the crowded coffee and pastry outlet, but found no sign of her.

I moved back to the gaming-tables and did my best to locate Estelle, but in all likelihood, she'd finished her shift and left for the day. I thought about calling Victoria's mobile, and then I remembered that it was still in my pocket. I considered contacting the Fifty-Fifty and asking to be connected to the telephone in Victoria's room. It seemed like a sensible move, but before I could do anything about it I felt a hand grip me by the shoulder and haul me around.

"Looking for someone?"

Ricks stood with his fists on his hips and the tails of his blazer hooked behind his forearms. The whites of his eyes had yellowed, as if he was low on vitamins as well as sleep. Grayish stubble had grown up on his jowls, blurring the lines of his goatee and giving it a smudged effect to go along with his eyes. There was a fuggy, decayed stench to his breath, and when he exhaled it took a good deal of self-control not to cover my face with my forearm as though a canister of tear gas had been tossed at my feet.

"I'm trying to find Victoria," I said.

"We have her in a room."

I felt my nose crinkle as his breath washed over me once more. "A hotel suite?"

"That's funny," he told me. "She's asking for you."

There was nothing futuristic about the back room set-up at Space Station One. The room Victoria was detained in was as close to a prison cell as you could get without adding bunk beds, graffiti and a seven-foot man-ape called Crusher. The door was constructed from painted metal, with a wire-glass insert about the size of a hardback novel and a multi-pin lock that would be a real challenge to pick. Fortunately, Ricks had the appropriate key on a sizeable ring, so there was no need to test myself.

Victoria was slouched in a gray plastic chair at a gray plastic table that had been fixed to the gray concrete wall. The Houdini biography was open in her hands, and when we entered the room she laid it carefully down onto the table with the pages splayed.

She offered me a tired smile, then raised her hands to clear her hair from her eyes. I noticed that she'd acquired some yellow plastic bracelets to go along with her blue cocktail dress.

"Handcuffs." I shook my head and clucked my tongue at Ricks, as though he'd let himself down very badly.

"It's fine, Charlie," Victoria said. "The dummies left me here reading my Houdini book. In another three chapters, I'll be able to release myself and sneak out through that door."

Ricks grunted, and stepped around the table to approach Victoria. He was carrying a cardboard folder in his hands, and he set the folder down onto the table before snatching at Victoria's wrists and raising her arms above her head. He parted her hands and used a gadget from his trouser pocket to snip the cuffs away.

Victoria rubbed the skin of her wrists, wincing at the red

striations that had appeared. I sat across from her and chucked her under the chin.

"Okay?"

"Never better."

"You look tired."

"So do you." Her eyes slid sideways. "So does Mr. Ricks, for that matter."

"Did they treat you okay?"

"Well, I didn't get the room upgrade I requested."

I gave her hand a squeeze and she squeezed back. If we hadn't been sitting in a detention cell with a security agent watching over us, it might have passed for an affectionate moment.

She said, "You didn't answer my mobile."

I thought back to the withheld number that had appeared on the screen when I'd been inside Maurice's office. "Bad timing, I'm afraid."

"You said you'd only be gone five minutes."

"That was the plan."

"They took our money," she told me, and swallowed hard. Her eyes were getting a little swimmy. "Every last dollar. I'm sorry, Charlie."

"Oh well. House always wins, right?"

She bowed her head and sniffled, and I was just reaching for a hanky when I saw that Ricks had passed one across. Victoria accepted it with a murmur of gratitude, and while she dabbed her eyes and blew her nose, I leaned one arm over the backrest of my chair and faced up to her knight in shining armor.

"So, let's hear it."

Ricks twisted his lips, as if he was tasting around the various ways in which he could begin, and then he reached inside his blazer and removed a clear Ziploc bag. He tossed the bag onto the table and awaited my reaction. I lifted the bag and stared at its contents, working an elaborate shrug.

"You recognize that?" he asked.

I checked on Victoria. She peered at me from beneath her

fringe, her eyes smoky and vague. It was hard to read anything from them.

"Absolutely," I said. "It's my ring."

"Your ring?"

"My lucky ring, to be exact. I asked Victoria to wear it when she was playing blackjack."

"Lucky ring." Ricks shook his head at the words and ran his hand over his oily scalp. He freed the bag from my fingers and emptied the ring into his nut-brown palm. "It's a damn twinkle."

"Excuse me?"

"A twinkle." He gathered the ring between his forefinger and thumb and pointed the flattened face toward me. "An improvised mirror. Your friend here was playing blackjack and she had the ring angled so that she could read the dealer's cards."

I squinted at my warped reflection in the polished surface of the ring. My head looked out of proportion—my cheeks bloated and eyes swollen, as though I'd just stepped out of an orbiting shuttle without my spacesuit on. Even so, I had to admit that I could see myself quite clearly.

"Well I never. This is the first time I've noticed that the surface is reflective." I blinked, as though utterly mystified. "I'm sure Victoria hadn't noticed it before, either. Right, Vic?"

Victoria contemplated me for a long moment, then shook her head almost imperceptibly.

I offered Ricks a neutral smile. "It's a little unfortunate if this is all you have."

"She was past posting."

"Past wotsying?"

"Posting. At the roulette-table."

"You'll have to forgive me, but I have no idea what you're talking about."

Ricks snarled and rested his bunched fists on top of his cardboard folder. He leaned his weight onto his fists until his knuckles popped and then he sighed his morning breath all over me.

"She was staking triples. Three blue chips, five dollars each.

Only, when she hit a number straight up she pulled a switch. Suddenly she had two blue chips sitting on top of a two-hundred-dollar black marker."

"That was my bet," Victoria told him, in a manner that suggested it wasn't the first time she'd run the argument.

"Oh, sure. And it just so happened that the one time you hit your number was the one time when you laid that particular stake. That exact pattern of chips."

"I was lucky."

"Yeah? Maybe it was your ring."

Victoria steepled her fingers and pressed her fingertips to her lips. Color flushed her cheeks. "As I've already said a number of times, you should ask the croupier if you don't believe me. He didn't have a problem with my bet, and neither did his pit boss. At least, not until you came over and started levelling accusations."

"You want me to pull the tape? You want us all to watch the move?"

Ricks pushed his face toward Victoria and held it there. I heard a faint whistle as he inhaled through his nose. I didn't envy Victoria the outbreath she was about to experience.

"So I ran your passport through our system," he added, curling his lip. "Made an interesting connection."

Victoria grimaced and backed away from Ricks, as if he was a drunken Lothario in a pick-up bar.

"I told you I knew a guy called Alfred Newbury," he said. "One of the best casino cheats I ever met. He's your father, right?"

I heard myself scoff.

"Er, Starsky, I hate to tell you this, but Victoria's father is a High Court judge."

His head swiveled and he beamed a disarming grin. His teeth gleamed quite brilliantly against his dark skin.

"No, friend. You're thinking of his nickname."

Ricks slid the cardboard folder in front of me as if he was laying down a winning hand at the end of a marathon poker game. I delayed for a moment before opening it. The folder contained a number of printed pages. Clipped to the top page was a headshot of a distinguished-looking gentleman with thick white hair and a bushy, snow-white beard. His gaze was bold and discerning, but there was a mischievous sparkle in his eyes, as if he'd known at the moment the image was captured that it would one day be clipped to a typeset report just like the one in Ricks' folder.

I lifted the photograph clear of the page. Beneath it was a printed sheet listing some personal details. Name, age, date of birth, permanent address. The report gave the man's home town as St. Albans, near London, and it stated that he was married to a woman called Joyce.

I recalled Victoria mentioning that she'd grown up in the London commuter belt, and I knew for a fact that her mother's name was Joyce. And hell, I couldn't deny that there was a likeness about the face in the picture and the features of my good friend Victoria. I nudged the folder aside with a dismissive snort.

Ricks said, "He was known as The Judge on account of he always knew when to make his move, plus when to quit. Guy worked Europe, mostly. The Riviera. Monaco. Spent some time in Eastern Europe. He didn't play Vegas often, and so far as anyone knows he hasn't been back here in years. I tracked him my second year in the job. He ran a crew at the Sahara and hit us for a couple hundred thousand. Got away with it too."

"That doesn't sound like a member of Victoria's family."

I fixed on Ricks' eyes. His pupils danced left and right, as though he was running calculations in his mind.

"Oh, he's her father, all right. Looks like he passed on a few pointers, too. Maybe we should try to get a hold of him, see if he's feeling mighty proud?"

Victoria's head snapped around as though she'd been jabbed in the neck with a pointy stick.

"You can leave my father out of this."

Ricks grinned, and showed her his palms. "Well, what do you know? Seems I was right all along."

"You have some dirty allegations," I said. "Congratulations."

"Oh, that's something, coming from a lousy crib-man."

I put my head on my shoulder and did my best to appear

bemused. "I'm a writer, Mr. Ricks. I think perhaps you're confusing me with the lead character in some of my mystery novels."

"Oh, come on, you think we didn't check you out back at the
Fifty-Fifty? You think we don't have access to your records?"

"Record," I corrected him. "A single, youthful mistake. Nothing more."

It was Ricks' turn to scoff. He poked a finger at my lap. "You
want that I should ask you to turn out your pockets again?"

No, that wasn't a suggestion that I was altogether keen on.
For one thing, I had my burglar tools on me. But worse still, I
also had Josh's wallet.

"Didn't your mother ever tell you it's rude to point?"

"Guess she was too busy teaching me not to steal other folks'
possessions."

"That's enough," Victoria said. "Can't you just tell us what it
is that you want?"

"Want?" Ricks straightened and cupped the back of his neck.
"Gee, I don't know. I guess I want you to quit cheating my
casinos."

Victoria scraped the legs of her chair backward and stood
abruptly. She paced to the far wall in a measured fashion and
pressed her hands flat against the painted surface. She kicked the
toe of her shoe against the plastic skirting board.

"Am I right in thinking that you know about the ultimatum
we're facing?" she asked.

"He knows," I said.

She turned her head and scowled hard at Ricks. Her back was
arched and her teeth exposed. She looked like a cat with its hack-
les raised—one that was ready to pitch itself into a claw fight.

"Hey," Ricks said, and raised his spread hands like a shield. "I
don't only work for the Fifty-Fifty. My agency watch over a
number of resorts. This here is one of them."

"Oh, really? And what hours are you required to work? Because forgive me if I'm mistaken, but I was beginning to form
the impression that this was personal to you."

"Lady, I don't punch in and out. My job doesn't work that way. I'm employed to stop casino cheats. You were cheating one of my casinos."

"Because our lives are in danger."

Ricks sucked his lips inside his mouth and shook his head, as though the situation wasn't playing out in the way he'd intended. He rested his hands on his hips and looked toward the ceiling. His tone dropped to something approaching confidential.

"For the record, miss, I happen to believe your father was one classy guy. Maybe the best casino man I ever went up against. And maybe I'm not altogether comfortable watching his daughter pull the kind of routine that would make her old man blush. Leastways, not with a petty housebreaker who's too dumb to know when he's in over his head."

I guess I should have been offended by his assessment of my abilities but right at that moment I was rather more interested in his attitude toward Victoria's dad.

"You have the money Victoria won," I said, speaking carefully, as though there was a voice-activated bomb in the room and I was doing my best not to detonate it.

"She cheated that money."

"That may be," I told him, in the same measured tone. "But the fact is this casino hasn't lost anything. So there's really no harm done."

"Is that so? You expect me to believe you haven't been tossing guest rooms for the money you need?"

I shook my head. "No tossing. I'm studiously neat. And you can rest assured that my night didn't go nearly so well as I might have hoped."

Ricks looked from me, to Victoria, then rested his chin on his chest and shook his head.

"We don't have a great deal of time left." I checked my digital watch and scared myself with how true that happened to be. "Can't you at least give us a chance to save ourselves? Don't keep Victoria locked in here."

Ricks firmed up his jaw, then released a gasp of air and pinched the bridge of his nose. "I don't know why I'm even listening to this."

"We won't gamble again," I went on. "Not one bet at one table."

"Charlie, be serious." Victoria moved across from the wall. "You can't promise him that."

"Sure I can. After all, not gambling is a Newbury family rule."

"If I even catch you with one chip in your pretty English hand," Ricks warned Victoria, before letting the words trail off and allowing his shoulders to sag. "Lady, you should know that your father is the only reason I'm even entertaining this."

"Do we have a deal?" I asked, and offered Ricks my hand.

"Shoot," he said, and shook my hand wearily, like a man doomed to confront the fate he has just set in motion.

"Victoria?"

"Okay, fine." She snatched up her ring from the surface of the table and held it between her thumb and forefinger, thrusting it toward Ricks' face. "But I'm keeping my lucky ring."

Ricks shook his head some more and gathered up his cardboard folder. "Way I see things, you may just need it."

He approached the heavy metal door and unlocked it with his key, then heaved the thing open and motioned for us to leave. I guided Victoria outside with my hand on the small of her back, where the sequined material of her cocktail dress met with her skin. I was crossing into the hallway when I paused and leaned close to Ricks' ear.

"There is one more thing," I said, in what could have passed for a whisper.

"You don't know when to quit, do you, guy?"

"An address," I went on. "And a name. For the croupier working the roulette-table Josh was fixing. The one likely to end up with a hook where his hand used to be."

"That all?"

"That's the last of it."

Ricks pouted, and tipped his head to the side. "I'll have some-one look into it."

"Terrific." I patted him on the shoulder. "You're a gentleman. And you've done a very noble thing here today."

"Save it," he said. "Quit trying to work me, and get out of my sight before I change my mind."

"Consider it done," I told him, and with that I whisked Victoria away along the corridor without a backward glance.

TWENTY-FIVE

"I can't believe you're smoking again," Victoria said.

"Really?" I exhaled. "That's what you want to lead with?"

We were sitting across from one another in a cushioned booth in the Fifty-Fifty's Starlight Eaterie. Our table was a landfill of crockery. When we'd first joined the queue for the breakfast buffet, I hadn't felt hungry. Then I'd seen the mountains of food on offer, and my stomach had begun to plead its case. I'd loaded my plate with cooked meats, eggs (scrambled and poached), hash browns and grilled tomatoes, then returned for pancakes, waffles, fresh fruit, maple syrup and cream. I'd washed it all down with orange juice and enough coffee to see around time, and then I'd begun to debate whether I should loosen off my belt buckle and assess the muffins. After a good deal of thought, I'd concluded that it might be more appropriate to ignore the No Smoking signs and light a cigarette, and it was this decision that had prompted Victoria to speak for the first time in more than ten minutes.

"But you were doing so well."

"I was a walking nicotine patch."

"I just hate to see it."

"Well now, we can't all be perfect, can we?"

Victoria slumped in her chair and crossed her arms over the scooped neck of her cocktail dress. If we'd been anywhere other than Las Vegas, I imagine she would have felt kind of slutty to be eating breakfast in (it must be said) a rather revealing outfit.

But in a funny way, it seemed entirely fitting, and if only I'd been sporting my tux I could have convinced myself that we'd spent the night playing high-stakes baccarat and were now the disheveled stars of a quintessential Vegas moment.

Victoria kicked me in the shin. "You might as well go ahead. I can see you're dying to goad me."

"I'm shocked, is all." I placed my hand on my heart and widened my eyes. "It's not every day that you learn a dark secret about your best friend."

"So I lied to you, Charlie. *Whoopee!* And yes, I get that you think that it's not terribly different from how you lied to me about the way you really look. And in your eyes, that makes me a hypocritical bitch for the way I reacted. So I guess you're entitled to crow about it before you grow up and realize that we're even."

"Even? You had me believe your father was a bastion of respectability. A High Court judge."

"Well, what would you have had me say?"

"The truth. Christ, out of everyone you know I'm probably the most likely to understand."

"It's not something I'm especially proud of."

"Well, from what Ricks said, maybe you should be. Your father must have been good."

Vic squinted. I raised my cigarette to my mouth and did likewise. The brand I'd stolen was stronger than I was used to. I was starting to like it.

"Oh, give me one of those," Victoria said, and reached for the packet.

"You're kidding me."

Victoria offered me an insincere smile as she removed a cigarette. She struck a match from a book with the hotel's logo on it and raised the flame toward her face. Sounds corny, but I was beginning to see her in a whole new light (and I don't just mean the one from the match).

"I didn't know that you smoked."

"Oh Charlie. There's an awful lot that you don't know about me."

She drew expertly on the cigarette, her chest expanding as her cheeks hollowed out. She held the cigarette very elegantly between her fingers, with her bare elbow cupped in her palm. How someone smokes can be such an intimate, revealing thing. Watching Victoria, I could almost picture her back in her university days, sitting on a windowsill with a college scarf around her neck, a volume of poetry in her hand and a faraway look in her eyes.

"So tell me something else that I don't know about the mysterious Victoria Newbury."

She leaned her head back and exhaled smoke toward the ceiling. A doped smile stretched her mouth.

"Dad's still active, for one thing."

"He is?"

She pointed at me with her cigarette. "You remind me of him in that way. Can't help himself. Enjoys the life too much."

"And he's successful?"

She nodded. "Very. He works in the Far East these days. Likes to go where the casinos and dealers are new. Says they're vulnerable while they're learning the trade."

I blew a plume of smoke from my lips. "And what does your mum think of all this?"

"She dislikes the risks involved, but at the same time she enjoys the lifestyle. It used to be she was raising us while he was away in Europe and America, so she never got to experience it for herself. Nowadays, I'd say she's a lot more understanding."

"And does he work alone?"

"Nuh uh." She took another hit on her cigarette. "You need a good team. Dad works with five or six like-minded people around his own age. Mostly they card count. The other moves— past posting, for instance—it's too easy to get caught." She exhaled and wafted the smoke away. "As you saw for yourself."

She reached across and tapped some ash into the saucer I was using. I took another draw myself. The smoke and the coffee were beginning to make me feel a touch light-headed. If it wasn't for the weight of all the food in my stomach, I might very well have floated up from my seat.

"So how much do you know about cheating a casino?"

"More than the average person." She cocked her shoulders. "Less than an expert."

"Your father taught you?"

She nodded, and her eyes lit up, as though she was recalling a fond memory.

"He wasn't home as much as I'd have liked. Partly it was the work, but you could always tell he relished the travel too. That's another way in which you remind me of him. A wandering soul." The skin crinkled at the corners of her eyes. "I suppose it made the times he was home more special. He had a den—still has, in fact—and it's like a mini-casino in there. He has a French roulette-table and a blackjack felt, a little faded and frayed these days. When we were kids, he used to play with us."

"And did he play fair?"

She grinned. "Fair wasn't anything he cared about, or anything he taught us. He just liked to win. And counting cards, or using a twinkle, those were simply ways of achieving that. To him, the entire life is a game. He's just very thorough in the way that he plays." Victoria stubbed her cigarette into a smear of ketchup. "To be honest, I wasn't as interested as he wanted me to be. It's like your lock-picking. I can understand the theory, but to get good at something, you really have to practice. I just didn't care enough."

"So what happed at Space Station One?"

Victoria slumped back against the vinyl booth cushion. "Desperation. We needed money fast and I didn't see the sense in leaving it to luck."

I blew the last of the smoke from my lungs and stubbed out my own cigarette. I twirled the packet on the table.

"Quite a risk."

"You're telling me. Ricks was right. Dad would have been mortified."

"How come?"

She sighed. "Twinkles? They went out of fashion around the era this hotel is meant to represent. And past posting without a team behind you? Well." Victoria threw up her hands, as if it was explanation enough. I wasn't sure that I followed her.

"Did you think you'd be caught?"

"I realized there was a reasonable likelihood I might be."

"So why try?"

"You mean aside from the fact we might be killed tonight?"

"Yup."

She reached for the sugar dispenser and tipped sugar granules into her palm. "It was Josh, actually."

"Masters? What did *he* have to do with it?" I searched out her eyes and peered hard into them, trying to pick up on what she was saying. She smirked a little, as if I was being altogether too slow. "Wait. You knew he was cheating, didn't you?"

"There you go."

"But how?"

She ditched the dispenser and dusted her palms together, sprinkling sugar over the table. "I was watching him, while you were playing poker. He was being so brazen about what he was up to. It intrigued me."

"You could see he was using one of those bottle tops to trade up his chips?"

"Not to begin with. The first thing I noticed was that he was palming some of the chips that belonged to the woman sitting across from him—the sweet old lady with the gold lamé jacket? Then I noticed that he was past posting too."

"The cheeky rogue. And you were willing to help him?"

"Not with the old lady. I told him to put her chips back."

"And did he?"

"He didn't have much choice. I would have exposed him if he didn't."

"Christ. No wonder he gave you free tickets to his show."

"Oh, I imagine he enjoyed it. All men like to show off, right?"

"I've heard it said."

Victoria stretched her arms way above her head. She yawned and groaned somewhat indulgently.

"Charlie, we're really stuffed."

I put my hand to my belly. "I know. I think it was the pancakes."

"No," she said. "I mean, we're screwed. I messed up and got caught and now we can't gamble any more."

"Doesn't matter," I told her.

"Like hell. I suppose we could head downtown to Freemont Street."

"Seriously, Vic. I've found a way to make the money we need."

She propped her elbows on the table and pushed her face toward me. "Then I'm all ears."

I checked over my shoulder. "Can we discuss this upstairs in my room?"

"Works for me. I have something to tell you myself, as it happens. But let me just ask you one thing. Is it legal?"

"Oh, Vic," I said. "Sometimes I wonder if you know me at all."

TWENTY-SIX

"Ah, sweet, sweet bed. It feels so good to have found you again."

Victoria flopped onto my bed as if she'd been crawling across an arid desert for many days and had finally chanced upon a glistening oasis. She spread her arms wide, luxuriating in the thick cotton bedcovers, lifted her legs into the air and kicked off her shoes.

"Oh, that feels good," she said.

I dropped into an easy chair beside the mini-bar and rested my face in my hands. "I'm shattered."

"Me too. So come on, tell me how you're going to save our hides before I'm completely unconscious."

She commando-crawled up the bed, turned and collapsed onto the pillows and cushions propped against the headrest. Her cocktail dress had ridden up on her thighs and she tugged the sequined material down at the hem, before covering her legs with a spare pillow.

Her legs really weren't at all shabby. And there was a dizzied fatigue to her eyes that was sort of endearing. In other circumstances, at another time . . .

I rubbed my face, clearing my mind of the notion.

"I tracked down Maurice," I said, with sudden focus. "The guy from the note we found in Josh's suite."

"You did? How?"

"Long story. The short version is that there's a show at the

Atlantis resort, a circus-type revue that features our friends from upstairs—the giant and the midget."

Victoria winced.

"The giant is called Kojar. The midg—Sorry, *the short one* is called Sal. And Maurice is a chap called Maurice Mills. He produces the show."

"And what's this Maurice character like?"

"In a word? Strange. He likes everything to be white. His clothes, his house, his furniture—all white. It's kind of like meeting an angel with a personality disorder."

"And is he on the side of the angels?"

"Hard to say. But he is the source of the money we need."

"So he's rich?"

"He certainly has a bob or two. And he has a plan to make an awful lot more."

"And is that where we come in?"

I laced my fingers together behind my head and yawned rather flamboyantly. "Pretty much," I said, and from there I went on to explain as much as I could.

I began by telling Victoria how Maurice was looking to make the step up from Vegas show producer to casino impresario, how Kojar and Salvatore were part of his crew, and how Josh had been promised the key role in the Magic Land theater in return for helping them to obtain the necessary "juice" to build the casino. I started to expand on what was meant by the term juice, but it seemed that Victoria was ahead of me on that score, and so I skipped forward and told her about the blackmail list that the Fisher Twins had compiled, and how Josh had failed to get his hands on it. From there, I told her that I'd been hired to steal the list in return for the one hundred and forty thousand dollars that we needed . . . and I was all set to go on and address some of the detail of what stealing the juice list would involve when Victoria interrupted me.

"Hang on, let me get this straight," she said, with a face as tart as lemon juice. "Your solution to paying off the Fisher Twins is to steal something from them that's more valuable than the money they're after us for in the first place."

"In a nutshell, yes."

Her eyes bugged out of her head and she gazed at me as if I was certifiable. "Don't you think it might be better if we stole from somebody other than the people we actually owe money to?"

"It would have been nice if things could have turned out that way."

"Charlie, if we get caught, I really don't see it going down too well."

"They've already said they're going to kill us, Vic. I don't know how much worse it can get."

She lowered her face and picked idly at the cotton pillowcase. "Hmm."

"Is that a 'Hmm, yes, I can see how you've offered us the best possible solution to a tricky situation and, while I don't feel altogether comfortable about it, I realize it's the only shot we're going to get?'"

"No, Charlie. It's just a 'Hmm.' I really don't know what to say."

"Nothing *to* say." I craned my neck and read the alarm clock on the bedside cabinet. "We have something like eleven hours left to pull it off."

"Eleven hours." She grimaced. "How difficult is this going to be?"

"Well, it ain't easy."

"I had a feeling you'd say that. Where is this juice list?"

It was my turn to grimace. "I'm told the twins keep it in their office. In a variety of safe that I've attempted to open three times before in my life."

"Just attempted?"

"I got close once. If I'd had another hour or two, I'd have cracked it no problem."

"Oh good grief. And what does this juice list look like exactly?"

"Maurice didn't know for sure. But the likelihood is that it'll be in electronic format, rather than a little black book, say."

"And just where is the twins' office to be found?"

"On the top floor of this hotel."

Victoria's eyes swiveled toward the ceiling, as though she could see through the forty or so stories that separated us from our goal.

"Please tell me it's dead easy for us to get to."

"What do you think?"

"I think ignorance could be bliss, but I suspect I should really know what we're up against."

I retrieved my hands from behind my neck and contemplated my nails, playing the part of a man barely troubled by the obstacles that confront him.

"Well, for starters, there are just three ways to reach the twins' office. The most direct route is a private express elevator that only the twins and a handful of staff are entitled to use. In order to operate the elevator, you have to swipe a key card and type in a six-digit code. There are security cameras fitted inside the carriage, and the cameras screen footage to two personal assistants positioned outside the twins' office." I glanced up from my nails. "Actually, there are six personal assistants—they work a shift pattern so that two of them are always on duty at any one time."

"And the other ways?"

I clicked my teeth. "Option B involves the service stairs leading up from the floor below, where a security desk is manned twenty-four-seven and the door is protected by another six-digit code."

"Or?"

"Option C—I start on the roof and get to perform my world-famous cat burglar routine."

"Christ."

"Only I have vertigo."

"Christ."

"And I'd need to know how to abseil—which I don't—and I'd have to be able to break through a triple-pane glass window without making a sound—which I can't—and it would really help if I could get out the same way and find a plausible escape route—which may involve a helicopter. Oh, and then there's the challenge of doing it all without being spotted by the thousands of tourists outside this building at any one time, and with the kind of money and equipment we simply don't have."

"We're not filming *Ocean's Eleven* here, Charlie."

"More like *Ocean's Two*, on a really tight budget. Assuming you're prepared to help, that is?"

"Of course I'll help. You know I'll do what I can."

Victoria smoothed her hands over the pillowcase and her brow wrinkled in a way that showed me she was clearly troubled by something. It wasn't very long before she told me what that something was.

"Do you really believe that Josh was planning to steal this juice list?"

"I'm not sure I care. Right now, all I'm bothered about is paying off the Fisher Twins and getting out of Vegas alive."

"It bothers *me*."

I found myself smiling. "That's because you're a stickler for tying loose threads together. And I appreciate it when you're reading one of my manuscripts, but in a situation like this, you have to let some things go."

"And what if I don't want to?"

"You could sleep on it. You said you were tired, right?"

"I can't sleep with all this running around my head, Charlie."

"Vic, you should see yourself. I reckon you could sleep through a hurricane about now. In fact, I wouldn't be altogether surprised if you're not already asleep and this is just a bad dream. Why don't you close your eyes and find out?"

She gave me a skewed look, as if her patience was running very thin indeed.

"If it helps you to relax," I went on, "we can't try anything before four o'clock this afternoon. Maurice tells me the Fisher Twins play golf at that time every day. There's a course on an Indian reservation in the middle of the desert. It's a half-hour drive from the Strip. So even if they only play nine holes, it should give us enough time."

"Will you at least hear me out?"

I gritted my teeth and cradled my forehead, as if someone was twisting a screw inside my brain and I wasn't entirely thrilled about it.

"Fine. Go ahead and put doubts in my mind. After all, there's no sense in making any of this easier on ourselves."

Victoria curled her lip and drew my attention to the middle finger on her right hand. Then she showed me her other fingers and began counting them off.

"Point one, why would Josh do it? He already has a show that's doing very well. The Fifty-Fifty is a prestigious casino and he's making a lot of money."

She held onto her index finger, poised to curl it down and move on to her second concern.

"You want me to answer these one by one, or all at once?"

"Point two," she went on, ignoring me, "he's an illusionist, not a burglar. From what you say, the safe this juice list is stored in is difficult to open."

"Not if you have the code."

She glared at me. "Obviously. But Josh wouldn't have the code because it's not his safe. So why would anyone think he could get hold of the list?"

"And point three?"

Victoria closed her hand into a fist and studied her knuckles, as if she was wondering what kind of imprint they might leave on my face.

"I don't have a point three," she said, stiff-jawed.

"So what's with the finger-counting?"

"Does it matter? Aren't those two questions enough to be going on with?"

I shrugged, somewhat half-heartedly. And if only I could have summoned another yawn, I would have added that too. Because the truth is, the same concerns had been nibbling away at the back of my mind, and I'd been trying my hardest to ignore them.

"Well," I said, "as for your first point, I'd say that you can never underestimate the ego, ambition and greed of a cretin like

Josh Masters. Okay, he had a pretty comfortable set-up here, but he wasn't performing in the main theater, and he wasn't the casino's headline star. So I reckon it was a status thing, not to mention a money thing."

"That sounds a little weak, Charlie."

"And as for your second point, it could be he *does* know his way around a safe. Maurice was telling me that Josh has some escapology built into his show. And granted, a lot of magicians use gimmicked cuffs and locks, but if Masters was even halfway serious, he'd have taught himself the basics of lock-picking and safe manipulation. Look at me. As a kid, I was into card tricks, and yes, as time went on, I became more interested in locks, but there's nothing to say Josh didn't have a similar background. And a lot of the stuff you see in magic carries over into the work I do. Dexterity, sleight of hand, misdirection."

"Even weaker."

I stood up from my chair and paced the carpet. Pacing the carpet didn't help a great deal. I moved over to the window and gazed out at the Strip. Traffic was as busy as ever. The sidewalks too. Opposite, the hotel towers of Caesars Palace thrust upward into the white-blue sky as if a little piece of Benidorm—the worst piece of Benidorm—had been transplanted into the middle of the desert landscape.

"All right," I said, tapping a finger on the window glass. "Ask yourself this. Why did he run away in the middle of his show? True, the Fisher Twins knew about his gambling scam, but that's the kind of thing they could have resolved among themselves. God knows, there are enough stories about Vegas stars indulging in excess."

"So what are you suggesting?"

I turned and flattened my back against the window. "I'm suggesting that maybe he'd made a real mess of trying to get his hands on the juice list. If he'd screwed up so badly that the twins had found out what he was trying to do, then he had good reason to be scared."

"But if that's the case, wouldn't they have quizzed us about the list?"

It was a good point, and yet another one I hadn't been able to reconcile in my mind.

"All I can think, Vic, is that the twins assumed we were only a part of the gambling fix. Perhaps they believed we were just a distraction. So that's more misdirection. And then there's the twins' sister, of course."

"Who?"

I stared quizzically at Victoria. It took me a while to realize that I'd forgotten to fill her in on that particular connection. I must have been more tired than I thought.

"Caitlin. The dead girl in the bath—it turns out that she was their sister."

"Are you serious?"

"I'm afraid so. And when you factor that in, it's another very good reason why Josh might have felt like he had to run. Hell, she could be the primary reason. Think about it—they worked together, they were friends. What's to say Josh didn't tell her what he was planning? What's to say he didn't ask her to help him and join him at Magic Land? Say he did, and say she couldn't handle the idea of her brothers being duped, and so she told them what Josh was up to. That would explain why he killed her. And that would make sense of why he ran."

I spread my hands against the window glass and waited for Victoria to acknowledge the logic in what I'd just said. She didn't look entirely convinced. She didn't appear all that comfortable either. She was squirming on the bed and chewing her lip and contorting her face in a most unseemly manner. Eventually, she patted the space beside her.

"Sit down a minute."

"Eh?"

"There's something I need to show you."

I remained standing. Victoria reached for her handbag and patted the bed once more.

"Sit down, Charlie."

Despite my better judgment, I skulked across the room and climbed onto the bed, shuffling backward until I was sitting with my back resting against the stacked cushions and my knees raised up by my chest. I gripped hold of my shins.

"Victoria, your voice is sounding funny."

"I'm sorry. I meant to tell you this earlier, but then you started to talk about Maurice and the juice list, and . . . well, I forgot."

"Forgot what?"

Victoria gave me a searching look, chewing her lip some more, then said, "Charlie, are you absolutely certain she was dead? The girl in the bath, I mean."

"Of course."

"You checked for a pulse?"

I scratched the back of my head. "Well, no, not exactly. But there was no need. She wasn't moving."

"Did you touch her?"

"I didn't want to, Vic."

"So what did you do exactly?"

I sighed and shook my head, as though everything Victoria was asking me was entirely inconsequential.

"I put my hand in the water and found it was cold. Then I watched her for a while. She didn't move the whole time I was in the bathroom."

Victoria smiled glumly and removed the Houdini biography from her handbag. She passed it over to me, saying, "Look at the inside cover."

I did as she said. There was a message written there.

Caitlin. Some inspiration for your new act. Doesn't hurt to learn from the best. Love always, Josh.

"Okay, so it was Caitlin's book. Big deal."

"But somebody has made notes throughout the book, Charlie. They've also highlighted certain passages. It was annoying me when I was reading it, but it was something I could live with. And then I saw *this*."

Victoria flipped through the book until she found a right-hand page with its top corner folded down. It was headed with the words *The Domestic Magician*. She pointed at a particular passage that had been highlighted in yellow ink. An asterisk had been scrawled beside it in pencil.

I read the highlighted lines and a hollow queasiness began to form in the pit of my stomach. I gulped, and it felt as though I was swallowing gravel. The words swam before my eyes, but there was no denying what they said.

Houdini's New York home was furnished to accommodate his passion for magic. Extensive shelving housed his numerous reference books, and whole rooms were devoted to his collection of stage props. The crowning glory was his bathroom, where a large, bespoke tub was installed so that Houdini could fill it with ice-cold water and discipline himself to hold his breath for long periods of time, by way of preparation for the rigors of his Chinese Water Torture Cell.

TWENTY-SEVEN

"Oh boy," I said.

"You think she might not be dead?" Victoria asked me.

I turned my mind back to the scene in the bathroom. How long had I been inside? A minute? Maybe two? If Caitlin was well-practiced at holding her breath, there was every chance she could have lasted that long. It would explain why she hadn't moved, because staying absolutely still would have helped her to preserve oxygen. And with her head and ears submerged, there was no reason why she would have sensed me standing over her or heard me moving about. True, I'd put my hand in the tub to test the water, but I'd done it away from her feet, and since I was under the impression that she was dead at the time, I'd been really quite delicate.

"Maurice told me that Caitlin had been working on a new act," I said, my voice a little shaky. "He said it would be perfect for the Atlantis. I didn't make the connection at the time. He must have been talking about the water theme."

"Wowzer." Victoria freed the book from my hands and scanned the passage again for herself. "So it sounds like you're not a suspect in her murder any more."

"Maybe."

"Though it doesn't explain why Josh went back to his suite after he disappeared. I mean, if she wasn't dead, then he didn't have a body to dispose of."

"Perhaps he didn't go back."

"Then where did the key card go?"

I glanced toward the receptacle on the wall near the door to my suite. My own key card was there, enabling the air-con to function.

"Think about it. If Caitlin was alive, and she was using Josh's bath to practice holding her breath, then when she was finished she could have taken the card with her."

"Oh, I get it. She dries herself, gets dressed, empties the bath, takes the room card, and leaves."

"Precisely."

"Though it doesn't fit with your theory about Josh confiding in Caitlin about the juice list, and Caitlin telling her brothers."

"It doesn't?"

"Come on. She'd hardly be using his suite to practice holding her breath while all that was going on."

"Maybe she was really serious about practicing." I reclaimed the Houdini book from Victoria and fanned the pages. "Any other revelations in here?"

"Not that I found. I checked the other highlighted passages but nothing leaped out at me."

"So no mention of how to crack a Schmidt and Co safe?"

"No mention of juice lists, either."

"Typical." I lifted the book before my eyes and frowned at it. "Call yourself a plot device? One lousy clue, that's all you're offering us?"

Victoria barely laughed. Maybe she was too tired. Or maybe I wasn't quite as funny as I liked to believe.

"At least we can contact the police now," she said.

"How's that?"

"Well, if Caitlin's not dead, you're not a potential murder suspect. So we can call them in and avoid getting killed."

I shook my head. "Ricks and the twins have enough evidence to have us arrested for casino theft. Two counts, in your case."

"I'd rather that than be killed."

"But we don't know for certain that Caitlin is alive."

"Charlie."

"What? She looked dead when I saw her, Vic. And yes, maybe we have a possible explanation for that now. But we don't know for certain one way or the other. It could be she was practicing and it went wrong."

"So what are you suggesting, exactly?"

I considered our options for a moment. It seemed like there were a couple of things we could do.

"I think you should look for Caitlin. If she's alive, she might not be too hard to find. People here at the casino must know her. Someone will be able to tell you where to look."

"And what about you?"

"If Ricks hurries up and tells me where I can find the croupier with the one-hand card shuffle, I'll go and speak to him and see if he can put us in touch with Josh."

"And if that doesn't work?"

"I'll steal the juice list."

"Just like that."

I tapped my temple. "Positive mental outlook, Vic."

"Inspirational. So when do you want me to begin looking for Caitlin?"

I studied her face. The only way she could have looked any sleepier was if an anesthetist had just jabbed a syringe into her rump and asked her to begin counting down from ten very slowly.

"Listen, we're both shattered. I say we take a nap for an hour, then get started. It'll be much better if you're thinking straight when you find her."

"*If* I find her. But I suppose getting some rest does make sense. Would you mind if I stayed here? I don't think I have the energy to get off this bed."

I told her that was fine.

"And Charlie, if we get close to the deadline and none of this has worked out, will you promise me we can call the police?"

I locked onto her eyes and held them, nodding as sincerely as I could. "If the time comes, we'll call them. But that's not going to happen."

Victoria turned her back on me and reached for a pillow, tugging it beneath her head. She sighed and flexed her toes, wiggling a small hollow in the covers.

"You know this positive outlook thing . . ." she said, in a dozy voice.

"Yeah."

"Well, I was thinking—at least you have plenty of material for your short story."

I couldn't sleep. I tried stretching out and nodding off but it wasn't happening. I was too wired.

After a good deal of huffing and complaining, I propped myself up on my elbow and looked down at Victoria. Her eyes were closed and she was breathing steadily. One hand was curled on her pillow, barely holding a coil of her hair. Her jaw wasn't locked, she wasn't grinding her teeth, and so far as I could tell she was enjoying some respite from it all.

It's funny how mistaken you can be about somebody. I never would have guessed that Victoria's father was a crook. The idea that he was a judge had seemed to fit so well with everything I knew about her, that I'd never had any reason to doubt it.

I can't say that I was troubled by the revelation. In some ways, I was even quite glad. She obviously cared about her father, in spite of his faults, and knowing that made me a little more comfortable in my own skin.

The sad truth is that I don't have many friends. I move to new cities too often to build lasting relationships, and since I spend most of my time writing novels or stealing from people, I'm not the most social of creatures. I don't like to be interrupted when I'm working on a new book, and I most certainly don't like to be disturbed when I'm breaking into somebody's home, and that doesn't leave me much scope to forge close friendships. I suppose I don't have the inclination, either. But I did have Victoria, and I trusted her implicitly, and she was the one person in all the world that I didn't want to let down.

With that in mind, I stopped watching over her and moved to the other side of the bed, where I reached a hand into my holdall and removed a spiral notepad and a pen. Turning to a fresh page in the notepad, I pulled the lid from the pen and went through the motions of preparing to write. But who was I kidding? I couldn't write with everything that was happening. Sure, I might have had plenty of new material, but who wants to spend a half-hour sketching out an idea for a short story if there's a chance they might be dead before they get an opportunity to write the damn thing?

I put the notepad down and picked up the Houdini biography. It was a weighty volume, and the text was quite small, so it wasn't something I'd be able to read in a hurry. I returned to the highlighted section Victoria had shown me and I read over how Houdini had practiced holding his breath in the oversize bath. I guessed it was a good way to learn. After all, you had to put yourself in a position where it was impossible to breathe, because otherwise it would be too tempting to cheat. And how else could Caitlin do that from the comfort of a hotel suite, short of constructing a glass tank and having a couple of burly friends standing nearby to hoist her inside and watch over her with safety axes?

So it struck me as plausible that she'd been holding her breath, and that I'd leaped to the wrong conclusion in thinking that she was dead. And while that made me look rather stupid, I have to confess that I was relieved. Victoria was right to say that I'd run into more than enough corpses just recently, and it would make a refreshing change if I was able to leave Vegas without adding to my personal body count.

I sighed, rather theatrically, and fanned the pages of the Houdini biography. The sheer amount of highlighted text surprised me, and I could understand why it had bugged Victoria. I also knew that she hadn't found anything of significance beyond the reference to Houdini's bathroom activities, but I figured it would be remiss of me not to take a look for myself.

I started at the back of the book and worked toward the beginning, for no other reason than it seemed the contrary thing to do. Nearly all of the highlighted passages related to illusions that Houdini had performed, and some sections were accompanied by handwritten notations. The handwriting was difficult to read, and on the few occasions when I managed to decipher it, I didn't learn anything of significance.

Some way toward the front, I found a passage that tweaked my curiosity, but it wasn't capable of telling me where I could find Josh, or why exactly he'd run, or where his glamorous assistant might be found (assuming she wasn't dead). I sighed again, as if to bookend my reading experience, and then I set the biography aside and consulted the time on Josh's watch.

Just for a change, his watch had stopped, and I asked myself if perhaps it was a magic timepiece that only worked when it was attached to his particular wrist. I loosened the strap and freed it from my hand, and then I wound the mechanism tight and set the time to match my cheap, reliable, digital watch. Finally, I turned Josh's timepiece in my hand and studied the back of the casing, and what I saw there caused me to pull the type of face I tend to pull when I see something that doesn't altogether surprise or disappoint me.

I added a shrug, then fastened the watch on my wrist again and turned back to Victoria. It was time for me to wake her, and I was about to do exactly that when I heard a shuffling noise over by the door to my suite and jerked my head around just as a square of paper was pushed underneath.

TWENTY-EIGHT

The slip of paper contained a name and an address, written in a very neat hand. The black ink had smudged from where the paper had been folded, and I was reminded of the fountain pen Ricks favored. I snatched open the door as soon as I'd read the note, but by the time I poked my head out into the corridor, whoever had delivered it was nowhere to be seen.

"What is it?" Victoria mumbled, and I turned to find her peering over her shoulder at me from the far side of the bed.

I held up the square of paper. "Contact details for the croupier." I shrugged. "At least, I think that's what it is."

"From Ricks?"

"Must be."

Victoria rubbed her eye with the heel of her hand and stifled a yawn. "You could call him and check. He gave you his card, right?"

"I could, but I'm not going to. I think this is his way of helping us without drawing attention to what he's up to." I squinted at the note. "What else could it be?"

Victoria raised her hand to her head, as if she was coming around from a concussion.

"How long have I been asleep?"

"A little under two hours."

"I feel awful."

"See? Didn't I tell you that a quick nap would help?"

She groaned and shifted her legs sideways until she was perched on the edge of the bed, facing away from me.

"So what's his name, this croupier?"

"Jared Hall."

"Huh. Sounds like a university residence. Does he live far away?"

"No idea. This is just a street address."

I approached my holdall and dug through it for a pair of battered jeans and some baseball shoes. Wriggling out of my black suit trousers, I pulled on the jeans and the baseball shoes, then transferred my wallet to my left pocket and Josh's wallet to my right. I dived into the holdall again for my denim jacket, slipped it on over a clean T-shirt and dropped my trusty spectacles case and plastic disposable gloves into my jacket pocket.

"I have a couple of hours before the twins leave for the golf course," I said. "I'm going to head to the taxi rank and see if I can get a ride to this address."

Victoria stood up and turned to appraise my new outfit. "Would you like me to come too?"

"Honestly? I think it'd be better if we split up and you try to find Caitlin. I thought perhaps you might begin with the theater staff?"

"Okay." She nodded. "I can do that. You still have my mobile, I think."

"Do I?" I gathered my black trousers from the bed and checked the pockets. She was right. "You want it back?"

"No. You keep it. That way I can call you if I learn anything."

I pushed the telephone down into the back pocket of my jeans, then glanced up and met her gaze.

"Sure you'll be okay?"

"I'm a grown woman, Charlie. I can look after myself."

"So I don't need to worry about you being detained for cheating another casino?"

"Go," she said, and waved me toward the door. "Meet me back here at two o'clock, unless I call you beforehand."

"Okay, Boss. Be good."

I had no idea that the neighborhood Jared Hall lived in was known as Naked City until my cab driver told me as much. I suppose I could have asked him to explain the source of the name, but the closer we got to the address on the scrap of paper, the more giveaways I saw. Like, for instance, the flashing neon signs for gentlemen's clubs and strip joints, the lurid pink billboards featuring dark silhouettes of shapely dancers in high heels, the low-rise buildings advertising sex toys and smutty videos, and the women with high skirts and bare legs, soliciting from outside a failing burger franchise.

Naturally, there was more to commend the area to your average tourist than mere sex. There were also twenty-four-hour liquor stores and bail bond businesses, tattoo parlors and gun shops, EZ Loan credit outlets and Auto Spas. Heck, we even passed the Elvis-A-Rama Museum and Gift Shop.

Jared Hall's condo was located on a cross street leading away from (or perhaps more accurately fleeing) the neighborhood in the direction of the Strip. It was positioned in the shadows of the Stratosphere Tower, behind a bleached concrete sidewalk, a chain-link fence and a rusted and wheel-less station wagon. The building was two stories in height, dirty cream in color, and laid out on three sides around an oval swimming pool. There was no water in the pool, only a brownish sludge of mud and fallen leaves.

A faded sign on one side of the building directed me up a flight of concrete steps and along an open balcony toward an apartment in the far corner. The windows of the apartment were guarded by metal bars and obscured by dirt. I knocked on the front door and the door swung open. I didn't like that very much. The neighborhood didn't strike me as the kind of area where an unlocked door went unpunished for long, and I'd written the scene enough times myself to know just how perilous it could be. For your average hero of a mystery novel, an open door invariably turns out to be a trick invitation. And if I played my role to the letter, I'd be expected to step inside and creep along the hallway until I found something very nasty indeed—like, perhaps, young Jared in a deathly mess, stinking of a foulness too loathsome to describe, with a swarm of flies circling his mutilated corpse.

I guess I must be a sucker for a classic set-up, because I shoved the door aside and moved forward into the hall. There was no loathsome smell or insect buzz—just a cramped, empty kitchen on my right and a lighted doorway at the end of the hall. I cleared my throat and delivered my line.

"Hello? Jared? Anyone home?"

To my enormous surprise, there was no answer. I edged closer to the pearly sunlight up ahead.

Still no smell. Still no flies.

"Hello? Is anyone dead in there? Are the cops on their way? Am I shortly to become a fugitive from justice?"

I took another step forward, readying myself for what I might find behind the open doorway, and was within striking distance of the next room when something thudded into my shoulders from behind and I accelerated so fast that my nose butted the wooden doorframe.

A brilliant pain lit up the space between my eyes and an enormous pressure swelled in the bridge of my nose. I blinked, and watched in horror as a torrent of blood gushed from my nostrils. Cupping my hands to my face, I moaned somewhat redundantly, and turned to see what the hell had just happened.

Jared Hall had happened, and I could almost have believed that he was more shocked than me. His mouth opened and re-opened wordlessly, his eyes bulged, and he staggered backward down the hallway with his bandaged right hand in front of his face as though he was warding off a demon from his cruellest nightmares.

He wore bright orange beach shorts that exposed his spindly legs in all their glory, and a crumpled Yankees baseball shirt. His lank hair was uncombed and messy, a long way removed from the Brylcreem side-parting he'd sported at the Fifty-Fifty. His pimpled jaw quivered manically.

"Who are you, man? What are you doing in my place?"

"Ywa dwaar wzz aupan," I said, through my bloodied nose and cupped hands.

"I can't understand you, man. What are you doing here?"

I would have liked to have explained myself, but just at that moment I gagged on the blood running down the back of my throat. I did my best to swallow and breathe normally but my airways were blocked. I coughed, and coughed again, and a bubble of blood and saliva burst from my lips to coat my chin and spatter my T-shirt.

Now true, I'm not an avid fan of the sight of fresh blood, but when the blood in question belongs to yours truly, and when I happen to be choking on it, my usual reserves of composure and consciousness have been known to desert me. I remember being conscious of that fact, and reminding myself that the absolute worst thing I could do would be to faint in front of the one person who'd caused me such grievous harm in the first place. In fact, I can recall remonstrating with myself quite severely as my eyesight lost focus, my head went slack and I found myself pitching forward into the very blackest of black holes.

I came around with a start, and a damp flannel on my face. The flannel was fragrant (and not in a good way), but it was welcome all the same. I pressed it against my brow, then bunched it in my hand and dabbed at my nostrils.

A dry gust of wind tugged at my hair. I cracked open my eyes and squinted against harsh sunlight. I was sitting on a thin carpet with my back propped against a wall and my head resting on the aluminum frame of a sliding door. The door was open and looked out onto a concrete balcony surrounded with corroded iron railings. Beneath the balcony was a scrub yard and in the yard was a rabid dog. The dog was chained to a washing line, but it was straining at its leash, giving every indication that it planned to break free and scale the wall so that it might feast on my bones. I had no idea what breed the dog was—modern science couldn't tell you what breed the dog was—but it had taken a clear and quite severe disliking to me.

I yanked at the sliding door until it closed with a puff of air.

It didn't stop the dog from barking, but at least the noise was muffled.

"Who are you, man?"

I turned my dazed head in the direction of the question. Jared was sitting in a folding canvas chair, his hairy legs splayed, with his bandaged right hand resting on his knee and what appeared to be a barbecue fork in his left fist. A slanting rectangle of sunlight framed him in, as if he was in the glare of a spotlight at the end of a television quiz show. The light emphasized the acne bumps on his cheek and drained the color from the dice tattoo on his neck—making it look like a drunken prank with a magic marker.

I peered beyond Jared toward the shadowed corners of the room. It was all but empty. A wooden crate was positioned beside his feet—he was wearing battered espadrilles—and the crate appeared to be filled with a random collection of kitchen utensils and crockery.

"My name's Charlie," I croaked. "Don't you recognize me?"

Jared leaned forward and peered at me over the glinting tines of his fork. The look of puzzlement on his spotty face failed to resolve itself.

"I was at your roulette table yesterday evening."

His confusion persisted.

"With Josh Masters."

Ah, that did the trick. His grip tightened around the fork.

"What are we having, by the way? Sausages?"

He looked from me, to the fork, then back again. A deep crease settled into his brow and the skin pulled taut around the corners of his mouth, stretching his pimples.

"You know Josh?" he asked.

"He's more of an acquaintance, really."

"Know where he's at?"

I let go of a sigh and raised a fingertip to the base of my nose. When I pulled my finger away, the tip was wet. At least I hadn't been unconscious long enough for the blood to clot.

"I was hoping you might be able to tell me," I said, sounding nasal. "I've been trying to find him."

Jared lowered the fork a fraction. "How come?"

"He didn't tell you?"

"Tell me what?"

I shrugged. "Your ruse with the casino markers and the bottle top. Josh was palming me chips at the table."

"Bullshit."

"I really wish that were so." I paused as a wave of pressure passed through my nose. I got the feeling that speaking was making the bleeding worse, but I didn't have a great deal of choice. I tipped my head back and said, "I hear he made off with your cut. Mine too."

Jared stuck out his bottom lip and turned the fork upside down so that he could prod at the skin of his thigh. His eyes slid sideways and he contemplated his broken hand.

I said, "I was there when the Fisher Twins did that to you. They made me watch through the glass in the wall."

He tensed. "You work for them?"

I held up the taped fingers on my right hand. "Not even close. I guess I was lucky. They just broke two of my fingers." I turned my hand in the light coming through the window, so that Jared could see the arthritic curl that my fingers had taken on. "Who knows? Maybe I'll be able to use them again some day."

His jaw loosened and his arms went limp. He dropped the fork into the wooden crate and followed it with his eyes.

"I haven't seen him, man."

"I need to find him."

"Can't help you." He looked up and fixed me with a plaintive, broken smile. "Guy screwed me bad. I'm gone. Vegas is over for me now."

I frowned. "But there are other casinos."

He shook his head, like he'd run the argument with himself already. "Nah, man. They put my face in the book. And my hand," he said, gesturing at it with his pitted chin, "it ain't worth shit anymore."

He lifted his hand in the air and considered it for a long moment, gazing at it in a detached way, as if it was no more than a prosthetic.

"I'm sorry," I said. "Truly."

He sniffed, and wiped his nostrils with the webbing of his bandage. "Yeah, and I'm sorry about your face. I didn't mean for that to happen. Guess I just freaked, you know? Finding you here, an' all. My bad."

Funny, it hadn't worked out so great for me, either. I re-folded the flannel beneath my nose and pointed my chin at the room we were sitting in.

"I don't know what you were worried about. You can't have thought that I was a burglar—it doesn't look like you have anything to steal."

He considered the room himself, then picked at the bandage on his hand. "A buddy of mine has a breakdown truck around back of here," he told me. "Guess I was loading it when you arrived."

I nodded carefully. It seemed to make sense.

"Where will you go?"

"My buddy'll be back soon. He's driving me to Reno."

"Reno?"

"My hometown."

"Well, that doesn't sound too bad."

"It sucks, man. Vegas is where it's at for me. Was, anyways."

I pushed myself up from the carpet with a groan, using the wall to aid my balance.

"Any suggestions where I might look for Josh?"

He shook his head. "Some place other than Vegas if the guy has smarts. I never should have listened to his fix. I was set, man. I was good."

"And Caitlin? His assistant?"

His mouth twisted. "Casino, maybe? But don't mess with her, dude. You know who she is, right?"

Jared was about to say more when he was interrupted by an electronic ping. I thought of Victoria's mobile in my back pocket and was poised to reach for it when Jared fumbled in his shorts and removed a cellphone of his own. He pressed a button with his thumb and read over the screen without a great deal of interest.

"That's my ride." He sniffed again. "I gotta go. You gonna be okay? You feeling dizzy?"

"Oh, I'm feeling dizzy," I told him. "But I'll be all right."

"You can rest awhile, if you need it. Doesn't bother me no more."

I held my left hand out to him and he did likewise. We shook awkwardly, in the manner of two men who are naturally right-handed, and then he shrugged his shoulders and lifted the packing crate, resting it on the padding of his bandage. He was halfway to the door when he turned to look back at me.

"You should get out too, man. Find someplace else to start over."

"I'll give it some thought."

"Yeah, well think fast. The Fisher brothers ain't just today's bad news. They're tomorrow's too."

TWENTY-NINE

I watched Jared slouch off along the concrete balcony and down the stairs to the street, and then I ducked back inside his apartment. There wasn't much to see. The living room and the room next to it were empty, and the only thing the bathroom contained was a roll of toilet paper. I tore off a couple of sheets, twisted them into knots and stuffed them up my nostrils. I grimaced at how ridiculous I looked in the bathroom mirror, then ran the cold tap over the flannel and did my best to scrub away some of the blood that had stained my T-shirt. All I succeeded in doing was making the T-shirt bloody *and* wet, which was really quite brilliant of me. Tossing the flannel into the sink, I went to check the kitchen.

The kitchen was much the same as the rest of the apartment. Every cupboard and drawer was empty, except for the drawer beneath the sink. The drawer didn't contain anything of value. I found some wooden barbecue skewers, a roll of baking foil and a box of matches. I also found a carton of used playing cards from the Circus Circus casino. I didn't pause to count the cards, but I did ease the pack into a spare pocket on my jeans by way of consolation for a wasted trip.

I suppose I could have used my picks to lock Jared's apartment as I left, but there didn't seem much point. And anyway, I was far more interested in flagging down a passing cab and making my way back to the Fifty-Fifty as soon as possible. My excursion hadn't taken as long as I'd feared, and I had a couple of errands to run.

I was approaching the door to my hotel room from the direction of the service stairs when I glanced up and saw Victoria coming along the corridor toward me. She'd changed out of her cocktail dress into a mauve sweater and gray corduroy trousers. Her face brightened when she saw me, then knotted an instant later.

"Christ, Charlie. Are you okay?"

It took me a moment to remember the bloody stain on the front of my T-shirt.

"I'm fine. It's no big deal."

She put her head on one side and studied me curiously, stepping closer to look up at my nose. "Where have you been? You haven't been walking around the hotel like that, have you?"

"It's just a bit of blood, Vic."

She raised her hands and plucked the two corkscrews of tissue from my nostrils.

"Ah," I said. "I'd forgotten about those." I grinned sheepishly and hefted the plastic shopping bag I held in my right hand. "Thought the sales staff were treating me a little strangely."

Victoria broke into a tremendous grin. She held it for all of two seconds before glancing down and registering the blood on the toilet paper. "Eugh," she said, and pressed the tissues into my hand. "My God," she went on. "What happened to you? Your nose looks like somebody stepped on a grape."

"Charming. I got pushed into a doorframe, as it happens."

I fumbled in my pocket for the key card to my room and slid it into the lock. I reached for the handle and a static charge buzzed through my fingers. I cursed under my breath, then kicked the door open and held it aside with my foot.

"Who pushed you?" Victoria asked, as she moved past me. "Was it Jared?"

"Yup. But it was sort of an accident."

"An accident? How can that be?"

I entered the room behind her and mumbled a reply. Unfortunately, Victoria didn't consider my mumbling to be quite good enough.

"I can't hear you, Charlie. Speak up."

"For some reason," I said, "he formed the opinion that I was an intruder."

Victoria twirled around and planted her hands on her hips. "You broke into his home?"

"Kind of."

"You bloody idiot. Don't you think we're in enough trouble already?"

"The thought had occurred to me."

I moved across to my holdall and searched through it until I found the gray record bag I sometimes use to carry my laptop. I filled the record bag with the contents of my shopping bag, then added my spectacles case, Victoria's mobile, Josh's wallet, my cigarettes and one or two other items for good measure.

"What did you buy?" she asked, with an exasperated sigh.

"Just a few bits and bobs. Oh, and some chocolate."

I threw a Hershey bar to Victoria, then ripped open my own snack and inhaled the sickly-sweet delight in a shade under three mouthfuls. I was still chewing as I peeled off my bloody T-shirt and moved into the bathroom. I soaped my chest with the complimentary hotel body wash, then patted myself down with a towel.

Victoria appeared in the bathroom doorway, nibbling on her chocolate bar.

"See what I mean about the squashed grape?"

I contemplated my swollen nose in the mirror above the sink. It was sore and tender, but I didn't believe it was broken. "I guess that's why I'm the writer," I said. "It looks pretty normal to me."

"It's ginormous."

"There's a tiny amount of swelling."

"And it's all squished. As if you're pressing it up against a window."

"It's not that bad."

"Yes, it is."

I abandoned the mirror to go and find a clean T-shirt. The one I chose was hooded with long sleeves, and it was green in color. I thought it would complement my grape-like nose.

"Should I ask how things went with Jared?" Victoria went on. "Or is your nose answer enough?"

"He talked to me, if that's what you mean. But I didn't get a lead on Josh."

"Bummer."

"And his hand . . ." I shuddered. "Let's just say Josh has messed up Jared's life good and proper. He's leaving Vegas as we speak."

"Poor guy."

"What about you? Any luck tracking down Caitlin?"

Victoria took another bite of her chocolate bar. "I hung around by the theater, as you suggested," she said, before swallowing. "There was no one there, so I tried the same thing outside the Rat Pack show and managed to speak to a couple of the dancers."

"And?"

She belched and covered her mouth with her hand. "Gosh," she said. "Excuse me."

"You're excused. Provided you hurry up and tell me what they said."

"They said that the Fisher Twins have a cabin at a place called Mount Charleston. It's an hour outside Las Vegas, and apparently it's where Caitlin spends a lot of her time. I don't have a telephone number or an address, but I'm told it's impossible to miss—it's the largest place by quite some distance."

I looked at my watch and scratched the back of my head. It was shortly after two o'clock, so there was no way I could get out there and break into the twins' office all in the same afternoon.

"It's okay," Victoria told me. "I've been down to the concierge and hired myself a car. I can go by myself. I'll do my best to find her, Charlie."

"Thank you," I said, and meant it. "I'll keep my fingers

crossed." I lifted my hand and frowned at my taped digits. "Not that I can do much else, of course."

Victoria smiled. "Are you ready for what you need to do?"

"As I'll ever be. I've just been up to Floor Forty-nine on a scouting mission."

"And? How did it look?"

"Honestly? It looked as if I'm going to need some help."

THIRTY

I hadn't wanted to involve Kojar or Sal in my attempt to get my hands on the juice list. In fact, when Maurice had suggested the notion back at his home, I'd gone to great lengths to explain why I needed to work alone. I was an expert at sneaking into and out of places unnoticed, I'd told him, and it wouldn't do to have novices along for the ride—especially ones as conspicuous as those two. Besides, I'd added (somewhat misleadingly), if I was by myself and I happened to get caught, there was no danger of the Fisher Twins linking Maurice to the job.

I must have been more convincing than I realized, because when I changed my mind and telephoned Maurice to say that I couldn't do the job alone, he was more than a little reticent. Eventually, though, he agreed that Kojar and Sal could be excused from the matinée performance of their circus revue to lend me a hand, so long as I didn't "screw up" and land us all in a "shit storm" of trouble. It seemed an odd kind of bargain to me, but I thanked him anyway, then slung my record bag over my shoulder and accompanied Victoria downstairs to claim her hire car. I watched her drive away in a Chrysler PT Cruiser, eager to make sure that she didn't veer onto the left-hand side of the Strip, and afterward I cooled my heels in the grand hotel foyer as I waited for my accomplices to arrive.

My wait had barely begun when I became aware of a commotion over by the check-in desks. A group of women in gaudy outfits were arguing with the hotel staff. Their language was every bit as colorful as their clothing, and their waistlines were very nearly as big as their hair. The loudest of the women was familiar to me. She was still wearing the Dalmatian-print blouse that she'd discarded on the floor of Dirty Harry's hotel room, and she held a padded brown envelope in her hand.

As I watched, she pulled a wad of notes from the envelope and thrust them across the counter, instantly extinguishing the objections of the hotel staff. I heard her demand three adjoining rooms, and while the staff complied with her instructions, her companions smacked gum, cocked their hips and brazenly stared down anyone unfortunate enough to look in their direction.

I held back until the women had strutted away with their room keys before moving close and tapping Harry's girl on the shoulder. She turned sharply, full of aggression.

"Yeah? What now?" she snapped.

"Easy," I told her, and pointed to the envelope. "I just wanted to say that I know where you got that."

She looked from me, to the envelope, and back again. She tipped her head onto her shoulder and squinted hard at my face. In the bright lights of the foyer, she appeared older than I'd previously thought. A flock of crow's feet marked her face.

"I know you?" she asked.

"Nope."

She eyed the envelope again, then glanced over her shoulder to where her group of friends were passing through the casino. By the time she turned back, she seemed to have decided that I was no more than a fantasist. "You don't know nothing," she told me, with an ugly snarl.

"I'm afraid that's not so. For instance, I know enough to call Space Station One and ask to be put through to Harry's room."

She clutched the envelope against her bosom, as if she feared I might reach out and snatch it from her.

"Who are you?" she asked slowly.

"That's not important."

"Then what is it you want?"

I didn't know what I wanted. Truth be told, I didn't know

why I'd confronted her in the first place. Yes, getting some of the money would have been nice, but I couldn't see her handing it over without a fight, and right now was hardly a good time to draw attention to myself. And the talk of calling Harry's room was simply a bluff. I wasn't outraged by her crime—I was just irritated that she'd taken the money before *I'd* had a chance to.

So I guess what it came down to was spite—a desire to make things difficult for her. But now that I'd seen how she was destined to spend the money—entertaining her friends, maybe paying for a meal and a show, maybe losing it all at the craps table—any desire I'd had to cause trouble for her began to desert me.

"Only to tell you to have a good time," I found myself saying.

"Huh?"

I backed off, abandoning her to her confusion. "Oh, and to recommend that you don't leave all that cash in the safe in your room. Believe me, it's really not as secure as you might imagine."

It was nearing three o'clock by the time Sal and Kojar finally showed up, and so without further ado I led them upstairs by somewhat more, and somewhat less, legal means until we reached a locked store room located on Floor 49.

Once I'd picked the door open and closed it behind us, I cleared a space on the tiled floor and used my finger and a helpful layer of grime to explain what I needed Kojar and Sal to do. In truth, I'd seen Wile E Coyote sketch out more complicated plans, but I still had to go over it twice before they were happy. Fortunately, my scheme didn't involve anything so difficult to obtain as Acme Dynamite, and I had only to arm myself with my questionable acting ability as I stepped out into the corridor and set things in motion.

The security guard on duty was perched on a high stool behind a curved wooden counter, just a couple of meters from the door I was aiming to access. He was a squat fellow, with bulging, ruddy cheeks and a well-cultivated mustache. He had on the same vintage cop uniform as the guards downstairs, only his polyester shirt was pulled very tight across his drooping pecs and fatty shoulders. The brim of his angular hat was tilted so low that I could barely see his eyes, and I found myself talking to his mustache as I hurried toward him.

"Security? Thank God. I just heard a woman scream back here."

I jerked my thumb over my shoulder and did my best to appear spooked. The guard's mustache twitched and squirmed, and he reached out toward the two-way radio on his counter.

"You need to come right away," I added. "I really think she's in trouble."

I turned, as if to jog back in the direction I'd come from. The guard stepped down from his stool, but he was still uncertain. His head turned toward the stairwell door, and he snatched up his radio and raised it toward his lips.

"You need to hurry."

I grabbed him by the wrist, preventing him from speaking into the radio. He obviously didn't work out too often, because he was panting by the time I'd dragged him as far as the store room.

"Listen," I said, and pushed his bulky frame toward the door.

A high, squeaky mewling became audible.

"Sounds like a cat," the guard commented.

He was right—it did sound like a cat—and I began to realize that Sal's acting range was even more limited than my own.

"Don't you think you should check?"

Sal picked up my cue and gave it his best shot. His voice came out sounding midway between Shirley Temple and a Smurf.

"Oh, help me," he wailed. "Please, help me."

"Gee, I don't know," the guard said, and fiddled with a knob on the top of his radio. "I better call this in."

I'd had enough of his dawdling, so I kicked open the door, grabbed him by the tie and yanked him inside the store room. Kojar welcomed him with a crushing embrace, picked him up, turned him around and dropped him clean on his head.

"Holy crap," I said. The guard was a crumple of uniform and mustache on the floor. "Did you just kill him?"

Kojar shrugged, as if he wasn't entirely sure, and then he lifted the guard by the ankle, bent at the waist and sniffed around his face. He seemed perplexed for a moment. Then he snapped his head away and covered his nose with his hand, as though he'd just chanced upon something foul-smelling in the back of his refrigerator.

"He breathes," Kojar announced. "But he eat bad eggs for breakfast."

"You weren't meant to knock him unconscious," I told him. "Remember? I need the code to get through the door."

Kojar and Sal looked up at me for a moment, wide-eyed, as though this was news to them.

"Forget it," I said. "You might as well go ahead and remove his uniform."

Sal looked dubious. "You want us to undress the guy?" he asked, in his high nasal drone.

"We've been over this already."

"Yeah, but I ain't no fairy."

"Fine. I'll do it. Kojar, lift him up."

I must say, I could get used to having a brainless giant at my beck and call. On my command, Kojar let go of the guard's ankle, cupped his hands beneath the man's chin and held him aloft at around chest-height (or head-height for a normal human being) with his feet dangling in mid-air. It struck me that Kojar looked a lot like an athlete preparing to throw the hammer, and that perhaps the guard was lucky to be unconscious, after all.

Since I was afraid that the guard's head might come off in Kojar's hands, I did my best to remove his clothes as quickly as possible. Once I was done and the guard was stripped to a white cotton vest, paisley boxer shorts and navy socks, I worked with Sal to bind his wrists behind his back with his necktie while Kojar secured the man's belt buckle around his ankles. I had to remind Kojar not to pull the belt so tight that the guard's feet would be severed, but by the time we were through he was neatly trussed up.

I went through the guard's pockets until I found a swipe card and then I gathered his radio and threw it to Kojar. He caught it in his meaty hand, giving the device the appearance of a child's toy, and at that point it finally dawned on me that part of my plan was fundamentally flawed.

My original idea had been for Kojar to dress in the guard's uniform and to stand watch at the security desk. But if Kojar tried pulling on the guard's trousers or buttoning his shirt, he'd wind up looking like Dr. Bruce Banner soon after transforming into the Hulk.

I tossed Kojar the guard's hat. "This'll have to do," I said. "No point in you putting on his clothes."

I looked at what he was wearing. From behind the security desk, nobody would be able to see his sweat pants or his athletic trainers. His vest was a different story. Sure, it was blue, but it was also sleeveless in order to show off his muscles, and combined with the hat, there was a real danger he might look like a Chippendale midway into a themed strip.

"If anyone asks, just tell them that you're new and your uniform is on order."

Kojar nodded, and set the hat onto his head at a jaunty angle.

"And if you hear anything on the radio that suggests we're in trouble, well, do what you can."

He touched the peak of his hat and smiled inanely.

I looked over at Sal. He was crouched beside the guard, monitoring his breathing.

"How's he doing?"

"Still out cold."

I nodded at his diagnosis, then rooted through my record bag and removed a strip of sticking plaster and a pair of nail scissors. I cut a mouth-sized patch of the plaster, peeled off the paper backing and smoothed the makeshift gag over the guard's mouth, making sure that he could still breathe through his nose.

I returned to my bag for my spectacles case, a small make-up compact and two latex masks.

Now admittedly, when I'd walked along the corridor to lure the guard toward the store room, I hadn't been able to hide my face. And on top of that, I'd directed Kojar and Sal through some restricted areas in the hotel. So it stood to reason that any number of cameras could have recorded our features. But even so, I thought that wearing a mask was still a worthwhile precaution.

On the downside, a desert town wasn't the ideal place to buy ski masks at short notice, and the best alternative I'd been able to find had been on sale in the souvenir store outside the Rat Pack theater show.

"You're kidding, right?" squeaked Sal, when I passed him one of the masks.

"I'm afraid not."

I pressed my own mask against my face and snapped the elastic strap onto the back of my head, jiggling the thing around until I'd aligned the eyeholes properly.

"How come I don't get to be Frank?"

I cocked my head on my shoulders. "Glad you asked. We're doing this My Way."

Sal grimaced and showed me his crooked teeth, as if someone had just whistled in his ear at an unbearable pitch. Then he lowered his face to fix his own mask. When he looked up again, he'd been transformed into a pint-sized Dean Martin.

I opened the make-up compact in my hand and used the circular mirror to check on the smiling rubber visage of one Francis Albert Sinatra.

"This is real dumb," Sal told me.

"You're probably right. But it's non-negotiable."

I peered out at him from behind the slits in my mask. The slits narrowed my vision in a way I wasn't especially keen on, making it seem as though I was looking through a letter box.

"Talking of non-negotiable," I said, and tossed him a pair of scrunched-up plastic gloves. "I'm afraid they don't make them any smaller."

"Are you for real?"

"If you plan on touching anything, you'll wear them." I worked my own gloves onto my hands, taking care not to snag the plastic on my taped fingers. Then I pointed at the door. "Gentlemen, shall we?"

I locked up behind us and followed the pair of them along the corridor, stationing Kojar behind the security desk and Sal where he could keep watch for anyone who might be approaching. Then I crouched down to confront the locking mechanism on the stairwell door.

Thanks to the security guard, I already had the appropriate swipe card in my possession, so the only obstacle that remained was the electronic combination keypad. The numbers on the keypad ran from zero through to nine, and Maurice had said that there was a six-digit code. Originally, I'd hoped that Kojar would be able to extract the code from the security guard, but since all Kojar had managed to extract from the security guard was a faraway look and a long series of zzz's, I was going to have to fall back on a trick that had worked for me once before in Amsterdam.

The make-up compact, you see, had been emptied of foundation powder and re-filled with fingerprint powder, of the kind that certain resourceful individuals are willing to sell over the Internet. By the by, certain even more resourceful individuals are willing to sell talcum powder over the Internet and claim that it's fingerprint powder, but since I'd taken the precaution of testing my latest batch, I was hopeful that it could help me to narrow my odds of getting through the door.

With that in mind, I used the tiny brush fitted inside the compact to apply a fine layer of powder to each numbered key before shining my penlight over the results. I was somewhat dismayed by the mass of prints that materialized. They were adhered to every single key, a whole spectrum of whorls and arches and loops. I sighed and shook my head. I was still shaking my head when a thick finger appeared from over my shoulder and punched in a six-digit sequence.

I turned and scowled at Kojar from behind my mask. Of course, he couldn't see my expression, so maybe that explained the beatific smile on his face.

"What the hell are you doing?"

"I enter code."

"You can't just guess, Kojar. This thing is wired to detect false numbers. You enter too many, and it locks down completely."

Kojar frowned at me, then held up a piece of laminated pink card with Sellotape around the edges. Printed on the card was the following information: *Door code 5-8-8-3-2-6.*

"Where did you get that?"

"On counter."

I looked from Kojar, to the security desk, and back again.

"Why didn't you just tell me it was there?"

Kojar shrugged, and looked genuinely perplexed by my question.

"Oh, never mind. Give it to me."

I snatched at the laminated card and went through the routine of swiping the key card and tapping in the numbered sequence. A green bulb lit up, the locking mechanism buzzed and the door sprang open on its hinges.

I held the door open with the toe of my shoe, wiped the fingerprint powder from the keypad with the hem of my shirt and whistled at Sal.

"With me, Short Round. We have work to do."

THIRTY-ONE

The service stairs were deserted and I led Sal straight up to Floor 50. Another magnetic card reader and combination keypad barred our way. I reached into my pocket and pulled out the swipe card and the door code and put them to good use. The door clunked open and I set my eye to the crack. I could see a slither of corridor, a frosted glass partition and two security cameras. A fire hose and an axe were set into the wall on my left, and the ceiling contained air vents and a smoke sensor.

I scoped the area behind the door. The corridor ended just a few feet away in a solid-looking wall. I wound my head back in and reacquainted it with my shoulders, then wedged my record bag into the gap between door and jamb.

Sal was trying to look out from behind my legs. I lifted him to one side and turned my attention to the service stairs. This was supposed to be the top floor of the main hotel tower, but the stairs appeared to continue upward. I climbed as far as a half-landing, then turned and faced up to two double doors with daylight visible around the edges. A sign attached to the wall warned me that they were wired into an alarm system. I gave the alarm some respect to begin with, but I was soon able to disarm it with a steady hand and a strip of lead taken from my spectacles case.

I pushed the doors open and squinted through my mask against the mid-afternoon sun, shielding my eyes with my hand as I peered up at the giant 50-cent coin twirling overhead. From

street-level, the coin had seemed to move with a soundless effi-
ciency, but up here it creaked and screeched as though it was sorely
in need of some oil. Below the spinning coin was the glass exterior
of the counter-revolving, rooftop restaurant. The glass walls were
tinted, but I could see the outline of people on the inside, and
since I was afraid of being spotted, I ducked back into the stairwell and swung the door closed behind me.

I was still blinking away the sun glare when I made it back
down to Sal. He had his hands on his hips and was tapping the
toe of his yellow sneaker on the floor in an impatient rhythm.
His Dean Martin mask was the only part of him that seemed
happy.

"What's next?" he asked.

I crouched toward my record bag and undid the zip, saying,
"You heard Maurice. The twins' office is just along this corridor.
They should be on the way to their golf club by now."

"Sure, but they have staff, right?"

"Two personal assistants, at the very least."

"So what gives? You have guns?"

I stopped what I was doing and searched out the blacks of his
eyes from behind Dean's face.

"That's not how this is going to happen."

"Knives, then?"

I sighed, and felt my breath wash back from the inside of my
mask.

"So what—you have a Taser in there?"

"I have cigarettes."

"Huh?"

I pulled out my box of cigarettes and waggled them in the air.
It took me a couple more minutes to bring Sal fully up to speed,
and I can't say he was altogether convinced by my approach. He
even went so far as to check my bag to make sure that I really
wasn't in possession of any concealed weapons. Once he was
convinced that I didn't have a machete or a compact nuclear
device squirreled away in a zipped side-pouch, he went on to

suggest that perhaps he could arm himself with the fire axe from the corridor and "go native on their asses."

Thankfully, I was able to dissuade him from adopting that particular approach, and after a good deal of coaching, he finally seemed to grasp the notion that it would be really quite neat if we could get our hands on the juice list without anybody knowing a thing about it.

I stabbed a cigarette through the slot in Dean's mouth.

"I ain't sure I can smoke through this thing," Sal whined, the cigarette jostling from side to side.

"Sure you can," I said, and set the flame of my lighter to the end of the cigarette.

He inhaled, then coughed, and a plume of smoke emerged through the mouth and eye slits of his mask.

"How about you do the smoking?" he croaked.

"You want me to stand on your shoulders and show you why that's a terrible idea?"

The eyes behind the mask narrowed but Dean's expression didn't alter in the slightest.

"You sure this'll work?"

"Only one way to answer that."

I eased the door open and sneaked into the corridor, then beckoned Sal toward me with an exaggerated sweep of my arm, as if I was welcoming the real Dean Martin onto the main stage at the Sands. Sal shuffled over and I dropped to my knees and bowed my head.

"Need a boost?"

"Nah," he squeaked. "I can handle it."

Two tiny hands gripped onto my neck, followed by the tread of a toddler-like shoe on the small of my back. A second shoe thumped into the rear of my left lung, and then his right foot was up on my shoulder. He teetered for a moment and clawed at my hair.

"Steady?"

"Just hurry it along, already."

I straightened, with my hands supporting his ankles. Tipping my head back, I saw that the top of his head was brushing the ceiling. The smoke alarm was off to his right, and I moved toward it with the kind of stride he obviously wasn't used to.

"Whoa, buddy."

He overbalanced and circled his arms, and I had to step backward to stop us both from tumbling over.

"Better?"

He coughed, and a great cloud of cigarette smoke rolled across the underside of the ceiling.

"Perfect," I whispered. "Give it some more."

Before too long, Sal really got into the swing of things, and he became so confident that he was able to stand on tiptoes and cup his mouth over the smoke sensor before exhaling. The smoke enveloped the plastic moulding, wafting back over his masked face. He pulled away, then drew on the glowing cigarette and exhaled again. The fresh burst did the trick. After a moment's hesitation, a small whine started up, followed seconds later by a great droning clamor.

I rolled my shoulders and caught Sal in my arms like a baby, then stooped to collect my record bag and backed out through the door. I carried Sal up beyond the half-landing and set him down on a step beside the doors to the roof.

"I could have walked, you know," he said.

"Of course you could."

"You didn't have to carry me."

"Hush. I hear people coming."

It wasn't true. Above the whap and whop of the alarm, I could barely hear myself speak, but I was hoping to hear footfall and I preferred to wait for it in silence.

Not long afterward, the door to the service stairs thudded back against the wall and I heard female voices and the percussion of stiletto heels. Flighty chatter echoed upward as the women made their way downstairs. They didn't appear to be distressed and I thought that was understandable. Short of seeing flames, most people would assume that the alarm was just an exercise, and I guessed there was a muster station just a couple of floors below, where they'd congregated during routine tests in the past.

Sal shuffled forward and tried to force his head through the railings. I hauled him back and held him at bay with an outstretched arm pressed against Dean's latex forehead.

"Hey!" he shrieked.

"Ssshh."

"They gone?"

"Ssshh."

It was difficult to know how many people to wait for. Moving before the office was evacuated was a sure way to get caught, but if we waited too long, hotel security would be on the scene and we'd have missed our opportunity.

"I think we're clear."

The moment the words were out of my mouth, the door thumped into the wall again and a pair of high heels clattered down the stairs.

"That was close."

"You figure she's the last one?"

"Here's hoping."

The alarm was much fiercer out in the corridor. I winced and bent at the waist, scurrying forward as though running from a mortar attack. The wailing swelled inside my head, pushing all sense and caution out through my ears. I bundled into the frosted glass partition and craned my neck around to survey the area. Sal did the same thing down by my waist. I couldn't see anyone and apparently neither could he, because he squirmed past my legs and moved on before I was able to stop him.

The reception had the feel of a private gentlemen's club. It was styled with leather couches and chairs, low mahogany coffee-tables spread with golfing magazines, polished brass standing lamps, cigar boxes, whiskey decanters, and a large oil painting of a hunting scene.

On the opposite side of the room was a long wooden counter (also mahogany), which was empty aside from a pen-set and guest ledger. Behind the counter were two cushioned swivel chairs where I imagined the twins' personal assistants were usually to be found, as well as two laptops and two telephones that looked complex enough to navigate warships. Between the telephones was a television monitor. The on-screen images were divided into quarters, with the uppermost segments featuring the empty interior of an elevator carriage. In the bottom-right segment, I could see Kojar fussing with his new hat, tugging it down over his ears as though he was aiming to convert it into a cravat.

To my left was a solid-looking door. Two brass plates were affixed to it, bearing the names *Mr. R. Fisher* and *Mr. G. Fisher*. I didn't know if the twins had fought over the order in which their names would be positioned, but once I tried the brass handle I did at least know that the door had been locked.

I was glad that the door was locked because it reduced the likelihood of anyone being on the opposite side. The variety of cylinder that had been fitted beneath the handle was familiar to me, and while opening it wasn't entirely straightforward, it didn't take much more than a minute to select the necessary implements from my spectacles case and pick my way through.

The first thing I did once we were on the other side was to lock the door behind us. The second thing was to remove my mask, since I couldn't imagine the twins allowing surveillance cameras inside their office. Lastly, I let go of a sigh of contentment, because by happy coincidence, the alarm had just stopped.

THIRTY-TWO

To describe the twins' office as grand would be an understatement. I'd been in airport departure lounges that were more modest. The view from the floor-to-ceiling windows at the end of the room took in the Strip, the geometric McMansions of suburbia, the peaks of the Red Rock Mountains beyond, and very possibly infinity too. Beneath the picture windows was a sleek conference table that could seat at least twenty-five guests, while the middle ground was filled with an extensive collection of lounge chairs and sofas, upholstered in plush fabrics and leathers, and separated from one another by standing lamps and exotic houseplants. The wall behind the seating area had been clad in large slate tiles, and was dominated by a huge, unlit fireplace. Another oil painting featuring a hunting scene was positioned above the limestone mantel.

Closer to us (and by closer I mean within driving distance), were a pair of curved, cherrywood desks that had been arranged beside one another to form a horseshoe. They were free of all clutter, aside from matching pen-sets with tiny American flags poking out of them.

A circular mosaic was located on the floor just in front of the desks. Unlike your average mosaic, this one had been created with casino chips. The outer rim was made up of white chips, with a black concentric border, and the centerpiece was a 50-cent coin fashioned from neatly arranged silver markers. If I could have prised the chips out of the mixture of mortar and resin that contained them, and somehow replaced them with worthless replicas, I could have made myself very rich indeed. Sadly for me, the best I could do was to drop to my knees, run my fingers over the pattern and emit a low whimper, before at last turning my attention to the thin, dark crevice that ran around the perimeter of the coin.

Now that I knew there was a good chance that Maurice's information had been accurate, I found my feet and walked around to the opposite side of the desks. I'd been led to understand that it didn't matter which desk I started with—they were both as identical as the men who owned them—and from what I could see, that certainly appeared to be the case.

The desks were very fine pieces of furniture, made with obvious skill. The aged cherry timber had been turned and finished with great care, so that every join appeared utterly flawless. Each desk contained a number of locked drawers arranged on either side of the central knee-hole, and the locking furniture and handles had been manufactured in a becoming shade of brushed steel.

I wheeled aside the leather swivel chair from the desk on the right, ducked down into the knee-hole and clicked my fingers at Sal. Sal had tipped his mask up onto the top of his head, so I could see just how much he relished my snapping my fingers at him.

"Go and wait by the door," I whispered. "See if anyone is moving around out there."

As Sal muttered and mumbled across to the door, I delved inside my record bag for my penlight and cast the beam around the underside of the desktop. After some searching, I spied a tiny keyhole, about half the size of the nail on my little finger. I ran my fingertip over the opening and screwed up my face in disgust, and then I reached for my spectacles case and hunted for one of the smallest picks I carried.

It wasn't that the lock was especially difficult to open—desk locks rarely are—it was just that it was so damn fiddly. I guess a guy in my line of work should learn to get used to these things, but miniature locks are one of my bugbears. True, they tend to offer up less resistance to being forced, but if you want to do things right, it can be frustrating as hell trying to hold your hand steady enough to defeat one of the little buggers, and this particular example was truly dinky. If my first impressions were correct, none of the pins would be any bigger than the mechanics in the stolen watch that was struggling to keep time on my wrist, and I could already tell it was going to vex me.

Imagine facing up to an average-sized doll's house and trying to poke a scaled-down key into the lock on the front door. Tricky, right? Well, maybe not so tough if you happen to be the same size as Sal, but teeth-grindingly, stomach-clenchingly, hair-pullingly infuriating for me.

Then again, if it had been simple, I don't suppose I would have experienced the warm, fuzzy feeling that coursed through my veins when the itsy-bitsy pins eventually succumbed to my charms and the teeny tumblers turned and the little cherrywood hatch dropped down from above.

I have to admit it felt good. Mind you, that was nothing compared to the sweet sensation I experienced when I repeated the entire process beneath the second desk and a matching hatch eased down. I called Sal back from the door and waited for him to join me (without, I noticed, any need to bow his head), and then I guided his hand up inside the hatch and rested his teeny finger on the plastic button I found there. That done, I scrambled back to the first desk and located my own button. On the count of three, we pressed down, and I watched from below the three-quarter height kickboard as the floor mosaic popped up on a soundless, concealed hinge to reveal a circular orifice.

I squirmed beneath the kickboard on my belly and crawled on my hands and knees as far as the edge of the hole. I peered over the rim and a classic Schmidt & Co combination-lock safe stared back.

The safe was buried in hard-set concrete to a depth of approximately three feet. It was round in shape, with a green metal fascia, a reinforced steel door and an eighty-digit combination dial. The cylindrical space that led down to it was just large enough for a grown man to poke his head and shoulders inside, and I did just that.

"Pass me my bag," I said, into the hole.

My bag thumped onto my back. I wriggled out and turned to see Sal dusting his hands off.

"Thanks."

"Hey, no problem."

I removed a pad of graph paper and a pencil. Since I'd been forewarned about the type of safe I'd be dealing with, I'd already gone to the trouble of drawing some hasty graphs on the opening pages. Normally, completing the graph was something I liked to do myself, but since I was going to have my head stuck down inside a cramped hole, it seemed that I would have to entrust Sal with the job.

"Take these," I told him. "I want you to put a pencil mark on the graph for every number I call out."

I beckoned to him and demonstrated what I meant. He snatched the pad away with an attitude that suggested I was vastly underestimating him.

"Pass me the pencil already. You can trust me."

I hate it when someone says that, but I handed the pencil across anyway before returning to my bag for a physician's stethoscope. As a general rule, I don't like to use a stethoscope. In theory, it's supposed to make it easier to hear the click of the contact dials on the wheelpack engaging, but I find that it just makes me aware of other noises coming from the inner workings of the safe, or even my arthritic finger-joints. I much prefer to use my naked ear and my gut instinct, but the location of this particular safe made that impossible. So the stethoscope was a necessary evil, as was the penlight I gripped in my teeth. I flashed Sal a smile, along with a beam of light, and then I dived down into the hole and set to work.

Safe manipulation is the purest and neatest way to defeat a locked safe, but the downside is that the technique requires a good deal of time and patience. It relies on the application of practical maths, a keen ear and a sound understanding of safe mechanics. And on top of all that, it involves a dose of good fortune, because while it's usually possible to identify the numbers that make up a particular combination, there's no way of knowing what order those numbers should be entered in.

Just to add to the challenge, the wily technicians at Schmidt & Co had constructed nearly all of their moving parts from plastics and nylons. That made it about as hard as it could get to hear any tell-tale clicks and clunks, and next to impossible to feel any resistance through the combination dial, especially when I was hanging upside down with my head and upper body in a space a little smaller than the drum of a tumble-dryer.

Twenty minutes in, and all the blood in my system seemed to have collected in my head. My temples were buzzing and my face felt hot and prickly, as if it had been jammed inside a vegetable steamer. I backed up out of the hole and lay flat on my back, yanked the stethoscope from my ears and held my hand out for the pad. The graph that Sal had produced was made up of a series of jagged peaks and troughs, representing the possible ranges of just two numbers. I wafted the pad above my face and tried my best not to groan.

"How much longer you think this will take?" Sal asked.

"An hour. Maybe more."

"Are you kidding me?"

"It could be less. But then we have to run the combinations."

"And how long will *that* take?" If anything, his voice had become even higher than usual.

"At a minute per combination? You don't want to know."

Sal put his face in his hands, and I was left to consider Dean Martin's inappropriately smug demeanor.

"We have, like, an hour and forty-five minutes, max."

"In that case, we'd best crack on."

If he picked up on the pun, he didn't show it. Instead, he gripped onto the pencil with both hands and sat quite rigidly at the edge of the hole.

I worked as swiftly as possible for the next half-hour, not

even pausing when my head began to pound. It felt like I'd called out a good many numbers, and so far as I could tell, most of them were accurate. A couple of times, Sal tapped me on the back and told me to cool it while he investigated a suspect noise on the other side of the door. The reception staff had returned soon after I'd begun manipulating the safe, and usually he reported back to say that he'd heard a telephone ring, or the whirr of a document shredder. I can't say I was staggered by his revelations, though I was always relieved to be able to continue. With each number I called out, we were moving steadily toward the next stage of the process and, just maybe, an improbable triumph.

Of course, as soon as a thought of that nature entered my head, things were bound to fall apart, and it wasn't long before Sal tapped me on the shoulder for perhaps the fifth time and I hauled my head out of the hole to give him a piece of my mind. It was bad enough to be interrupted, I was about to tell him, but to be interrupted just to hear that somebody was using a photocopier was really beginning to wear on my nerves.

As it happened, I didn't say anything, because it was immediately apparent from the haunted expression on Sal's face that something was about to go very wrong indeed. He pointed toward the bottom of the door, where the bar of light had darkened in the middle. I heard a throaty chuckle, followed by the noise of a key being fitted into the lock.

I've heard it said that some people find themselves paralyzed in dangerous situations, but I'm most certainly not one of them. In the seconds that followed, my brain considered and discounted a number of possible hiding spots, and before the door was even halfway open, I'd selected the right-hand desk and dived for its cover. I even had the presence of mind to toss my equipment and my record bag into the crawl-space ahead of me, but as I dragged my legs and my feet under the kickboard and grunted with the final, heroic effort of snatching my toes out of harm's way, I realized with a sudden dread that I'd overlooked one trifling detail. The mosaic hatch was still open.

THIRTY-THREE

Listening to people enter a room without being able to see them was fast becoming a nasty habit for me. These particular individuals paced directly to the hole in the floor.

"Christ, get Stacey," said a man's voice. "And call security too."

"Has the safe been compromised?" asked a second man.

"I can't tell yet. Just go get Stacey."

Feet pounded toward the door and I risked peering out from beneath the kickboard until I could glimpse the legs and back of a man with his head buried inside the hole in the mosaic. His khaki trousers and blue knit sweater gave me a fair idea of who I was looking at, but when he pulled his ginger head out of the hole I knew for certain. The Fisher Twins were back from their golf game much sooner than I'd been led to expect.

The twin I could see looked even paler than normal and his many freckles stood out distinctly against his whitish skin. He seemed low on patience as well as iron, and he plunged his arm into the hole and yanked fruitlessly on the door to the safe.

He was still tugging away when two sets of legs appeared alongside him. I guessed the tan chinos and brown loafers belonged to the second twin. The nylon stockings and black, medium heels seemed likely to be Stacey's.

"Anything missing?" asked the twin who was standing.

"I don't know. You have today's code?"

"On my PDA."

The second twin crouched down beside his brother and reached

inside his trouser pocket. He removed a compact electronic device and began to poke at it with a metal pointer.

"Stacey, what's going on?" asked the first twin. "Has anyone
been in here?"

Stacey shifted her weight between her feet. "I don't think so."

"Anything unusual happen?"

Her feet quick-stepped some more. "We had another fire
drill."

"A scheduled fire drill?"

"Gosh, I don't know. I don't think so."

The twins shared a look.

"Get Ricks up here. *Now.*"

Stacey scurried away, and the twins shook their identical
heads at one another.

Watching them from beneath the desk, I was conscious that
I'd made a couple of errors. In my hurry to dive for cover, I
hadn't seen where Sal had ended up, so I had no way of knowing
if he was likely to be found anytime soon. On top of that, my
own hiding spot was far from ideal. Yes, there was a danger I
might be seen beneath the kickboard, but more to the point, I'd
sought refuge in the exact spot where one of the buttons that
opened the mosaic was to be found.

On the plus side, I hadn't managed to crack the safe. Ordinarily, I wouldn't have been too thrilled by my professional short-
comings, but as the twins were about to discover that their safe
hadn't been compromised, I really hoped they might not feel the
need to activate a full-blown security procedure.

"I have the code," said the twin with the PDA.

"Give it to me."

He read the sequence aloud, and I felt a smile tug at my lips as
I committed it to memory. Could it be that I might find myself
with an opportunity to access the safe, after all?

I was still feeling dazed by the possibility when I glanced
down at the graph on the pad in my hands. At least two of my
numbers had been wrong. I couldn't remember if that was my

fault or if Sal had been careless with his record-keeping, but I felt mighty peeved all the same.

I guess I would have beaten myself up a little more if I hadn't been distracted by the metallic clang of the safe door being thrown back against the sides of the concrete hole. Any second now, and the twins would be a lot more relaxed.

"Goddammit!" one of them screamed. "They got it. They took the damn list."

Huh?

"Are you shitting me?"

Oh, thank God. He had to be messing with his brother.

"Do I look like I'm shitting you?"

Actually, he looked a lot like a man on the far side of angry. His jaw was clenched, his eyes were dark swirls and he slapped his palm down hard against the floor, like a wrestling judge counting off a bout. He stood and lashed out with his foot at the mosaic hatch. A half-second later, he let go of a howl of pain, clutched at his toes and hopped around in a circle.

Meanwhile, his brother stuck his own head into the hole. His arm moved feverishly in and out, until he'd placed several stacks of dollar notes beside the opening.

"That's all they took?"

"It's all they wanted."

His brother dropped heavily into a club chair and hauled off his shoe to consider his foot. His mouth puckered with discomfort and I found myself wincing in a similar manner. It wasn't sympathy pains—as he'd fallen into the chair, it had skidded sideways and I'd glimpsed the fingers of Sal's hand.

The twin in the chair gingerly flexed his toes, sucking air through his teeth.

"So what do we do?" his brother asked.

"I'm thinking."

"You have a back-up, right?"

"Sure, but that's not the issue. The list is out there now." He nodded toward the picture windows overlooking the Strip.

"But it can't bite us, yeah?"

The twin with the busted toes stared at his brother. "You think these people know how to apply that kind of information? They push too hard and the whole thing comes down."

"Maybe they're smart. They were smart enough to get the list."

The twin in the chair shook his head ruefully. "We need to close down on this fast. Where in hell is Ricks?"

"Relax. He'll be here."

If anyone could relax, it certainly wasn't me. I was struggling to understand the implications of what I was hearing. If the juice list had already been snatched, then I'd never had any chance of claiming my fee from Maurice. What's more, I was stuck at the scene of the crime, my hiding-place was about as stupid as you could possibly imagine (unless you could conceive of a teeny man cowering behind a club chair where a seriously hacked-off casino impresario happened to be sitting), and if I didn't somehow escape and pull together a serious amount of money in a handful of hours, I was destined to die a quite horrible death. Was that everything? Did I even want to turn my mind to what else could go wrong?

"What's happening?"

Ricks strolled into the room behind his question, flipping open a pocket notepad. The twins brought him up to speed while I peeked out from my hiding-space and watched him squat down beside the hole in the mosaic. He'd changed his clothes since I'd last seen him—he had on a dark blue blazer over a white shirt and pressed gray trousers—but his eyes retained the glazed look of a man low on sleep, and when he raised a hand to his silver-thread beard, he stifled a yawn.

"No cops, right?" he muttered.

"No cops."

Ricks nodded once, as though recalibrating his approach. "I'm going to need names for the people who might want the list."

The twin in the club chair made a gargling noise that suggested he didn't rate the idea. "You want that I pass you the damn telephone directory? Come on, Ricks, you know what was on that document."

"Some of it," Ricks said, and I thought I could almost detect a hint of regret in his voice.

"So you know what we're dealing with. I want this thing shut down. I want it stomped on."

Ricks turned sideways and held the twin's eye. "I'll have to speak with your staff. *All* of your staff. One of my team will review the fire alarm. Another guy will run the security tapes."

"That's going to take time."

"Sure is." He pointed his pen at the lid of the mosaic. "You touch anything?"

The twin shifted uncomfortably. "How do you think we knew the list was gone?"

"We'll run it for prints anyhow. And I'll have somebody sweep the room."

"You did that last week."

Ricks straightened, his knee joints popping. "That was for bugs. I want to be sure that whoever did this is gone."

The twin stiffened in his chair, eyes wary. His brother glanced over his shoulder, as if he feared he might be in the presence of a ghost.

"You think they're still here?"

"It's possible."

"I figured they left already."

"Could be. But my guess is the job was carried out during the alarm evacuation. When was the last time you checked the safe?"

"Two days ago," said the one who was scared of ghosts.

"Time?"

He was about to answer when he was interrupted by a sharp, unexpected trill. Cold panic flushed through me. The chirping was coming from right beside me. To be exact, it was coming from my record bag. The awful truth was, I'd forgotten to set Victoria's mobile to silent. And now the damn thing was ringing.

Of all the asinine mistakes I'd made in my life, this one really topped the list. I lurched for my bag and plunged my hand inside, groping desperately for the stupid contraption. It twittered and vibrated gaily, and still I couldn't find it.

At last, my fingers touched upon the treacherous hunk of plastic, but the telephone slipped from my sweaty palm like a bar of wet soap and shot out from beneath the desk. I thrust an arm out after it, only to stub my fingers on the toe of Ricks' shoe.

I gazed slowly up and Ricks gazed slowly down. He clucked his tongue and said, "Why don't you crawl on out and answer your cell? Must be an important call."

I looked from the telephone, to Ricks, and back again. I didn't dare look at the Fisher Twins. The telephone was chirping like a deranged cricket, skittering across the floor. I flipped it open and angled the screen toward me. *Withheld Number*. I raised the device to my ear.

"Charlie? It's Victoria. Good news. I just found Caitlin and she's willing to talk with us. We're on our way to the Fifty-Fifty. Where are you exactly?"

THIRTY-FOUR

My exact location was somewhere close to "thoroughly screwed." I didn't say as much to Victoria. Instead, I gambled and told her in a rather strained voice that it would be helpful if she and Caitlin could meet me on the theater stage where Josh had performed his show.

"The theater? Are you sure that's safe?"

"Absolutely."

"Charlie, are you all right? You sound a little strange."

"Never better," I told her, and snapped the phone closed.

I locked eyes with Ricks. There was a coldness and a stillness in his pupils. He was breathing heavily and his ears seemed to twitch, as though they were resonating with the angry thoughts banging around his mind.

I heard movement to my left and was in the process of turning when one of the twins introduced me to the toe of his right shoe, spinning my head around on my shoulders. My vertebrae made the sickening noise of a football rattle, which didn't strike me as a good sign, and my sight had already blurred before the pain even registered in my temple. I yelped and clutched my hands to my head, trying to protect myself from a follow-up blow. The next two chipped at the base of my skull, as if he was aiming to split my head like a coconut. I tried to roll under the desk but he stomped on the small of my back, then grabbed me by the ankles and heaved me onto the edge of the mosaic.

"That's enough," Ricks said, but the twin didn't agree.

A couple more digs were aimed at my kidneys. I wrapped my arms around my chest, curling in on myself. It maybe wasn't the most heroic of reactions, but I found it impossible to think beyond the instinct.

"Stealing from us again, huh, guy? What is it with you anyway?"

"I didn't steal," I yelled, as he kicked at my elbow. "Ouch. Stop it. It wasn't me."

"Where's the list? Where is it, you prick?"

My arm came loose and I snatched it back beneath my body, afraid that he might stomp on my fingers.

"Aarrgh. Will you listen to me? I don't have your damn list. I couldn't get inside your safe."

The twin shaped to kick me again and I rolled away from the blow. The strike never came. Cautiously, I peered out from under my bicep. The twin was standing on one leg with his foot in the air.

"What's that you say?"

"It wasn't me. I couldn't crack your safe."

"Oh, sure." His face darkened and his foot ratcheted backward.

"It's true," I told him. "You can search me. I don't have it."

The twin watched over me for a moment. I could tell he was tempted to strike me again, but maybe his foot needed a rest.

"Do it," he said to Ricks. "Search the prick. Find out if he's lying."

Needless to say, after I'd staggered upright, Ricks didn't find the juice list inside my record bag or on my person or even beneath my Sinatra mask. He did find plenty of evidence to suggest that I'd been tampering with the safe, but there was nothing to prove that I'd been the one to get inside it. Well, nothing other than the fact that the juice list was gone.

One of the items Ricks found among my things was Josh's wallet, and he flipped it open and checked its contents. As soon as he saw the name printed on the credit cards, he treated me to a suspicious glare and a wag of his head.

"I found it," I told him.

"Where?"

My face shrugged. "His pocket."

"You want to explain that?"

"It was from before he disappeared. The two things are wholly unconnected. I give you my word."

Ricks snarled, as though he didn't rate my word very highly, and meanwhile he tucked Josh's wallet into the inside pocket of his blazer. He pushed my record bag and the Sinatra mask to one side and twirled his finger in the air, gesturing for me to turn. I summoned up my strength and did as he asked, spreading my palms on the surface of the desk. Ricks patted me down until he found my own wallet and the pack of Circus Circus playing cards that I'd taken from Jared's apartment. When he was satisfied that there was nothing unusual about either of them, he returned them to me.

"I know who took the list," I said.

I leaned against the desk and rubbed at the back of my neck. It felt uncommonly warm, as though I'd ripped a good many muscles. I couldn't turn it all the way to the right, and if I tried to turn it to the left I feared I'd pass out from the pain. At least it distracted me from the wet gash on my temple, and the way my ribs felt as though they were puncturing my lung each time I breathed. And it sure put my earlier nosebleed into context.

"Go on," said the twin in the club chair. He was still rubbing his toes from his battle with the mosaic hatch. I was almost sorry he hadn't been the one to start kicking me. I could only guess what injuries he might have sustained.

"I think it was Josh Masters."

The twins looked at Ricks. Ricks stroked his beard, turning over my response.

"What makes you say that?"

"He was the one who told me about the list." I raised a hand to my temple and winced, as though processing the thought was more painful than the ache in my forehead. "When we were planning the roulette fix," I gasped. "He told me where it could be found."

"That all?" asked the twin in the chair.

I met his gaze, which wasn't easy considering I was seeing two of him. Or was that his brother?

"He disappeared, didn't he? He ran when you turned up to his show. He must have thought you were onto him."

He quit rubbing his toes and sniffed his fingers, recoiling from the smell.

"You have our money?"

"Not yet."

"So let me get this straight. You figured the smart play was to rip us off?"

"I was getting desperate."

"No shit."

"What about your lady pal?" Ricks cut in. "She here too?"

I shook my head. "That was her on the phone. I came here alone."

"Yeah? Then how'd you open the mosaic?" He gauged the distance over to the second desk. "You're kind of wiry, but your arms ain't that long."

"I used a Band-Aid to stick down one of the buttons. You saw the box in my bag, right?"

Ricks walked around the rear of the desk I was propped against, checking behind and beneath it. He did the same with the second desk, then moved on past the twin with the up-tempo feet and approached the fireplace. He crouched down and peered up at the chimney, as if he suspected my back-up was Santa Claus. When he didn't find anyone, he approached the rear of the club chair the twin was sitting in.

"Listen," I said, trying to keep the urgency from my voice. "I think I've figured out where the juice list is. Where Josh is, too."

Ricks was still moving toward the space behind the chair. I really didn't want him to find Sal. It would only complicate matters if he did.

"Did you hear what I said?"

He smiled benignly and looked down behind the chair. I braced myself for his reaction, not knowing what explanation I could possibly offer. He frowned and bent at the knees and straightened a moment later with something in his hand.

"This yours?" he asked, and held up my pencil.

I nodded.

"You really came here alone?"

"Cross my heart." I gulped. "And if you'll only let me, I really think I can find Josh for you too."

THIRTY-FIVE

I experienced a mixture of emotions as I stepped inside the Fisher Twins' private elevator. On the one hand, I felt relieved, perhaps even elated, to have got the twins away from their office without Sal being discovered. True, I had no way of knowing how he'd moved from behind the chair without any of us seeing him, let alone whether he'd be able to escape without being caught, but at least something had gone my way, and more to the point, I had a little more flexibility in what I could say to try and dig myself out of the pit of trouble I seemed to be in.

On the other hand, my wrists had been bound in front of my waist with a pair of plastic tie-cuffs, the twins and Ricks were surrounding me, and I was about to lead them all to Victoria. I was tired and beaten up and more than a little scared, and I wasn't at all sure that I was capable of thinking very clearly.

"What happened to your golf game?" I asked, if only to break the awkward silence in the elevator.

The twins turned and looked past me at one another.

"It's just that I heard you play golf at four o'clock every day," I went on. "That's why I thought it would be safe to be in your office."

The twin on my left (the one who'd kicked the mosaic hatch and had limped as we'd entered the elevator) cleared his throat. "Today is our birthday."

"We don't play golf on our birthday," added his brother.

"Your birthday? Wow." I stuck out my bottom lip. "I did not know that."

"We like to keep it low-key."

"Huh." I shuffled my feet. "Well, Happy birthday, I guess."

"Yeah," Ricks said, hefting my record bag awkwardly. "Congratulations."

"Appreciate it," the twins responded, just as a timely *ping!* and a sudden loss of momentum signaled that we'd arrived at our chosen floor.

The theater was in complete darkness, aside from a collection of dusty footlights pointed in at the stage itself. Otherwise, everything was as it had been when Josh had abandoned his show. The battered cabinet was still in the center of the stage, its doors flung open to reveal the beach mural and the coarse sand spilling out from its base. The straw sunhat Victoria had worn was hanging over the top of one of the doors. Her other prop, the pink daiquiri glass, was resting on the wooden floorboards close by.

Victoria was sitting at the front of the stage with her legs dangling over the blackened auditorium below. She glanced around skittishly when she heard us approach, and so did the redhead sitting alongside her. The redhead was really quite something. Sure, I might have seen the YouTube video of her performance, and I might even have stood over her while she lay naked in the bath, but nothing could have prepared me for my first real glimpse of her face.

Her skin was creamy white and seemed almost to glow in the glare of the stage lights. Her lips were full and lush, her nose lean and neatly upturned, and her sparkling green eyes had an almost feline quality. Her hair topped it all. It fell around her face in luxurious loops and curls, collecting around her shoulders and her delicate neck like a blood-red shawl.

She had on a scooped yellow top over a pair of admirably pert breasts and some figure-hugging jeans. True, I'd only seen her rear profile in the bath, but there was no doubt in my mind that this was the same woman.

As we drew near, the redhead stood and wiped the dust from her hands. She treated me to a watchful assessment, then glanced at Victoria before finally flicking her eyes toward her brothers. Bewilderment clouded her features and I thought I could understand why. How could a beauty like this be related to the Fisher Twins?

"Charlie, my God," Victoria said. "Are you all right? What have they done to you?"

She hurried across the stage and cupped my bruised face in her hands, yanking my head toward the light and prodding a finger at the swollen welt on my temple. I winced, then moaned as my rib flared with pain.

"I'm fine," I told her through gritted teeth. "Don't worry about it."

"Don't worry about it? Are you mad?" She spun to confront Ricks. "Are you responsible for this?" She did a double-take when she noticed that my record bag was knotted in his fist. "You're despicable."

"Is that right?" Ricks said flatly. "And what do you suppose he was doing upstairs when we found him?"

"Nothing that could have justified this, I'm sure."

"How sure?"

Victoria paused, then re-doubled her attack. "You should be ashamed of yourself. You should be locked up."

"It wasn't him." I touched her arm, as if to confirm the information, and then I stepped toward the redhead, aiming to take control of the situation before somebody else did it for me. "You must be Caitlin. My name's Charlie. I'd offer to shake your hand, only . . ." I lifted my cuffed wrists and spread my fingers.

"I guess that's okay," she replied. "Victoria told me you might know where Josh is at."

Her voice was cautious, a lot like her manner. She looked past me and checked on her brothers, as if she expected them to forbid her from saying any more.

"Actually, I was rather hoping you could explain his whereabouts."

"Me?" She raised her hand to her chest and opened her mouth, as though breathless. "But I don't have any idea where he's gotten to. I wasn't at the show when he went missing."

"Believe me, that much I'm aware of."

She backed off a fraction, perhaps unnerved by my response and only half-sure she wanted to know the reasons behind it. I gestured at the scarred wooden cabinet in the middle of the stage.

"I'm guessing you know your way around this thing better than anyone."

I approached the cabinet, my footsteps echoing out into the auditorium. I reached for one of the doors with my bound hands and stroked the lacquered wood.

The Fisher Twins stood blinking against the stage lights, peering fixedly at me with grim expressions. I didn't doubt that they were annoyed with me for involving their sister in the entire mess, and from the way they were leaning forward on their toes, I got the impression they weren't inclined to grant me a whole lot of time to explain myself.

Hell, they could crowd me all they liked. Standing on that theater stage, in front of the magic cabinet, I felt a sudden rush of confidence. It wasn't simply a renewed belief in the theory I'd been developing. It was also that I'd done this kind of thing before—in my burglar novels as well as real life—and there was something oddly fitting about gathering together the key players in a mystery before explaining what had happened and why. It was like a magic trick, in a way. First the build-up—the confusion, and the misdirection. Then the puzzle—the confounding of your audience. And now, the final flourish—the delivery of a solution so elegant that my culpability for what had happened might just be overlooked.

"The last moment that anyone saw Josh," I announced, in a clear, confident voice, "he walked around the back of this cabinet in the middle of his show."

"Jeez," Ricks said. "Enough with the routine. You told us you knew where he was at. Let's hear it."

"Patience." I stepped inside the cabinet on the coarse sand and turned to face my audience. "Victoria, when Josh disappeared, you were in my current position, helping out with the show. You were quite helpless inside the cabinet. You'd been strapped in securely and steel blades had been inserted on either side of you."

"The blades are just a diversion," Caitlin explained, walking closer to me.

I nodded. "I suspected as much. And normally, you'd be the one in the cabinet, correct?"

"That's right."

I smiled at her. "Do you mind my asking why you weren't performing last night? Josh told us you were ill—but that was less than a day ago, and you look perfectly healthy to me."

I could feel Victoria's eyes boring into the side of my head, but I willed myself not to glance in her direction.

"I wasn't sick."

"No?"

The young woman threw up her hands. "I was just beat, I guess. I'd been bitching about doing another show since the matinée. And Josh, well, he told me to take a break. Said he didn't want me to give a flat performance. Plus, I've been working on a new act, a water stunt for the show. I was kind of glad to have the opportunity to do some training."

"Indeed." I straightened my shoulders and lifted my chin, bracing myself against the rear of the cabinet. "Just so that I understand, you'd normally be standing where I am now, and at a certain point in time Josh would move behind the cabinet. Then, very quickly, the two of you would switch positions. That's the pay-off, as it were?"

"Sure. But before we do the switch Josh has to cover the cabinet. He drapes a black curtain over the entire thing. It's only there for, like, five seconds before I appear and pull the cover away."

"And by that time Josh is standing where I am?"

"That's right. And then he climbs out and joins me."

"In a bikini?"

She smiled demurely. "No, I tend to fill a bikini better than Josh."

I just bet that she did. I was poised to continue when one of the twins stepped forward and placed his arm in front of his sister, as though defending her honor in a high-school corridor.

"That's enough, Caitlin. This guy is stalling us." He glared at me. "You know where Josh is, or not?"

"You mean you really haven't figured it out?"

"Buddy, there's nothing to figure. He's gone."

I stepped down from the cabinet and peered at Caitlin, doing my best to gain her trust. True, I might never have cut it as a professional magician, but I was more than ready for my big reveal.

"How'd you do the switch, Caitlin?"

"Excuse me?"

"You and Josh. When you trade positions, it's because the cabinet is gimmicked in some way, right? We tried finding a secret door after he vanished, but we didn't look for too long. And I'm guessing if Josh had a talented carpenter build the cabinet, well, there are ways to conceal things that might otherwise be obvious."

Her cattish eyes narrowed and she sucked on her lips, as if wary of me all of a sudden.

"With respect," I told her, "there are bigger things going on right now than your stage secrets."

"Go ahead," her brother added. "You can tell him. If he screws this up, he won't be alive long enough for it to matter."

Caitlin drew a long breath through her teeth, then clasped her hands tight together and circled to the reverse of the cabinet. She dropped to her knees and flattened her palms against the base of the rear panel, just left of center, with one hand directly above the other. She levered down on her forearms, grunting faintly, and in almost the same instant a thin join appeared between two horizontal strips of wood. The strips were hinged in the middle and they began to swing upward, exposing an opening just large enough for a grown man to crawl inside.

"Wait." I nudged Caitlin aside. "Up here?"

She nodded.

"And there's what, a channel with enough space for someone to fit?"

"Yes. But first you have to release the sand through a small opening. Then, once you're inside, a second hatch lets you step through into the cabinet. I'm the one who has to open that."

I smiled glumly. "Can it be opened by the person inside the channel?"

"No. Why do you ask?"

"What about this hatch?" I went on, rapping my knuckle against the strips of timber Caitlin had released. "Can it be opened from inside the channel?"

"I don't think so. But then, it's never been an issue. Josh always made sure the hatch stayed open when we did the switch. There's a tiny catch on the outside, see?"

"I was afraid you might say something like that." I nodded to Ricks. "You might want to get a doctor in here."

And with that, I plunged my cuffed hands up into the darkened space above me and felt around for Josh's heels. It had taken a while for the penny to drop, but the logic now seemed inescapable to me. If Josh had succeeded in stealing the juice list, he'd had no reason to flee without handing it to Maurice first. But Maurice hadn't heard from Josh, and that suggested to me that he'd never left the stage.

The way I saw it, Josh had managed to steal the list at some point in the two days prior to his show. Feeling cocky, he'd indulged in the roulette scam. But when the twins appeared during his performance, he'd panicked and assumed that he'd been rumbled. So he hid in the only place to hand.

From what I could gather, nobody besides Caitlin knew how to access the hidden compartment, so he had only to remain quiet to escape detection. But cruelly, he had no way of getting back out. Once closed, the gimmicked hatch couldn't be opened from inside the channel where he'd concealed himself. And if my thinking wasn't completely flawed, I was afraid that he might well have suffocated.

"Oh Lord, is he there?" Caitlin covered her face with her hands. "Please tell me he's not there."

I forced my hands higher, clawing desperately at the wood with my fingertips. Having my wrists bound wasn't making the task any easier, so I pulled my arms clear and thrust my head up into the space. I scrambled and I pushed until I was half-standing in a nook just large enough to contain a grown man.

And I was the only man inside it. Josh Masters was nowhere to be seen.

THIRTY-SIX

I dropped out of the cabinet and rolled onto my side, gasping for air. It had been warm and stuffy inside the opening, and I already felt light-headed. I also felt crushed. Without a body, my theory was in serious trouble, and so, very probably, was I.

"That's it?" Ricks asked. "That's your explanation? You figured Josh was dumb enough to get stuck inside one of his own tricks. Jeez, we should never have come down here."

"I don't get it," I said, half to myself. "I don't understand where he went."

"No kidding. Guy was a magician. He could have vanished a hundred different ways."

"I really thought he'd be here."

"Yeah—well, he ain't." Ricks turned and checked on the twins' reactions before patting my record bag and addressing me again. "I think it's time we continued this conversation in private." He pointed at Victoria. "You too, miss."

"Trapdoors," Victoria replied.

"Excuse me?"

She stamped her foot on the stage. "Charlie, when we were here before, didn't you think he could have used one?"

"I suppose it's possible."

"Caitlin?"

Caitlin shook her head. "This stage only has one trapdoor. It's way over there." She jerked her chin off to the far right, close to where the twins had been standing during Josh's performance. It didn't seem likely that he could have made it to the trapdoor without being seen.

Victoria offered me a dispirited heft of her shoulders, then extended her hands and pulled me to my feet. She brushed some dirt from my shoulders, mussed my hair and kissed my forehead.

"Time's running out," she whispered. "I wish you'd put those pretty gray cells of yours to work."

"I tried, Vic."

"Then try again. You of all people should know the value of a good re-write."

She turned from me and knocked on the rear of the cabinet with her knuckles, working downward like a builder trying to locate a joist in a stud-wall.

"I showed you the only way in," Caitlin told her, in an apologetic tone.

Victoria crouched and contorted her neck to peer inside the concealed opening for herself. When she found nothing, she rocked backward on her heels and sat on her bottom with her hands spread on the stage floor.

"He must have left the theater. But how?"

"I'm not sure that it matters," I said. "He must be in Hawaii already."

"Hawaii?" Caitlin said. "What makes you say that?"

"We asked around," one of the twins told her. "People heard he was planning a trip."

"People?"

"Some girls from the revue. Some of the guys from the bar. You know how Josh liked to talk."

"And there's something else." I raised an eyebrow at Ricks and pointed a finger toward his blazer. "May I?"

"May you what?"

"If you'll just pass me the wallet."

Ricks tucked my bag under his armpit and extracted Josh's wallet from his pocket. He spread the leather compartments with his fingers.

"Hey," Caitlin said, stepping closer. "That belongs to Josh."

"I kind of acquired it," I explained, with a heft of my shoulders. "Before his performance."

"He means he stole it." Ricks stuck out his bottom lip and looked up from the wallet with a blank expression, as though it was just another dead-end.

"Oh, give it to me, will you?" I swiped the wallet from his hand and quickly removed the torn napkin with the telephone number on it. I uncurled the napkin and passed it to Caitlin. "That number is for the Hawaii Airlines booking line."

Caitlin let go of a withering breath and flapped the napkin in the air. She closed her eyes and pinched her nose with her finger and thumb, as if she was about to jump into a swimming pool.

"You're wrong," she said, in a fractured voice. "All of you. This was for our honeymoon."

"Your *what*?" demanded the second twin, stepping forward to tear the napkin from her grip. "What in hell are you talking about?"

She set her jaw and turned from one brother to the next. "Josh asked me to marry him. The ceremony was going to be in Oahu. He was arranging it all. Some guy he knew—a producer in town—had offered him a villa. We just needed flights."

"And you said yes to the bum?"

"We were going to tell you. We were just waiting for the right moment."

"After he'd ripped us off, maybe?"

"It wasn't like that."

"Perhaps he went ahead of you," I suggested.

"No," she replied, peeling her lips back over her teeth. "Not Josh."

"Then where is he?"

"The Cape," Victoria said, and clicked her fingers, as if snapping herself out of a trance.

"Cape Cod?" Ricks asked.

"South Africa?" I added. "Why would Josh have gone there?"

"No, you morons, the black cape. Caitlin said that Josh concealed the cabinet with a cape before they switched positions. And I seem to remember Josh having one just before he disappeared."

Now that Victoria mentioned it, I could remember that too. The way he'd twirled the cape had reminded me of a bullfighter.

"You're right," I said.

"So where is it?"

We all looked at Caitlin. She stepped toward the rear of the cabinet and moved her foot around in an arc on the stage.

"Josh didn't use it to cover the cabinet?"

I looked at Victoria. Victoria looked at me.

"No," we replied, in unison.

"Then it should be here."

"Could anyone have moved it?" Victoria asked, directing her question to the Fisher Twins.

"Lady, so far as we know, nobody's been here since Josh disappeared."

Victoria clicked her fingers and turned to me with a light in her eyes. "Then that's how he did it. Don't you see? Instead of covering the cabinet, he shrouded himself. In the darkness, he could have crawled away without being seen."

"Crawled where?"

"Anywhere. The trapdoor maybe. Or even behind this curtain."

Victoria paced to the black curtain at the rear of the stage, the one with the rope lighting in the shape of the Vegas skyline. She gathered the curtain near her feet and lifted it in her arms, ducking her head underneath.

"Where does this lead?"

"There are doors from the back," Ricks said. "Corridors that take you on a bunch of different routes."

"Then that's how he got away."

"Neat," one of the twins put in. "But now he's gone. And you still owe us our money."

As much as I didn't want to admit it, he was right. The moment Josh left the stage, he could have gone anywhere he pleased.

What puzzled me was why it hadn't pleased him to head to Maurice's white-on-white home and hand over the juice list. If he'd stolen the list purely for money, then I supposed it was possible that he might have tried to interest somebody else to spark a bidding war, but so far as I could tell he'd genuinely wanted to be the star turn at Magic Land. And the longer he delayed, the less likely that became.

There had to be something else, something we'd missed that would explain what was going on. And whatever it was, I needed to find it soon.

I felt a tug at my hand and looked down to see Caitlin prising my fingers away from Josh's wallet.

"It's not yours," she told me. "You have no right to keep it."

She clutched the wallet to her chest, shielding it with her hands, as though it were precious stone. I didn't know what she hoped to find inside it to justify her reaction. Maybe the autographed portrait shot. Because aside from that, there was just his credit cards, his hotel key card, the cardboard sleeve with the number of his suite, and the valet ticket for his car.

Hang on a minute . . .

"I have an idea," I said, not for the first time.

"Another one?" Ricks groaned.

"Hear me out. I really think I might be onto something."

THIRTY-SEVEN

We waited beneath the shade of some palm trees while one of the valets retrieved Josh's car. It was a bright, sun-drenched afternoon, the kind of weather that didn't fit with my mood. If I'd written the scene myself, rain would have been lashing down from a brooding gray sky, and Faulks would have been soaked clean through, with his clothes stuck to his skin like webbing.

In fairness, my underarms were perspiring rather heavily, but it wasn't quite the same thing. The audio didn't help, either. Birdsong and idle fountain splatter filled the air, along with the carefree conversations of tourists waiting in line for a cab and the hum of traffic out on the Strip. Hardly the stuff of nightmares.

At least the vintage automobiles parked behind us in the hotel foyer conjured up some of the atmosphere I might have expected. If I squinted over at the Packards and Buicks and Studebakers, I could even have believed I was in the middle of a hardboiled noir. Of course, if that was the case, I'd need to brace myself for a bittersweet ending that might not involve the neatly packaged solution for which I'd been hoping.

"What are you thinking about?" Victoria whispered.

"Oh, nothing."

"Nothing?"

"Too tired to think."

"Well, that's unfortunate, because I have a question. What do we do if the car is a dead end?"

"We could run."

"Think we'd make it?"

"No, but we might shed a few pounds from that breakfast buffet."

Victoria kicked me in the shin.

"Ouch. That's not going to make running away any easier."

She turned her back on me and looked over toward Ricks and the Fisher Twins. They were standing in a huddle with their hands in their pockets and their heads bowed in conference. Caitlin was close by, grinding her toe into the pavement. It might have been a good opportunity to make our escape, if only Ricks hadn't arranged for a group of security guards to watch over us.

"What about those cuffs you're wearing?" Victoria asked. "Could you loosen them?"

"Not without a pencil. Or better still, one of my picks." I nodded toward one of the security guards who happened to be holding my record bag.

"How about a biro?"

I grinned at her. "That might do."

Victoria delved inside her handbag, then acted as if she couldn't find what she'd been looking for and palmed a biro across to me. A purist would say she did it all wrong, but so far as I could tell, there were no purists watching.

"Houdini would be proud."

"Are you going to do it now?"

"Let's just see what the car brings first."

I'd barely finished speaking when a gleaming Lexus sedan pulled up and a young valet stepped out in a polo-shirt and pressed shorts. He went to hand the keys to one of the Fisher Twins but Caitlin hurried forward and claimed them for herself. She scrambled inside the Lexus and scanned the interior. The rest of us crowded around and watched through the open door as she searched the glove box and a selection of ashtrays and cup-holders and cubbyholes. She flipped down the sun visor. The car appeared to be empty, and one glance around the showroom-clean interior told me that things weren't likely to improve anytime soon.

"This is definitely his car?"

Caitlin nodded.

"Did he have more than one?"

"Not here. He kept a Porsche in storage. And a Harley."

"Maybe we should check those?"

"I don't think so." Ricks slapped his hand on the roof of the Lexus. "I think we're done here."

"Yeah, we're done," one of the twins agreed. "Let's go back inside and have that conversation."

"What about the boot?" Victoria asked.

"Huh?"

"The trunk," I said to Caitlin. "Can you open it?"

She searched beneath the dash for a likely mechanism, pulled a recessed handle and the fuel cap jinked out.

"Wrong lever."

"I'm kinda lost here." She held up her hands.

"Try the key." I turned the key in her palm, tilting the plastic casing toward the light. "Here."

I pressed a dimpled button, the indicator lamps flashed, there was a muffled clunk and the boot lid bounced up. I scurried to the rear of the Lexus and heaved at the lid with my cuffed hands. A puff of hot, moist air rolled out to greet me. It didn't smell nearly so pleasant as the scented freshener hanging from the rearview mirror, and as I covered my mouth with my arm and peered into the boot, I was unfortunate enough to see why.

A stiff, lifeless body had been wedged inside, legs bent at the knees. The face and torso were part covered by a black cloth, but I had a fair idea of who I was looking at. I peeled the cloth away and made absolutely certain.

Josh Masters stared back. His eyes were fixed and sightless, the left pupil misted with blood. His tanned face and neck were speckled a deep claret, and his capped teeth were arranged in a most unfortunate grin, as though he'd just performed his ultimate illusion and was awaiting the applause that was sure to follow.

Lower down, his arms were folded across his chest, fingers

clawed, and the downy hairs on his forearms were stained and matted with dried blood. Beneath his arms, his trademark white T-shirt was no more than a sodden, dark-red rag, torn and ripped. He looked to have been stabbed many times over, and the entry wounds were scattered from his neck right down to his lower belly.

I felt like I'd seen enough, and others seemed to agree. Rough hands shoved me aside and I stumbled on the tarmac before turning to see the twins crowding the rear of the car. They groaned and staggered backward, as though reeling from a small explosion, and one of them started yelling at a security guard to go fetch a medic. I wasn't sure that was strictly necessary. True, my track record was a little patchy, but I would have bet the house limit that Josh was dead.

I tried to catch Victoria's eye, but she was busy leading Caitlin away toward the valet booth. Meanwhile, one of the twins ordered his security detail to clear the area while his brother barked commands into a two-way radio. Something about the scene jarred with me, and it took me a good few moments to figure out why.

I forced myself back to the trunk of the Lexus. Josh didn't look a great deal healthier. I watched over him for just a short while longer and then I leaned into the trunk and shrouded his face with the bloodied black cape he'd used to make his escape from the theater.

Over at the valet booth, Victoria was clutching Caitlin's face to her chest and stroking her hair and making shushing noises. I beckoned Victoria toward me. She scowled, but when I repeated the gesture, she pressed a tissue into Caitlin's trembling fist, kissed her forehead and drew near.

"Where's Ricks?" I asked.

"Is that all you wanted? I have no idea, Charlie."

I turned on the spot and scanned the area. Ricks wasn't anywhere close, and I couldn't recall seeing him after the valet had pulled up in the Lexus.

"Don't you find that strange? He's one of their main security advisers."

"I'm trying to look after Caitlin here, Charlie."

There was a queasy sensation in my stomach, but it had nothing to do with the sights or smells I'd just experienced. The puzzle was beginning to assemble itself in my brain and I didn't like the picture that was forming.

"Charlie, it is Josh in the car, right?"

"The cabinet," I said, all of a sudden.

"Excuse me?"

"In the theater. He must have made for the stage."

"What are you gibbering about?"

"I have to go," I said, and started to run.

"Charlie?"

"It took me long enough," I called over my shoulder. "But I'm onto him now."

Of course, I hadn't been looking where I was going, and I ran straight into the twin on the two-way radio. I knocked the radio from his hand and stooped toward the ground, my knuckles grazing concrete. The twin snatched at my ankle but his reaction was slow and my momentum carried me free.

"Hey," he shouted. "Hey, quit running."

I didn't quit running. I zeroed in on the revolving glass doors at the front of the casino, bracing my cuffed hands out in front of me.

"Somebody stop that guy," the twin yelled. "He's getting away."

It didn't feel like I was getting away. It felt like I was running headlong into trouble. The criminal part of my psyche seemed to be having difficulty understanding what I was up to. The law-abiding part couldn't understand it, either.

Three security guards were ahead of me. They hunkered down with their feet spread and palms raised, as if I was a runaway freight train they were aiming to stop. I didn't have a lot of time to consider my options, but I did know that I couldn't dive through their legs without piercing a glass panel with my head.

I opted for a late swerve and dodged to my right. The guard nearest to me stuck out his leg but I vaulted his shin and crashed into a swing door, doing a good job of displacing my knee cap.

I hauled the door back, then toppled inside, lurching for the handle of a giant slot machine to stop myself from falling. The handle dropped, the drums spun, and the bride and groom who'd been posing for a photograph beside the machine looked appropriately startled.

I garbled an apology, then turned and kicked on without waiting to see if we'd won the sports car that happened to be revolving on the podium above them. I lifted my bound hands before my face and pumped my knees, hollering at the people in my way to clear a path. It didn't work. They froze and stared, perhaps asking themselves why the loony guy in plastic tie-cuffs was running into the middle of the casino instead of making for the exit.

The loony guy in plastic tie-cuffs wasn't entirely sure.

Facing me was a security guard with a nightstick. He wet his lip and raised his baton in a two-handed grip, as if he was a baseball player looking to strike a home run. I let go of an almighty scream and drove forward with my shoulder. The nightstick thudded against my bicep and my shoulder met with his chin. He went down hard and I lost my balance and pitched forward. An action hero would have pulled off a tumble roll and sprinted on. I belly-flopped onto the carpet, with my crotch smothering the poor chap's face.

"Sorry," I yelled.

"Geroff me," he mumbled.

I scrambled up from my knees but the idiot grabbed hold of my foot. I tried shaking him loose but he clung on until I was forced to tear my foot from my shoe and totter forward into a run. It was a lopsided kind of run. If I'd had time to haul off my other shoe, I could have balanced things out, but there was no way that was going to happen.

I glanced up and got my bearings. The high-stakes area was way off to my left. The keno pit was dead ahead. The theater was away to my right.

I veered toward it, skirting a craps table where all of the players were gawping at me, their game momentarily forgotten. A cocktail waitress blocked my way. I dodged left and so did she. We both went right. Her drinks tray teetered. I bent at the waist and hoisted her onto my shoulder. She yelped and slapped her tray against my back. Beer and soda rained down on me. I ditched her on an empty roulette felt and scurried on.

Behind me, the security guards were gaining, running hard in their vintage uniforms with their nightsticks drawn, like a motley crew of Keystone Cops. A pit boss in a sharp suit and trilby watched over me and raised a telephone handset to his ear. Two cigarette girls stood beside one another, their painted mouths frozen in a double "O." If only the sound system had been playing some jaunty piano music instead of mid-tempo jazz, I could have believed I was trapped in the chase scene from an old silent movie.

The crowds thinned as I neared the theater. The ticket booths were closed and laminated signs informed me that the show was temporarily canceled. The entrance was roped off and I would have been trapped if it hadn't been for the one door I could see that was slightly ajar.

Yanking the door back, I darted past a locked concession stand and burst through into the auditorium. Darkness embraced me and the carpet fell away beneath my feet as I ran between the rows of tiered seating.

I was halfway toward the lighted stage before I saw Ricks. He was on his knees at the front of the cabinet, with the sleeves of his blazer rolled up on his forearms and his hands buried deep in sand. The sound of my one-sock, one-shoe shuffle must have drawn his attention, because he flinched and peered out into the black. I wasn't sure if he could tell who was coming, so I shouted at him in my best English just to make sure.

"Hold it, Ricks. That's enough."

He ignored me and kept digging. I sucked air and tried to gather what was left of my strength. I had a stitch in my gut, my lungs were on fire and the plastic restraints were biting into the skin of my wrists.

The stage seemed higher than I remembered. I jumped up and hooked my arms and legs over the edge as if I was climbing out of a swimming pool, then picked my way between the footlights and cables and stood panting before Ricks.

"Security are coming." I pointed out into the darkness of the auditorium at the footsteps I could hear.

Ricks grinned disconcertingly and removed his hands from the sand. There was something wrapped in his right fist. His grin widened and he moved as if to get up from his knees.

I'd really had my fill of things by now. I'd been scared half out of my mind with the idea that I'd found a drowned woman; had a haul of casino chips taken away from me; been locked up, interrogated and threatened; trapped myself inside a closet; been ripped off by a hooker; got caught in the middle of a robbery; been kicked while I was down (repeatedly) and come face to face with the gruesome corpse of a mid-ranking magician. And now Ricks was grinning at me.

So sure, my hands might have been cuffed and my ribs bruised, I might have been struggling for air and to stay upright, but there was no way—*no how*—that I was prepared to stand it for a moment longer.

I bowed my head and snarled and went thundering across the stage. If Ricks had moved aside at just the right moment, I would have looked pretty stupid, but he didn't move and I didn't stop, and I hit him smack in the forehead with everything I had.

Ricks crumpled and let go of a croaking gasp. The item he'd been holding onto slipped free and arced through the air. It landed near to the black velvet curtains at the rear of the stage and before Ricks could react, I dived for it and gathered it into my hands.

I uncurled my fingers. In the middle of my palm was a computer memory stick, coated in soft rubber and rounded off at each end, like a rather eye-watering suppository. There were no markings on it whatsoever, aside from a few grains of sand, but I was as sure as I could be that I finally had a hold of the juice list.

I swiveled to see the security guards lumbering across the

stage, forming themselves into a semi-circle and closing in on me, eyes dark and chests heaving, like a pack of low-rent zombies.

"You've got the wrong guy," I said, and cringed at the line. "*He's* the one you should cuff."

They glanced at Ricks, unsure what to do. Ricks cupped his temple and glared at me the way a boxer glares at an opponent shortly before he removes his head from his shoulders.

"Throw that punk in a back room," he snarled.

"Throw them both in, why don't you?"

The security guards turned, and I squinted out into the darkness between their legs, watching in some confusion until the Fisher Twins moved into the light at the front of the stage.

"Yeah, do it already," the one on the left said. "They both have some explaining to do."

THIRTY-EIGHT

I found myself in the back room Jared Hall had occupied only a day before. It was just like the room where I'd been questioned with Victoria—same putty-colored walls, same plastic table screwed to the floor, same uncomfortable plastic chairs—the only difference being that I was on the mirrored side of the two-way glass. I guessed Ricks was in the room next door. Maybe he was even looking at me through the glass partition. I raised my cuffed hands to wave at him and my battered reflection waved back.

I sighed and paced the room. I smelled of the beer the cocktail waitress had spilled on me and I was still one shoe down, so I moved with a limp. While I paced, I stretched my arms up above my head, testing the sore spot on my ribs and scratching the polystyrene ceiling tiles with my fingernails.

I was on my third circuit of the room when the door was unlocked and the Fisher Twins walked in. They stood with their backs against the wall and their hands in the pockets of their khaki trousers.

"Sit down," one of them said, with a nod of his ginger hair and freckled face.

I studied him for a moment before doing as he asked. "Did Ricks confess?"

"To what?"

"Killing Josh."

The twin held my eye. He didn't answer in a hurry and I got a bad feeling about the delay. His brother cleared his stringy throat.

"He figures you for it."

"He's really playing that game?"

"You deny it?"

"Of course I deny it. I didn't kill Josh."

"Then how about the juice list? Ricks says you were the one who put it under the sand."

I spread my cuffed hands on the table and let go of a long sigh.

"You do remember that you caught me in your office? You do remember that I hadn't accessed your safe?"

"Then how'd the juice list get out?"

"I told you. It was Josh."

The twins shared a look. They offered me the same troubled expression.

"Ricks figures you hid the memory stick someplace when he searched you upstairs. Says you took us to the theater and planted the stick under the sand, so you could return for it later."

"Well, that's pretty dumb."

"Yeah? How else did it get there?"

I blew air through my lips. "If you want me to speculate, I'd say Josh was the one who broke into your safe, some time in the last couple of days. When you came to his show, he must have thought you were on to him."

"So?"

"So he must have been holding the memory stick at the time. At first, I guessed he'd hidden inside the cabinet and that he'd become stuck there. I was wrong about that, but not as wrong as I could have been. My thinking is that before he vanished, he lifted the gimmicked hatch in the back of the cabinet and hid the memory stick inside. Then, when the sand spilled out, the memory stick came with it."

"Why would he do that?"

"Same reason Ricks suggested I might have. So he could return for it later. Say his disappearing act hadn't worked. He wouldn't have wanted to be stopped with the memory stick on him."

"Yeah? Then how'd he wind up dead?"

"You'd have to ask Ricks that question."

The twin on the left approached the table and leaned his weight on his clenched fists.

"I'm asking you."

I stared at him, not wanting to glance away and have him interpret it as a sign that I was lying. "Maybe Ricks found out that Josh was ripping you off. Maybe he was watching Josh's show from the wings and saw him bolt. Then he confronted him."

"Why?"

"The list is valuable, right? Ricks would have known that. I understand he helped compile parts of it. He could have made a lot of money if he delivered it to the right hands."

The second twin left the wall and moved alongside his brother, stroking his chin.

"Maybe you were the guy waiting for Josh."

"Duh. I was sitting in the front row of the theater. And I was on stage just a couple of minutes after Josh vanished. You spoke to me. Then you locked me up with my friend next door."

The twins exchanged another look. They still didn't seem convinced.

One of them said, "Ricks was in here questioning the croup."

"The whole time?"

They didn't offer me a response. It seemed likely they didn't know for sure.

"What about cameras?" I asked.

They looked at me with question marks in their eyes.

"Surveillance cameras," I went on. "If there are cameras where Josh's car was parked, they might prove who killed him."

The twin on the right pushed up from his fists.

"Don't try anything smart while we're gone."

I scraped back my chair and lifted my shoeless foot onto the table. "Do I look like the type who could?"

Not long after the twins had left, I turned my back on the mirror-glass partition and reached inside my shirt pocket for the biro

Victoria had palmed me. Gripping the metal nib, I pulled the plastic casing away. Then, holding onto the flexible plastic tube containing the biro ink, I fed the nib down into the ratchet mechanism on my tie-cuffs. Once I was free, I dropped the cuffs and the biro parts under the table and sat rubbing my skin, luxuriating in the novelty of being able to move my hands freely again.

After a time, I stood and approached the door to the room. I tried the handle and found that it was locked. There wasn't a lot I could do about that. I didn't have my picks on me and the biro and plastic tie-cuffs weren't up to the job. And besides, I was pretty sure there was a security guard stationed outside, just waiting to beautify my face with his nightstick if I happened to cause any trouble.

I crossed to the mirror and pressed my face to the glass, cupping my hands around my eyes. If I focused right, I could just make out a dim murkiness beyond.

I returned to the plastic chair. A half-hour went by, and my head was just beginning to loll and my eyelids starting to droop when I was roused by the sound of the door being unlocked. The Fisher Twins walked back in.

"Well?" I asked. "Did you find anything on the surveillance footage?"

"Come on, smart guy. Why don't you just tell us why you did it?"

"Huh?"

"Don't play dumb with us."

"You've lost me, I'm afraid."

The twin nearest the door exhaled and rubbed at his eye with the heel of his palm, as though he'd just concluded a lengthy business meeting and was feeling especially jaded. "There is no footage."

"The recordings for the past day have been erased," his brother added. "The cameras in the parking lot were powered down."

I gulped. It wasn't what I'd been expecting to hear, but I wasn't about to give up that easily.

"Well, there you go," I told them. "Ricks is high up in your security detail. I'm guessing he must have had access to the recordings and that he deleted them to destroy the evidence. Case closed."

"Funny. He said the same thing about you."

"Given you're a burglar, and all."

I swallowed. My ears popped. "I didn't erase that footage. I wouldn't have known where to look or how to delete it."

"You knew where to look for the juice list, all right."

"Because Josh told me."

"So you say." The twin jabbed a finger at me. "Hey, where are your cuffs?"

I looked down at my hands, suddenly conscious that I'd been rubbing at my wrists.

"They were starting to chafe."

"They do that. How'd you get 'em off?"

It didn't strike me as the most opportune moment to draw attention to my ingenuity with locks and bindings.

"I rubbed them on the table leg."

The twin frowned at me. His brother frowned at the table.

"Is that so?"

"I'm afraid it is."

The twin on the right checked the time on his watch. He turned and made as if to leave the room. I spoke up before he'd got too far, saying, "What about Josh's body?"

"What about it?" he asked the wall.

"Why don't you have someone on your security team examine him—maybe take a look at the stab wounds more closely. It might give you a link to his killer."

The twin flexed his hands. "You think this is *CSI?*"

"I'm not suggesting an autopsy. But surely it's worth a try?"

He looked back over his shoulder and summoned a flinty glare. "Maybe we should leave it to the cops."

"If you were planning to leave any of this to the cops, I wouldn't be sitting here right now."

He glanced toward the mirrored partition and found his brother's eyes in the glass. "Man has a point."

The twins nodded at one another and moved toward the door.

"Can I use the bathroom?" I asked.

Three security guards accompanied me as far as the door to the bathroom, and one of them followed me inside. There was no door to close for my privacy and no window to prise open to make my escape. I unzipped my fly and peed. The guard watched me do it. He didn't comment on my technique and I didn't ask him for any assistance. I took my time washing my hands, smoothing the soapy water over the sore spots on my wrists. Then I was transported back to my room.

Just before I was locked inside again, a fourth security guard came along the corridor and handed me coffee in a Styrofoam cup. I turned to the security guard who'd watched me pee.

"Loan me a cigarette, Mac?"

It seemed like a Mac moment, on account of his period cop uniform.

"I don't smoke."

"How about your buddies?"

"They don't smoke, either."

He locked the door behind me and left me alone in the room, drinking my lukewarm coffee and thinking about the cigarette I wasn't smoking. Two hours went by. I counted them off on my digital watch, since Josh's watch had quit working again. I tore the Styrofoam cup into pieces. I became so hungry that I started to wonder if I should eat some of it. I'd got as far as tasting a piece by the time Ricks walked in.

THIRTY-NINE

Ricks entered the room holding an ice pack against his forehead. The ice pack was pale blue in color, complementing his navy blazer and crisp white shirt. He grunted a greeting, then stepped forward and sat down in the plastic chair across the table from me. He lifted the ice pack away from his face and revealed a dark, swollen lump just above his left eye. It looked as if a crazed plastic surgeon had implanted a golf ball beneath his skin.

"I hope you're not expecting an apology," I told him, and spat a mulched piece of Styrofoam onto the remains of my cup.

"Doc tells me I have a concussion," he said. "That accounts for the nausea. And the dizzy spells."

"And the compulsive lying?"

Ricks barely smiled as he covered the lump with the ice pack once more. He used his spare hand to reach inside his blazer.

"Guess you figured you were mighty smart."

"You'll have to be more specific than that, I'm afraid."

He removed his hand and I saw that he had a playing card pinched between his forefinger and thumb. The reverse of the playing card was pointed toward me.

"Aren't you supposed to shuffle the deck and invite me to select my own?"

A smirk flirted with his lips and the graying bristles of his goatee beard stiffened and stretched, like the fronds of a sea anemone. He held the card in front of his nose and turned it slowly. Two of Hearts.

"You want me to memorize it?" I asked.

"Like it's the first time you've seen this playing card."

"What do you want me to say?"

Ricks exhaled audibly. My response obviously didn't please him. I don't suppose the playing card had pleased him a great deal either. There was blood on the waxed surface, and I was confident that a forensic test would demonstrate that it belonged to Josh Masters. There was also a single word scrawled across the face of the card in a faint blue ink. *RICKS*.

"Seems you recommended the Fisher Twins have somebody take a look at Josh's body. Seems you suggested they might find something to identify the killer."

"Just trying to be helpful. I thought the slash wounds might give them a lead."

"Kind of clever, I guess. Laying the plant."

"Me?"

"Yeah. You."

He was right, of course—I had done it. The moment everything had fallen into place for me, when the twins had pushed me clear of the boot of the Lexus and I'd first noticed that Ricks was nowhere to be seen, I'd used the biro Victoria had palmed me to write his name onto one of the playing cards from the deck in my pocket. Then, when the twins had backed off and I'd stepped up to look down over Josh the second time around, I'd slipped the card into his hand before tugging the black cape up to cover his face.

I have to confess that I liked the symmetry of the move. When I'd first met Josh, I'd wanted to show him a trick that involved writing a name on a playing card. And once it had occurred to me that Ricks was the killer, I couldn't see the harm in doing something similar to give justice a nudge in the right direction—especially if it would take the heat off me.

"Odd, ain't it," Ricks said, turning the playing card in his hand and showing me the reverse. The words CIRCUS CIRCUS had been printed over and over on the flipside, in a slanted brown font. "I seem to recall you had a pack of cards just like this when I searched you upstairs."

"Coincidence is a funny thing."

"Huh. And how would you rate the coincidence if I asked you to count out that same deck of cards onto this table and show me the Two of Hearts you're carrying?"

I didn't say anything to that. There wasn't anything to be said.

"Or maybe we should arrange for a specialist to compare the name on this playing card with a sample of your handwriting?"

"Sounds complicated," I told him. "And more than a little unnecessary."

"Oh, it's unnecessary, all right. But not for the reasons you have in mind."

Ricks spread his right hand on the table, fingers arched, like he was about to play piano. He drummed his fingers and I watched him at it. The tune didn't strike me as anything Liberace would have rated.

"You have a screwy notion," he said. "Figuring me for the guy who killed Josh."

"Makes sense to me."

"Is that so?" His fingers tickled the missing ivories some more. "Then I don't guess I'll be buying one of your mystery novels anytime soon."

"Not to worry. I hear they have excellent lending libraries in the prisons over here."

Ricks curled his lip and pushed up from the table, wincing as his balance shifted and the pain flared in his forehead. He gripped the table edge to steady himself, then paced stiffly behind me. I waited for him to lean in close to my ear and treat me to a dose of halitosis. Instead, I heard him punch the power button on the television fixed to the wall.

"Turn around, why don't you?"

Why didn't I, I thought, and so I turned in my seat and leaned an elbow on the backrest of my chair. Ricks motioned toward the television screen with the remote.

"This here is your killer."

The picture on the television was of a hunched figure sitting in a room much like the one I was sitting in, behind a table much like the one I'd just turned my back upon. He had lank, tangled hair and a smudged tattoo of a pair of dice on his neck. He wore a Yankees baseball shirt, his right hand was heavily bandaged and he was nibbling at the fabric of the dressing with his teeth. If Jared Hall had really planned on leaving Vegas, he was taking one hell of a circuitous route.

"Casino security picked him up a couple hours ago," Ricks told me. "Fool sent some kid in to cash a stack of ten k markers at the high-stakes cage. Dumb move. Security red-flagged the kid and hauled him inside for questioning. Gave our friend up right away. Guy was parked in a breakdown truck outside of a Fat Burger two blocks from here."

"The fact he had some silver chips doesn't make him a murderer," I told Ricks. "He might have lied to the twins yesterday. He could have had the chips all along. He could have been willing to risk his health to hold onto them."

Ricks lowered the ice pack from his forehead and weighed it in his hand along with my words. The weighing took a few moments and it led him to suck on his lips in contemplation. Once he was through sucking and thinking, he dropped back into his chair and slapped the television remote and the ice pack onto the table before me. I willed myself not to fixate on the colorful swelling above his temple as he delved inside the front, left-hand pocket on his blazer.

"They didn't only find your playing card when they checked on Josh's body. They found the man's cellphone too."

He pulled a clear, Ziploc bag from his pocket. Inside the bag was an expensive-looking mobile phone—the kind with a touch-sensitive screen. He frowned as he prodded at it with his thumbs. After some considerable time, his face relaxed and he showed me the lit screen.

"Text message. Sent at one-seventeen this afternoon."

I took the phone from him and stretched the plastic bag so that I could read the message clearly.

Am stuck in trunk of Lexus in staff parking lot. Have your roulette cut. Can you come free me?

I offered Ricks a puzzled look. "How does this connect Josh to Jared? Did you trace the number this message was sent to?"

"Better than that." Ricks slipped a hand into the pocket on the right of his blazer. He removed another plastic bag and another mobile telephone. This time, Ricks negotiated the operating system with relative ease before passing me the bagged phone.

"Found this on the croup," he explained.

I compared the two messages and confirmed that they were identical. Then I scrolled down and found that Jared's telephone had received the message at 13:17. That was around the time I'd been in his apartment, and it seemed reasonable to believe that this was the text that had prompted him to leave me by myself.

"I can see that the messages match," I said. "But that doesn't prove that Jared is responsible for Josh's death."

"The dressing on the man's hand has blood all over it."

I shrugged. "Unless you can demonstrate that the blood belongs to Josh, that doesn't mean anything. His fingers were mashed with a metal bar only yesterday. I'd say a little bleeding is to be expected."

"The blood is on the outside."

I shrugged some more. "Even if what you say is true, it looked to me as if Josh had been stabbed to death. Your man there couldn't lift a pen right now."

"So he used his left hand. That would explain why the wounds were spread around so much. The blood on the bandage would rate as splatter."

I supposed that was possible. And I couldn't deny that Jared had a plausible motive. Josh had screwed him out of his cut from the roulette scam, sure. But factor in the damage to his hand and his banishment from Vegas, and who knew what he was capable of. Hell, I knew only too well that he had a tendency to lash out.

I slid the phones back across the table to Ricks.

"It would help if you had the knife he used," I told him. "Or better still, a confession."

"Oh, we'll get a confession."

"Without breaking his hand this time?"

"Relax. I have enough evidence to work the guy. The text message is good, but one of my team searched the Dumpsters out back of the parking lot. We found a crowbar he used to force open the trunk—it has paint fragments that match with the finish on the Lexus. We also found the weapon. It has a lot of blood on it. Prints too, I'm guessing."

"You have the knife?"

Ricks shook his head. "No knife. Whack job used a barbecue fork."

I exhaled hard and turned to look up at the television screen. Jared was still gnawing on a thread from his bandage, as if it was a stubborn hangnail.

"Then I guess you do have your killer," I said. "But that still leaves one matter unresolved."

I fixed on Jared, chewing hard, and I allowed my mind to do the same thing on the knotted logic I was struggling to untangle.

"I didn't like Josh Masters a great deal," I told Ricks, "but he didn't strike me as completely stupid. So I don't see him climbing inside the boot of his Lexus and waiting more than half a day to send Jared the text message you found. Then there's the fact that somebody erased the footage from the cameras in the parking lot. I don't imagine Jared was capable of it, and you haven't suggested as much. Which means someone else was involved."

"You think so, huh?"

"Absolutely. And when you put all that together, you're really only left with one question that matters."

"Oh yeah? And what's that?"

"*Who shut Josh in the trunk of his car?*"

FORTY

"You're honestly saying it was Caitlin?" Victoria asked me.

"Cross my heart. And Ricks admitted as much. Eventually." I lifted my eyebrows. "Mind you, he wouldn't say a thing until we were outside the hotel and walking up and down the Strip. We must have covered a couple of miles talking it through."

Victoria shook her head. "I did not see that coming. She seemed genuinely upset when we found Josh's body."

"She was genuinely upset. She had no idea that he'd been killed."

I reached for the bread basket and slipped a chunk of warm ciabatta into my mouth. The Italian restaurant we'd selected was a smart establishment, with well-dressed waiting staff, immaculately laid tables and an appealing menu. It also happened to be situated in a corner of St. Mark's Square—the indoor version at the heart of the Venetian resort-casino.

We were surrounded on all sides by the mock façades of pastel-colored grand palazzos, and above our heads a domed, Renaissance-style sky was marred only by the visible sprinkler system. From the far side of the square, beyond the gelateria stall, I could hear the warble of a gondolier navigating the chemical-blue canal. Above the canal, on an arched bridge, a bride and groom exchanged vows in the glare of tourist camera flashes.

Sure, it was kitsch, but I can't deny that I really quite liked it. And I especially liked that I was able to share a meal with Victoria without the threat of imminent death hanging over us.

"You're sure that Caitlin wasn't working in partnership with Jared?"

"As sure as I can be. I very much doubt that she even knows who Jared is."

"But Ricks knew?"

"He did. In fact, he probably had more information than anybody else. His problem was timing. And I'm afraid I have to shoulder some of the blame for that."

Victoria frowned, as if she was about to assure me that I was talking nonsense. I wagged my finger. She deserved all the facts before she made that call.

"By early this afternoon," I said, "Ricks had got around to reviewing the footage from the surveillance cameras covering the theater exits. He managed to catch a glimpse of Josh making his getaway. Once he had the timing right, he was able to follow his route out to the staff parking lot on the connecting cameras."

Victoria snorted derisively and reached for her glass of Pinot Grigio. "And he couldn't have done that before?"

I felt a tic in my cheek. "Don't forget, to begin with he was faced with questioning Jared about the roulette scam, and then he had you and me to contend with. And since nobody knew about the juice list back then, I'm pretty sure Ricks expected Josh to turn up after a few days with his tail between his legs."

"By which point we might have been dead."

"Maybe. But don't you think that's why Ricks focused on us to begin with? I know he didn't exactly make things easy on us, but he could have made them an awful lot worse. And I'd say we have your father to thank for that."

"Forgive me," she said, sipping some wine, "but it would have been a lot more helpful if he'd just talked some sense into the Fisher Twins."

I tossed my head from one shoulder to the other, then popped another piece of ciabatta into my mouth and spoke from behind my hand. "Easier said than done." I chewed, then swallowed, and pointed a finger at Victoria. "But let me get back to the surveillance footage. According to Ricks, Josh spent twenty minutes in the driving seat of his Lexus, talking on his mobile."

"Who did he call? Maurice?"

I shook my head. "Maurice never heard a thing from the moment Josh disappeared. No, he called Caitlin. The register on his mobile confirms as much."

Victoria's face tangled. "But why?"

"To say that her brothers were onto him."

"Over the roulette fix?"

I shook my head again. "Over the juice list."

"Right," she said slowly, and set her wine glass down. "Because Josh had it on him when he vanished."

"Actually, no."

Her brow furrowed. "No?"

"Caitlin had it."

"But wasn't Caitlin upstairs in the bath?"

"I'm guessing his call probably roused her. According to Ricks, when she appears on the footage she's wearing a robe and her hair is wet. And she doesn't seem terribly happy. They rowed. For eight minutes."

"Okay," she said doubtfully. "Then what?"

"Then she shut Josh in the trunk of his car."

Victoria showed me her palms and a puzzled expression. "We're missing a step. How did she get him into the trunk?"

"We're missing plenty of steps. But the trunk part is easy. Josh climbed in voluntarily."

"He did? Why?"

"It seems there's a manned security booth at the exit of the parking lot. Josh was afraid he'd be stopped. His idea was for Caitlin to drive him out while he hid in the boot."

"Ah."

"But once she'd closed the lid, she left him there and stormed off to Mount Charleston."

"Right." She scratched her head. "And why did she do that again?"

I smiled. "That's exactly what Ricks asked her. He telephoned her, you see, once he'd finished watching the footage."

"And?"

"And he told her he wanted to help. Said he was worried about the mess she'd got herself in. Then again, the last thing I'd want to do if I was in Ricks' shoes is to tell the Fisher Twins that their sister was the one who stole the juice list from them."

Victoria leaned forward over her wine glass, her confusion deepening. "But hang on a minute. I thought Maurice asked *Josh* to steal the juice list."

"He did. But come on, Josh didn't have the skills to get inside that safe." I poked my thumb at my chest. "Even I didn't have the skills to get inside that safe."

"So, what—Josh got Caitlin to help?"

"Don't sound so surprised. She wanted that gig at Magic Land every bit as much as Josh. Perhaps even more. Remember, I've seen with my own eyes how committed she was to developing her new act. And she must have believed that the juice list could offer her a way to escape her brothers' influence." I lifted my shoulders. "Maybe she thought Maurice could use the leverage to help her out."

Victoria backed off from me and swirled the wine in her glass. She scrutinized the oily vortex that developed. "Not forgetting, I suppose, that she was in love with Josh. They were getting married, after all."

"Oh, mush."

"You're saying she lied?"

I sucked on my lips. "I didn't see an engagement ring on her finger."

"Trust you to notice that."

"Just observant, I suppose. But ask yourself this: could you lock your fiancé inside a car boot and leave him to stew?"

"Of course not. But then, I'm not Caitlin. She must have been angry."

"Try furious. From what she told Ricks, Josh had kept her in the dark about his roulette scam. Not that I'm surprised by that. I still don't understand why he did it."

Victoria pouted and took another sip of her wine. "Maybe he wanted a little extra spending money in Hawaii."

"Yeah, or maybe he was simply arrogant enough to believe he'd get away with it. But instead, he drew the attention of the Fisher Twins. And that was the last thing Caitlin needed."

"Right. Because she planned on stealing the juice list."

I wagged my finger. "Because she already had it. Don't you see? Caitlin could visit her brothers' office when they weren't around without arousing suspicion. And she could get close enough to one of the twins to sneak a look at his PDA and locate the safe code. The twins told Ricks that they'd last accessed their safe two days ago. So at some point between then and when Josh disappeared, Caitlin stole the list. Actually, I imagine it wasn't long before I found her in the bath. She wouldn't have wanted to give the twins too much time to discover the list was missing. And that would explain why she didn't perform in the show yesterday evening. Perhaps her nerves were frayed."

Victoria pulled a face that suggested her wine tasted foul. "She didn't tell Ricks all of that, surely."

"So I'm filling in a few blanks. But she told him enough for him to convince her to come back to Vegas. That would have been shortly before you showed up at her house and asked her to do the same thing. No offense, but I think she was already planning on returning."

"I see." Victoria reached for her knife and spun it on the table-cloth, her mouth twisted in concentration. "She was quite easy to persuade, now that you mention it. At the time, I assumed that was because she was concerned for Josh."

"Yeah, concerned that he didn't screw up. Ricks was prepared to erase the surveillance footage and turn off the cameras in the parking lot. The idea was for him to meet Caitlin at the Lexus and release Josh. Then they were going to work together to return the juice list to the safe."

"Only Caitlin had me to contend with."

"There's that. But more to the point, it was soon after they finished talking that Ricks got the call to say that an attempt had been made on the Fisher Twins' safe. He had to head to their office right away. And that's when he found me, and the whole thing became a whole lot more complicated."

"More complicated?" Victoria blew a puff of air toward her fringe and twirled her knife some more. "Honestly. I know I'm tired, but it seems bad enough already."

"Imagine how Ricks must have felt. I'm kind of amazed his head didn't explode."

"He's one cool customer, all right."

"You don't know the half of it." I stretched across the table and grabbed her wrist, stopping her from spinning the knife. I smiled by way of consolation. "When we were all leaving the theater and the twins were arranging for Josh's Lexus to be brought around to the front of the hotel, Ricks pulled Caitlin to one side and asked for the juice list. That's when she told him that she'd been a little too clever for her own good. She'd hidden it under the sand in the cabinet when you were waiting for us to arrive."

A light seemed to go on in Victoria's eyes. "So *that's* why Ricks went back."

"Damage limitation. Plus, he had no idea that Josh was dead, of course."

"Oh yes. So when did that happen?"

I reached for some more ciabatta, then thought better of it and fortified myself with a mouthful of wine instead. "It would have been some time after Ricks turned off the security camera," I said, swallowing. "Josh must have believed that Caitlin wasn't going to return to release him. He'd been calling her from the trunk of the Lexus, but she wouldn't answer her mobile. So out of desperation, he sent Jared a text."

"Big mistake. He didn't know what the Fisher Twins had done to Jared. He basically sent the guy an invitation to come stab him."

"Yeah, with his damn barbecue fork. And then Jared stole Josh's chips and made the error of trying to cash them out."

Victoria shook her head and released a long breath. "He could have got clean away if he hadn't tried that."

"So you see, Caitlin really didn't expect Josh to be dead when the trunk flipped up. And you might remember that she did her best to avoid opening the boot in the first place. It was only when you suggested it, and when I pressed the button on the key, that she lost control of the situation."

"And suddenly he's dead."

"Exactly. So you can understand why she was completely thrown by it. I mean, he was never going to be in the best of conditions, but she really didn't suspect a thing."

"Hmm." Victoria folded her arms across her chest. "So what happens now?"

"Now?" I leaned back in my chair and laced my hands behind my head. "We let Ricks smooth things over. It seems like the twins are willing to buy the idea that Josh stole the juice list. They have his killer. So there's probably no need for Caitlin's name to be mentioned."

She gave me a disapproving look. "That doesn't sound right."

"She has to live with Josh's death on her conscience, Vic. And if she's even half as mushy as you believe, that's going to be tough."

"And us?" She winced.

"We're in the clear," I said, and watched her face begin to relax. "The twins wanted us to repay the money they lost on the roulette scam or have us find Josh for them. Well, they've got their casino markers back, and we did find Josh—although perhaps not in the state of health they might have preferred. And on top of that, we helped to return the juice list."

"We were aiming to *steal* the juice list."

"Originally, maybe, but they're pragmatists, Vic."

She let go of a dispirited sigh. "I'm not sure I like that they got their blackmail list back."

"I don't like it either. But maybe it's better that more people don't have access to the information. And the part I do like is where Ricks comes in. The guy did us more than a few favors, and I don't think we've left him empty-handed. He knows about

Caitlin. Maybe he was even smart enough to make a copy of the surveillance footage before it got wiped. I'd say that if he waited a while and played things right, he could enjoy a very comfortable retirement."

"And Maurice? He can't be very pleased."

"Disappointed, I suppose. But he didn't pay my fee upfront, so he's not out of pocket."

"Yes, but we don't know what happened to Sal. If he's still inside the twins' office, they could find him and connect him to Maurice."

"Ahem," I said, and pointed over Victoria's shoulder toward the back corner of the restaurant terrace. She hesitated, then turned and looked in the direction I was indicating just as Sal lifted his head from a bowl of pasta. I raised my wine glass to him and he wiped his mouth with the back of his hand before grasping his beer bottle and encouraging Kojar to join our toast.

"Is that really them?" Victoria whispered.

"You couldn't make it up, right?"

"Sal's even smaller than I imagined."

"I know. I had to specifically request that high-chair for him."

Victoria turned back to me and shook her head slowly. "You're awful."

"Not so awful. I am paying for their meal."

"I should jolly well think so. But how did Sal escape?"

"That would be Ricks again. After we'd finished talking, he went back to the twins' office and found Sal hiding beneath the conference table. He reunited him with Kojar and got the pair of them out of the hotel without being seen. Oh, and he also released the security guard we'd tied up and let him know that it would be a bad idea to mention that he saw anyone other than me."

"So there's really no risk to Maurice."

"Hardly any. But I'd still like to think that I can sweeten things for him."

"Oh?"

"I was hoping you'd come with me to Mount Charleston

tomorrow. I'm going to suggest that Caitlin should meet Maurice. He as good as told me he could build a show around her underwater endurance act, and I think having her perform at a dump like the Atlantis should be sufficient punishment for what she did."

Victoria's mouth puckered. "She won't agree to that, Charlie."

"She will if she has any sense, and she'll persuade her brothers too. After all, Ricks isn't the only one who knows what really happened, and I'm quite handy with a pen and paper. It wouldn't take me long to write it all down."

"But that's blackmail. Why, it's no better than their stupid list."

"Actually, it's more like that short story you've been nagging me to write. And I have it in mind to pull something together along those lines, anyway—with the relevant details changed—once we've moved on from Vegas."

"We?" She blinked. "Does that mean you're planning on flying back to London with me?"

I offered her a rueful grin. "Not this time, I'm afraid."

"So where then?"

I spread my arms wide and gestured at the square surrounding me. Victoria cocked her head in puzzlement.

"But you just said you were moving on from Vegas."

"I am, Vic. I'm going to Venice. The real one this time. And I'm going to do some real writing. I've had my fill of burglary for a while. My readers deserve better. You deserve better."

She flushed and glanced down at the table. "Oh Charlie, I am relieved to hear you say that. I've been so scared this last day or so." She raised her head and peered at the blue-faced clock-tower above my left shoulder—a replica of the one in the genuine Piazza San Marco. "You know, it's just a few minutes before the deadline the twins set us. At one point, I really didn't think we'd live beyond it."

"It was never in doubt."

"You can say that now." She tapped her nose. "But I know otherwise."

"No, you don't." I tried (and failed) not to smile. "You can't honestly have believed I'd put you in that kind of danger, can you? Listen, the bottom line was that the Fisher Twins wanted their money back. And my first edition of *The Maltese Falcon* is worth almost enough by itself. I'd have been distraught to lose it—I'm superstitious enough to believe that I can't write for toffee without it beside me—but I'd have handed it over if that's what it came down to. I would never have let them harm you, Vic. You mean far too much to me for that."

I reached for her hand from across the table. She stared at me, eyes agog, and then her eyes narrowed with menacing intent.

"You bloody idiot. I've been worried half out of my mind."

"But focused, right? Willing to help? I couldn't have done what I did without you. I'd have lost Hammett's novel for good. And you might have lost me as a writer for good, too. And I really want to improve, Vic. I want to write the kind of novel you can be proud of."

"I don't know what to say. I'm going to have to—"

She broke off as she gazed down to where our hands were touching. For a moment, I thought she was caught up in the meaning of the gesture. Then I saw her eyebrows fork and her lips press together into a thin line. She snatched her hand away and pointed an accusing finger at my wrist.

"What the bloody hell is that?"

"Ah," I said, and rolled back my shirtsleeve. "That's the other reason I wasn't too worried. This watch used to belong to Josh."

"Used to? Dear God, please tell me you didn't take it from the poor man's body."

"No," I said, as though scandalized. "I stole it when we broke into his apartment."

"Oh. And I suppose that's better?"

"Well, yes, I think so. And to my mind, Josh was really no more than a custodian of this watch anyway." I raised my hand to my mouth and coughed discreetly. "By the way, do you happen to have the Houdini biography in your handbag still?"

She scowled at me. "I sincerely hope you're not comparing the two thefts. I wasn't the one who stole the book, if you remember?"

"Please, Vic. Just pass it over and allow me to explain."

Victoria huffed and grumbled, but she did as I asked and un-hooked her handbag from the back of her chair. Once she'd re-moved the Houdini biography and handed it over to me, I turned the pages until I found the section I was looking for, and then I cracked the spine and tapped at a highlighted passage with my fingertip.

In order to commemorate the first modest performance of his Water Torture Cell illusion, Bess selected a gift for her husband—a gold wristwatch with a white pearlescent dial. She had the watch engraved to him, with a short expression of her love. "To my Upside Down Houdini, Love Always, Bess, 04-29-1911."

As Victoria studied the passage, I unfastened the fragile leather strap from my wrist and placed the watch face-down on my white linen napkin. I pointed to the back of the casing and Vic-toria looked across and read the inscription, her lips moving in-creasingly slowly as she mouthed the words.

She fumbled for her wine glass and took a huge gulp. "That must be worth a bloody fortune," she gasped.

"Not a fortune, no. But enough to fund a good few months in Venice. It turns out that there was an auction of Houdini memo-rabilia in Vegas a few years ago. The magic store in this very ca-sino sells copies of the auction catalog, so I know roughly how much Josh paid."

Victoria shook her head and reached for the wristwatch, but before her fingers made contact I whipped it away and folded it up inside my napkin. She frowned at me, but I smiled broadly.

"What would you say to a small trick?" I asked. "Seems fit-ting, doesn't it?"

Her face paled. "What kind of a trick?"

"You do remember *The Thief in the Theatre*, don't you? You know, the part about the opera diva's necklace being smashed inside a velvet bag?"

I leaned down to my side and removed my right shoe, then gripped it by the toe and held the heel above the folded napkin.

"I don't have a velvet bag or a claw hammer, so I guess this will have to do."

"Oh, Charlie." She waved her hands. "No. Don't do it. Please."

"It's just an illusion, Vic."

"I don't care. I don't want to see it. In fact, I forbid it."

I wiggled my eyebrows. "You forbid it?"

"That watch is too precious. Here, why don't you use mine instead?"

"Oh, relax." I hoisted my shoe up above my shoulder. "I mean, what do you take me for? A complete idiot?"

AUTHOR'S NOTE

As anyone who has been to Las Vegas will know, real estate is at a premium along the Strip, and some major construction work was required to accommodate the imaginary casinos in this book. For those with an interest in fictional geography, the Fifty-Fifty is situated on the current site of the Imperial Palace (with Harrah's on one side and the Flamingo on the other), while Space Station One occupies the plot taken by Bally's, alongside Paris-Las Vegas and opposite the Bellagio. The Atlantis is squeezed in between the Mandalay Bay and Silverado Ranch Road.

My heartfelt thanks go to Susan Hill and Jessica Ruston, who made Charlie's career in larceny possible in the first place. Thanks also to Jim Brimer of Pink Jeep Tours, who was willing to detour back from Mount Charleston through the outskirts of Naked City; to Allison, April and Colin; to my wonderful agent Vivien; my brilliant editors Kate and Hope; all at Sheil Land Associates, Simon and Schuster and St. Martin's Press; and especially to my wife, Jo, who accompanied me on three trips to Las Vegas without ever winning that elusive accumulator jackpot.